THE ENCHANTER'S WAND

THE ENCHANTER'S WAND

Sally Stewart

Severn House Large Print
London & New York

This first large print edition published 2008
in Great Britain and the USA by
SEVERN HOUSE PUBLISHERS of
9-15 High Street, Sutton, Surrey, SM1 1DF.
First world regular print edition published 2007 by
Severn House Publishers, London and New York.

British Library Cataloguing in Publication Data

Stewart, Sally, 1930-
  The enchanter's wand. - Large print ed.
  1. Fathers and daughters - Fiction 2. Venice (Italy) -
  Fiction 3. Large type books
  I. Title
  823.9'14[F]

  ISBN-13: 978-0-7278-7707-9

Printed and bound in Great Britain by
MPG Books Ltd, Bodmin, Cornwall.

One

He regretted having to shut out the view – even for someone who had no wish to live there, Manhattan's night-time skyline was magical – but he'd been instructed to draw what, even after forty years of being a New Yorker, his hostess still referred to as curtains, not drapes. He did as he was told, then went back to an armchair at Elizabeth Harrington's fireside.

The room reflected its owner perfectly, he thought; wealth used with exquisite taste, and understated luxury that made no claim to be noticed. To his French eye it also remained, like Elizabeth herself, essentially – if unintentionally – English. While she poured coffee into fragile Crown Derby cups there was time to register the fact that she was growing old. Unreasonably, he'd expected her to stay unchanged, the eagle-eyed, widowed guardian of Walter Harrington's media empire, still the terror and admiration of friend and foe alike. But then she looked across at him and smiled and he forgot the too-careful hands of an elderly woman. She remained beautiful after all, and vividly alive; he'd be able to tell her granddaughter that when he got back to Paris.

Elizabeth lifted her coffee cup in a little gesture of welcome. 'It's lovely to see you again, Jacques, but you didn't cross the Atlantic in mid-winter to check up on your wife's aged relative. What's brought you to New York? Don't say you've been away again visiting some war-torn corner of the globe – I thought you'd had your fill of horrors.'

'I agreed to go back to Africa;' Jacques admitted slowly. 'There are horrors there that have to be reported on. That's why I've been at the United Nations building all day, making people look at filmed evidence even they can't ignore.' He saw the expression on Elizabeth's face, and lifted his shoulders in a little shrug of despair. 'A forlorn hope, you think? Maybe, but they're all we've got to keep global madness in check.'

She nodded, sparing him her own opinion of an organization she knew a great deal about. He looked too tired for it at the moment.

'Tell me about Jess,' she suggested instead. 'She sounds cheerful enough on the telephone, but is she really all right?'

He hesitated, remembering his wife's joy at a long-desired pregnancy and then its bitter culmination in the delivery of a stillborn child. 'She mourns our lost baby and always will,' he said at last. 'And she knows that we can't try for another child. I think she works too hard, but it helps her to keep busy, and

6

we have each other, which is more happiness than I, at least, deserve.'

Elizabeth sat in silence for a moment or two. While not maternal herself, she could nevertheless understand the grief of a woman who'd met and married her life's love too late to be certain of giving him children. It would be fanciful to see Jessica's tragedy as some kind of penance for her own misspent past, and Elizabeth Harrington had no taste for such fancies, but she frowned at the memory of her teenage daughter left with cousins in London while she made a career for herself in New York. From that abandonment had been spun the complicated web of relationships that still held them all uneasily together.

Her daughter Gillian, then a promising young ballet dancer, had been seduced by a flamboyant Welsh painter called David Llewellyn Matthias, who hadn't even stayed long enough to learn that he'd fathered a daughter. She had given up dancing and become an embittered, sickly mother and the wife of her mother's cousin, Gerald Smythson. The vagabond artist had finally settled down in Venice, married a Venetian, and fathered three more children there, wholly ignorant of his daughter Jessica in London.

More than thirty years later, working as an interior decorator in Venice, Jessica had met her natural father for the first time. A brief, unfriendly hail and farewell might have been possible anywhere else, but not within the compact little world of the lagoon city. The width of a small *rio* and an alley or two was all that had separated the palazzo Jess was working on from the *pensione* that housed Llewellyn and an unruly brood who turned out to be strongly against the idea of welcoming an unknown English half-sister into their rumbustious family circle.

Not inclined to do anything by halves, Fate had also embroiled a Frenchman, Jacques Duclos, into the plot by sending him to Venice at the same time as Jessica was there. From then on the story had become complicated, and they were not, Elizabeth realized, finished with it yet. With that thought, she suddenly launched an abrupt question at her guest.

'Will you see Claudia before you go home?'

Jacques' lined, brown face relaxed into a smile that told her how easily he'd followed her own train of memories; they were both obviously seeing in their mind's eye the youngest of Llewellyn's daughters, Claudia Matthias, who'd come to New York with Jacques six years earlier. He'd returned to Paris and soon afterwards married Jess, but Claudia was still there, Elizabeth's protégée.

'She is my other reason for coming,' he admitted. 'It's time she visited her parents. Maria and Llewellyn are hurt that she seems determined to keep away.' He held up a thin hand, anticipating what Elizabeth was about to say next. 'You're going to tell me how busy and successful she is. We know that, and we're all very proud of her, but she mustn't forget

8

her family; it's a very un-Italian thing to do!'

'I wasn't about to tell you what you already know,' Elizabeth pointed out sharply, 'but I will remind you of something you might have wanted to forget. Claudia was hurt herself, deeply so, when you went home without her. I don't blame you for that – how could you go on with the pretence of loving her when Jess was the only woman you needed in your life? But Claudia can't change the way she feels about you any more than she can stop hating my granddaughter for taking what she thought was hers. That's why she stays here. Jess often visits Venice, but she never comes to New York.'

Elizabeth waited to be told, politely but very firmly, that she'd just invaded private ground. For once, though, Jacques seemed willing to forgive the intrusion. 'I haven't forgotten anything at all,' he insisted gently, 'and certainly not my debt to you. Claudia would have managed somehow on her own – she's Maria's and Llewellyn's daughter – but it would have been a dreadful struggle without your love and protection. You gave her what I took away.'

'Not quite that,' Elizabeth commented with her usual insistence on accuracy. 'But I won't labour the point; I've merely told you why I think she'd prefer not to see you.'

'Then I may not succeed, but I promised Jess I'd try.' His smile softened the failure to explain why a meeting with Claudia seemed so necessary, and Elizabeth knew him better than to ask the question outright, but the restraint came hard to a woman whose career had been in investigative journalism.

Frustration made her voice querulous when she spoke again. 'Bring Jess with you the next time you come – she's half my age and therefore twice more able to face the misery of a transatlantic flight than I am.'

'I'll tell her the arithmetic seems right to me!' Jacques glanced at his watch and stood up to leave. 'I've kept you up late, *ma chère*; it's time I said goodnight and *au revoir*. Don't get up – I'll see myself out.' He bent to kiss her hand, and then her cheek, and a moment later she heard the firm click of the hall door.

The large, familiar room felt empty without him but, as always when loneliness threatened to assail her, she spoke to the painted image of Walter Harrington hanging above the fireplace.

'Something's going on, Walter! I can't tell you what it is at the moment, and that is exceptionally frustrating. I interfered, of course, betraying Claudia's feelings to Jacques, but I don't regret that and he won't give me away. Still, dear, special friend that he is, I shan't forgive him if he upsets her all over again. She's spent the last six years here trying to forget that Jacques Duclos exists. Jess ought to know that better than anyone – after all she got to marry him herself! So why does she want him to see Claudia?'

No answer to this question came from Walter, although it seemed to Elizabeth that his expression now at least looked properly thoughtful. She smiled and said goodnight to him, promising as she'd done throughout their years of working together to keep him abreast of a breaking story. Jacques' unexpected visit had tired her, but she was smiling as she turned out lamps and left the room. She had a mystery to uncover again and, like a seasoned war horse scenting the smell of battle, she couldn't wait to begin.

At noon the following day, the hour when any girl with Italian blood in her veins would be thinking it was time for lunch, Jacques sat waiting in the *ristorante* he'd been directed to. Here at Gino's, the woman at the agency he'd spoken to had assured him, was where Claudia was most likely to eat when she was in the city.

Half an hour later he was on the verge of giving up when the door swung open on a fusillade of sleety rain and this time it was Claudia Matthias who walked in. From his corner table Jacques watched as she greeted the *padrone.* Then she turned round to find an empty seat and caught sight of the man who, now standing up, was beckoning her to his table.

She didn't move towards him and for a moment it seemed more likely, if she moved at all, that she would turn on her heel and walk out. But he'd never known her to refuse a challenge before and she decided not to do so now. A slender, elegant figure in coat and

11

velvet beret of bright red – always a favourite colour, he remembered – her knee-length black boots completed the picture of a thoroughly modern New York career girl: stylish, streetwise, and not unaware that she was the focus of attention of nearly all the men in the room.

'*Ciao, cara,*' he said as she reached him. 'It's very good to see you again.'

She sat down opposite him, unbuttoning her coat, but not shaking hands with him. There was no time to waste on asking him how he'd known she'd be there; instead she went straight to the point. 'If you bothered to tell Elizabeth you were coming to New York, she forgot to mention it to me.'

Her voice, she thought, miraculously held the right note of surprise and careless interest. She would eat the spaghetti with clams that she'd already ordered from Gino, sip a glass of wine, and then bid Jacques Duclos a casual goodbye for probably another six years. By then, please God, it surely wouldn't matter if she saw him again or not.

'Elizabeth didn't know I was in town until I paid her a brief visit yesterday evening,' Jacques confessed, offering Claudia a menu which she refused with a shake of the head.

'I've already ordered. You can safely choose any of Gino's pasta – it's all good here.'

Jacques spoke to the grave young waiter – the *padrone*'s grandson, he guessed – and then turned his attention to the wine list. Claudia watched his face, remembering how many

12

times in the past she'd waited while he chose a wine with the care that only a Frenchman was likely to insist upon. It was safe to look at him now, comparing what she saw with the tired, cross man who'd limped into her mother's *pensione* in Venice all those years ago. His face was still more lined now, and the close-cropped dark hair more silvered. Even when younger he hadn't been a conventionally handsome man, but he'd refused to believe her when she tried to explain that male good looks in Italy were too common to be worth noticing.

He now dismissed the waiter with a pleasant smile and turned to her again. 'Is an old friend allowed to say that New York suits you very well? You look beautiful, and very much at home here.'

She accepted the compliment calmly – it was no more than she was used to, he supposed – and that in itself underlined one change that was more than surface-deep. The young, sloppily dressed college student he'd first met had been impulsive, eager and kind, swinging mercurially as her father did between gaiety and sudden despair. He couldn't see much trace of that Claudia in the poised, sophisticated woman facing him now.

'Elizabeth says you're launched on a brilliant career,' Jacques went on. 'What an achievement, *cara*: columnist for the *New York Times* and an already established political commentator.'

She waved this praise away with a familiar

13

gesture that reminded him of her father. 'I owe most of it to Elizabeth. She opened all sorts of doors for me that I'd never have got near on my own. But I am good at my job, and I work hard. That's one of the things I love about America – effort pays off here; in Europe it seems to be despised or ignored.'

He smiled faintly at that. 'Too sweeping, I think. There are still small pockets of resistance to the idea that success can be had without merit and some honest slog! Your own family proves my point. No one's worked harder all her life than Maria has, or more effectively than your brother does now – Jess is the person to tell you what Marco manages to achieve.'

Jacques laid no stress on these words, but Claudia thought she heard a rebuke in them nevertheless, and resented it. 'I've just been deliberately reminded of your wife, I think. I haven't said I'm sorry for Jessica's disappointment ... I am, of course,' she said coolly.

He stared at her, trying hard to remember that he must blame himself for the woman Claudia had become. 'It was my disappointment too,' he pointed out in a level voice, 'if that's how you like to describe the loss of a much-wanted child.'

She didn't need the expression on his face to tell her that she'd have done better to say nothing at all. But she couldn't change it now, however much it hurt to make him angry, any more than she could change her heart's bitterness towards Jessica Duclos.

Jacques must know by now that if he'd wanted children he'd chosen the wrong woman for his wife. Claudia had dreamed often enough of meeting him again – sooner or later Fate would arrange it somehow, she felt sure – and then he'd realize at last the mistake he'd made. He prized quality in all things, and couldn't fail to realize what she'd striven so hard to become. The longed-for meeting had finally happened, but it was all wrong – something else her English half-sister had managed to spoil. With the width of the ocean between them she was still somehow at Jacques' side, blinding him to anyone else.

Claudia pushed her food away half-eaten and made a show of looking at her watch, but he stretched out his hand to keep her sitting there.

'Don't go; there's something I still have to say.'

She pulled herself free and began to fasten her coat. 'If it's to lecture me on not going home more often, don't bother, please. Nothing's wrong or Mamma would have told me, and they know how busy I am here.'

Again he heard Elizabeth's explanation for why she stayed away, but without referring to it he must let Claudia know that she still could and should visit her parents.

'Listen, *cara*,' he said gently, 'Jess goes to Venice when Marco needs her to do some design work, and I go with her when I can, but it isn't very often. We don't make up for you not going at all. *You're* Maria's daughter, not Jess, and she and Llewellyn miss you.'

Claudia shook her head. 'Mamma won't have said so; she knows how much I love living here, and how hard I have to work to stay ahead of the competition.' Even to her it didn't sound quite enough and she had to go on. 'What she and Llewellyn don't know, because I've never brought myself to tell them, is that *this* feels like my home now, not that decaying city in the middle of a dying lagoon! Empty in the winter, it's miserable enough to drive its remaining citizens to drink, and crawling with tourists in the summer it's unbearable.' She saw the expression on Jacques' face and gave a sudden little shrug of defeat. 'Oh, all right, I'll try to go at the end of September, when the ravening hordes have gone home. Mamma will have that to look forward to.'

'She'll need it,' he said quietly. 'Claudia, Llewellyn is going blind. He still paints a little, but he won't be able to for much longer.'

The restaurant's cheerful chatter seemed to have been stopped by the wave of some magician's hand. Isolated in their own little pool of silence, he was conscious only of her suddenly stricken face, and she saw nothing but the sadness in his eyes that said she must believe him.

'Tell me it isn't true,' she pleaded hoarsely. 'God couldn't allow him to go blind – not Llewellyn.'

Jacques didn't answer, and she spoke again

16

herself in a voice that had sharpened now with anger. 'They should have told me. Why didn't they tell me?'

'Because it was what your father wanted,' he explained gently. 'He made Maria promise. They're both so proud of you, you see. Nothing matters as much as knowing how well you've done; no one was to be allowed to upset you with news you could do nothing about.'

Claudia nodded, aware that it was exactly what her parents would say. 'So why am I let into the secret now?'

'Jess was in Venice recently while I was away in Africa. Marco told her – as Llewellyn's eldest child, he thought she ought to know. She insisted, and I agreed with her, that you love Llewellyn too much not to be told.'

Claudia stared at him, her huge eyes darkened with pain in the whiteness of her face, but for once he couldn't guess from her expression what she was going to say.

'So I owe the news to Jessica,' she murmured, almost to herself. 'Something to be grateful to her for at last ... or just one more thing to make me wish she'd never found her way into our lives?' But, knowing the question didn't need an answer, she stood up, suddenly anxious to leave. 'I must go now, Jacques; I won't irritate you by offering to pay my share of the bill.' Then she turned away and bolted for the door.

He caught a glimpse of her scarlet coat on the rain-lashed sidewalk outside, and then she was swallowed up in the crowd. He stayed where he was, sadly pondering what she would do now. Had he just altered for a second time the life of a girl whose only foolishness had been to imagine herself in love with him? Or would she listen to the sound advice Elizabeth Harrington was likely to give her, and allow herself to be convinced that her parents would want her to stay here?

No nearer an answer ten minutes later, he complimented the *padrone* on the *spaghetti con vongole* he'd scarcely tasted and walked out into the icy rain. Nothing left to do, thank God, but collect his luggage and get to the airport in time to catch his flight back to Jess and home.

Two

Saturday was normally a day to look forward to: with next week's material safely filed, Claudia could relax before starting work on another assignment, and there was time for the social life she avoided when there was work to be done. Today it didn't feel normal at all. She'd spent too many of the night hours trying to forget the memory of the previous day's meeting with Jacques. There had been anger in his face, then pity – emotions she'd never wanted to arouse in a man who was simply required to love her. But worse than that, much worse, was the news he'd given her about Llewellyn.

When faint, grudging daylight finally crept into her bedroom she could give up the pretence of sleeping and brew the day's first pot of coffee. Her attic kitchen window in the old brownstone house she shared with two other tenants gave her a privileged view by most New Yorkers' standards – she could see the trees of Central Park. But staring at the bare, wind-tossed branches as she sipped her coffee, it was hard to believe that they'd ever feel inclined to break into vivid leaf again. The temperature had plummeted during the night and, instead of yesterday's rain, the sidewalks down below were covered in snow.

The weekend stretched ahead, needing to be filled. Continual activity was required if Jacques' news was to stay buried in some dim, unvisited corner of her mind. No day for jogging in the park; she'd swim more lengths than usual at her club, take in an exhibition or two, perhaps even use her press card to get a seat at the Met. Pity it was *Tristan und Isolde* tonight – still, that was better than *Gotterdamerung* for a girl who reckoned opera should only be written by Italians. But at the club an hour later friends suggested a film instead, and Wagner could safely be postponed for another night.

Claudia rose the next morning calmly determined to give the apartment a long-overdue spring clean. Then, with vacuum cleaner, dusters and polishing rags laid out in promising array, she suddenly changed out of her working jeans and sweater, and slithered to the Catholic church two blocks away.

It was marginally warmer inside than out and, old habit asserting itself, easy enough to kneel and stand at the remembered ritual of the Mass. But she knew she shouldn't be there, having not come to pray. That needed a contrite heart, and all she had brought was the shocking urge to shout to God Almighty that life was pitiless and unfair. It had been a mistake to come, she realized, because in this candlelit, incense-laden place she couldn't fail to remember her mother's gentle, un-shakeable faith and Llewellyn's insistence that his children should at least try to follow her example. His image was so clear now that he could have been standing in front of her ... She imagined her larger-than-life, near-genius of a father, in broad-brimmed hat and theatrical cape, striding along at a pace her small child's legs couldn't keep up with until he'd notice, stop and smile at her and hold out his hand.

Unaware that the church had emptied, she was still sitting in the pew when a voice spoke from the aisle beside her.

'You're troubled, my child – can I help you?'

She smeared away tears that had dampened her cheeks and turned to look at the speaker – a small man, unmistakably Irish by the sound of his voice. She struggled to keep her voice steady as she answered him. 'Thank you, Father, but no help is needed. I was just about to leave.'

He accepted the firm refusal with a nod, but continued to look at her when she stood up. 'I don't remember seeing you in the congregation before. You are new to this parish, perhaps not quite at home here yet?'

She thought it would be futile to lie to this gentle, shrewd-eyed man who could probably see right through her. 'Not new, Father, but I'm often away,' she managed to say. 'As a journalist I have to travel a lot.'

Shorter by several inches, he continued to stare up at her. 'But not born here, I'm thinking. Don't I detect a little trace of something different in your voice?'

'I was born in Venice,' Claudia was forced to admit, 'but I belong in New York now.'

He ignored the note of over-emphasis and simply smiled at her. 'Then I shall hope to see you here again. Go with God, my child.' He stood aside with a little gesture of farewell and she was free to walk past him, out into a muffled world of freshly falling snow.

That evening she set out again, in a cab this time, for the more fashionable neighbourhood of Elizabeth Harrington's palatial apartment block. It was the last Sunday of the month, when between the evening hours of six and eight Elizabeth was always 'at home' to her friends and to anyone else she considered worthy of an invitation. Claudia had been introduced to these gatherings so long ago that they were no longer something to dread; tactfully coached by Elizabeth, she'd learned how to dress, who to copy, when to listen instead of talk herself and, above all, what were the passwords needed to let an intelligent, presentable observer into the fascinating world of the great and the good.

This evening she was glad to walk into Elizabeth's drawing room just as the first guests were beginning to arrive downstairs. She wasn't ready yet to talk about Jacques Duclos' visit, but there was only the usual warm affection in her old friend's smile, and it seemed safe to hope she didn't even know of the meeting with Jacques at all.

'You're looking tired, child,' Elizabeth said with her habitual directness. 'Working too hard, I suppose – unless it was too much carousing with friends last night!'

Claudia shook her head, able to smile easily now. 'Neither, *grand'mère.*' The courtesy title had been agreed on long ago and they no longer bothered to explain the actual oddity of their relationship – that she was the younger half-sister of Elizabeth's real granddaughter, Jessica Duclos. 'I rashly started to spring clean my apartment and, once started, couldn't stop. I was about to say "you know how it is", but in fact you probably don't!'

'God forbid!' Elizabeth's delicately tinted face expressed horror at the mere idea of housework, but there the conversation had to

22

end as her first guests walked in.

With the idea of tiredness put into her mind, Claudia had an excuse for the fact that for once she wanted the evening to end, and was grateful that Elizabeth never allowed guests to linger beyond the time appointed for them to leave. With only another half-hour to go the end was almost in sight when an unfamiliar voice spoke beside her.

'Claudia Matthias? I was instructed by our hostess to look for you and introduce myself – Leif Hansson is the name.'

She turned to confront the speaker, a large stranger with untidy fair hair and an ordinary face redeemed by blue eyes that any right-minded woman would have died for. He was dressed with just sufficient neatness to pass muster in Elizabeth Harrington's drawing room, but Claudia reckoned that his tie had been a last-minute afterthought, and his grey flannel suit wasn't last year's model or even the one before that.

'Yes, I'm Claudia Matthias,' she finally remembered to agree, still in the dark as to why Elizabeth had sent him looking for her. 'I don't think we've seen you here before, Mr Hansson.' The comment was meant to lead them easily to why he was there now, but, apparently unaware of the give and take of social conversation, he seemed more inter-ested in staring round the crowded room.

'Do these people enjoy milling around, smiling and shouting at each other?' he asked with a note of wonder in his voice.

She spared a thought for the multitude who remained outside their hostess's magic circle waiting in vain to be admitted. 'I think you can take it that they feel privileged to be here,' she said frostily. 'If you don't, why bother to come?'

'To bring Mrs Harrington my mother's greetings while I am in New York. They knew each other well, long ago, when my father worked here. But I thought she would be alone.' He looked over the crowd again, still weighing the enormity of his mistake, then suddenly stared at Claudia. 'I was told you were Italian – why do you have a name I can't get my Norwegian tongue round?'

'Mother Italian, father Welsh,' she answered briefly. 'Matthias is a Welsh name.' But Leif Hansson still looked blank. 'He was born in Wales – it's a small corner of the British Isles.'

She saw his mouth twitch, but he answered seriously. 'I've heard of it; people like to sing there, I believe.'

With the conversation now grinding to a complete halt, Claudia was framing an excuse to abandon him for someone – anyone – else when he spoke again himself. 'Your name was also mentioned to me by an Italian I know – Giancarlo Rasini; he said you could give me some advice about Venice.'

Poise all but deserted her and for a moment she wanted to shout and scream that he must not mention the one place that she refused to think about. But with every ounce of self-control that she could drag together, she even managed to smile. 'My advice would be not to go there at all, especially in the middle of winter.'

She thought she'd spoken the words lightly but the surprise in his face said otherwise and she had to find an excuse for what she'd just said.

'Venetians believe their rain is wetter than anyone else's, which is probably true, and it's pretty much all that happens there in the winter – it rains!'

Leif Hansson's eyes continued to examine her. 'Is that why you choose to live here? Rasini mentioned that you never seem to visit your parents.'

The Norwegian's persistence was almost more than she could bear, and so was the criticism she imagined she'd heard in Giancarlo's reported comment. 'He's your friend, I take it? There's something you should know about Venice, Mr Hansson. His grandparents' palazzo and my mother's *pensione* might be only a small *rio* apart geographically, but they're poles apart in other ways. Giancarlo Rasini wouldn't know whether I go to Venice or not.' She hadn't answered his question, she realized, but nor did she intend to. Instead, she returned to something else he'd said. 'Why do you need the advice about Venice that I'm not now qualified to give you?'

'I'm going to work there for a while. I'm an oceanographer – therefore accustomed, of course, to water!'

The gleam of humour came as a surprise,

but it came too late, and she was tired of the struggle to seem calm and mildly interested in a stranger she would never meet again. She held out her hand in a minimally friendly gesture. 'Then I wish you good fortune, Mr Hansson, and strongly recommend a pair of thigh-boots as protection against the *acque alte* – but perhaps they're a part of a water-man's wardrobe anyway!'

She smiled as she said it, and for the first time he glimpsed warmth and likeability beneath the studied gloss of sophistication she presented to the world. There had been a hint of something else as well – anger or maybe even distress – that had threatened to disrupt her for a moment or two, but even if he hadn't imagined it, it was too late to ask about it now. He watched her slender figure walk away and merge with the crowd. Now, thank God, he could seek out his hostess and say goodbye.

'You found Claudia, I noticed,' Elizabeth commented with a smile when he reached her. 'Was she helpful about Venice?'

'Very – she advised me not to go!' He saw Elizabeth's smile fade and added calmly, 'Too much rain, I gather, but I quite like the stuff myself, so that won't matter.'

She nodded, reassured by the grin tugging at his mouth. 'You'll meet her parents, Maria and David Matthias, because the Rasinis are neighbours and certain to introduce you. Give them my love, please, and tell them how beautiful their daughter looks even though she does work too hard.'

On the verge of asking if that was Claudia Matthias's only problem, he remembered that, whatever it was, it was nothing that concerned him. Elizabeth Harrington hesitated too, tempted to embark on more information about the Matthias family; but she had other guests to attend to. Instead, her legendary smile lit her face. 'We should have had more time to talk, my dear Leif, but too many other friends came tonight. Someone else your father used to know should have been here – Nathan Acheson – but, as usual, he's been quartering the globe trying to keep its financial institutions upright.'

'He knows Venice?' Leif asked.

'He has a second home there that he's deeply attached to – and so he should be since it was redesigned for him very beautifully by my English granddaughter, Jessica!'

She smiled at the confusion in his face. 'Claudia isn't a blood relative; Jessica is. But David Matthias is father to both of them, so they're half-sisters. If you get to know the family better, as I hope you will, you'll be able to sort it out. Enjoy your stay in the lagoon city but expect to be changed by it. The old "enchanter's wand" never fails!'

'A promise or a threat?' he asked with interest. 'No, don't tell me – let me find out!' He took her outstretched hand and kissed it with unexpected grace, then turned and worked his way through the crowd to the door.

Thankful to be out in the cold night air, he

27

walked slowly back to his hotel. A morning flight to Venice and months of interesting work lay ahead, among people he didn't yet know. That was enough to think about, but his mind was considering different puzzles instead. Why had Elizabeth and the girl given such a different picture of the Matthias family's relationship with the Rasinis? And if it wasn't really the rain that kept Claudia away from Venice, what did? Most curiously of all, why had he found her so unappealing? She was beautiful, but until the last moment when she'd smiled and allowed him to see warmth and humour in her face, he'd regretted having to meet her at all.

Wrestling with this final question, he stood stock-still until the freezing air and a curious stare from a passer-by forced him to start walking again. Five minutes later he was back at the entrance to his hotel, stifling a sigh of regret for the clean, silent emptiness of the northern lands he was used to. Then he walked once more into the hothouse temperature and blazing lights that life in New York apparently seemed to require.

With the last guest gone Elizabeth gave the signal the caterers had been waiting for – their task now was to remove all trace of the party and return her drawing room to its usual state of ordered serenity. While they worked she and Claudia went to the room next door where supper was being set out for them by Elizabeth's housekeeper. More

28

friend than servant after forty years in the Harrington household, she looked at her mistress with the disapproving air she always wore on 'at home' evenings. An octogenarian lady should know better, she was inclined to think and not above saying on occasion, than spend hours at a time on her feet providing entertainment for people quite capable of entertaining themselves.

'Beef consommé,' she announced as Elizabeth and Claudia sat down. 'Drink it while it's hot. There's chicken fricassee keeping hot on the sideboard.'

'Thank you, Ella; just what we need,' Elizabeth agreed meekly, and then smiled at her grim handmaiden as she marched back to the kitchen.

'Ella's right, *grand'mère*,' Claudia risked pointing out. 'These evenings are tiring for you. Isn't it time to think of giving them up?'

'So that I can do what – doze in my armchair for a year or two longer than I otherwise might? I don't think so, my dear.' A glimmer of amusement lit Elizabeth's face. 'If it will make you and Ella happy I'll appear next time reclining, suitably gowned of course, on an elegant *chaise longue*, like some eighteenth-century French king's mistress!' She spooned her soup in silence for a moment, then fired a sudden question at Claudia. 'What did you think of Leif Hansson by the way?'

'Not quite what he seems at first sight,' Claudia admitted. 'I decided in the end that the pose of backwoods yokel bemused by city

29

life wasn't quite convincing enough; I doubt if Mr Hansson is bemused by anything very much.' She laid down her spoon and looked across the table. 'Tell me about the Hanssons.'

'His parents were younger than Walter but already his friends when I first got here. Arne was a professor teaching International Law at N.Y. University. He and Walter got involved in exposing a big corporation scandal, and became close from then on. Leif, a late but adored arrival, opted to finish his education in Norway, and Inga went back there too after Arne died some ten years or so ago. We keep in touch by letter, but until this evening I hadn't seen Leif for a very long time. Now it happens that he's being sent to Venice to work alongside your *bête-noire*, Giancarlo Rasini!'

She waited for the comment she expected on this, but no reply came, and Claudia busied herself instead with serving the chicken left for them on the sideboard. When she was seated at the table again Elizabeth stared for a moment at her down-bent face, uncertain whether to introduce the subject of Jacques Duclos or not. She felt sure now that Claudia had seen him, in which case the girl must know that she'd been visited as well, and that being so it would seem very strange not to mention him.

'I had a surprise visit from Jacques,' she finally decided to say. 'He was looking haunted by what he'd just come from filming in Africa, and couldn't wait to get home after making a report to the United Nations.'

'He waited long enough to waylay me at Gino's,' Claudia admitted briefly. 'I was reminded that I'm being an unnatural daughter, not going home nearly often enough.' She looked across at Elizabeth, unable to hide her desolation at the memory of a meeting that had gone so badly wrong. 'He pretends not to know why I don't go, but that's dishonest, because he does know.'

'Did you say that?' Elizabeth asked gently.

Claudia shook her dark head. 'No. Instead, I told him what I've never told Mamma – that this is my home now, and I can't bear the thought of living in Venice again. But I said I'd go for a visit at the end of the summer. That ended our conversation and I walked out of the restaurant.'

She forked chicken around her plate instead of eating it and, knowing her very well by now, Elizabeth refused to prompt her to say anything more. Given that it was her own granddaughter, Jessica, who was at the heart of Claudia's grief, it was perilous to talk about the emotional tangle they'd been caught in, and she'd agreed with Claudia long ago that the subject of Jess couldn't safely be discussed between them.

But the silence in the room was suddenly broken when Claudia spoke again, slowly, as if the words were being dragged out of her against her will. 'Something else happened before I walked out: Jacques told me why he thought I should go home...' She looked up and Elizabeth saw that her dark eyes were filled with horror. 'Llewellyn's going blind, *grand'mère* – imagine him not being able to see to paint! He'd rather be dead,' she ended hoarsely.

After a stricken moment Elizabeth found something to say. 'It won't happen quickly,' she tried to insist. 'Darling, new drugs, new treatments are always on the cards – let's not assume that nothing can be done.' She waited for a moment, uncertain what to say next. 'I hope Jacques didn't suggest that you pack your bags immediately and fly home. I'm sure that's not what Maria and Llewellyn would expect.'

'They didn't even want me to know,' Claudia said dully. 'I've only been told now because Marco gave the news to Jessica, and she and Jacques between them decided I should know.'

'Rightly so,' Elizabeth insisted at once. 'Of course you couldn't be kept in the dark.' She winced at the ill-chosen phrase, then hurried on. 'But knowing is one thing; tearing up your own life here is another. They have Marco at home, Lorenza and her husband now living in Venice again, and visits from Jess as well. What could you do by going back except load them with the extra grief of knowing that the life you've built here has been thrown away? Your parents would recognize it for the futile sacrifice it would undoubtedly be.'

Claudia finally nodded her head. 'That's what I think too – not just because it's convenient for me to think it but because I know them better than Jacques and Jessica do. And anyway, what would I find to do there – become a cub reporter on *Il Gazzettino*?' She managed a faint smile at the absurdity of the idea, and then got up to walk round to Elizabeth's chair and drop a little kiss on the top of her head.

'I didn't intend to worry you with the news; I knew I had to make the decision myself. But I feel better for telling you, *grand'mère* – I always do! Now I'll go away before Ella pushes me out of the door.'

'Busy week ahead?' Elizabeth asked in order to give her a normal note to leave on.

'The morning flight to Washington tomorrow – interviewing senators for or against the Kyoto Agreement ... controversial stuff!'

Elizabeth nodded. 'But exactly what you're very good at, and Walter would have agreed with me if he'd still been alive, so let's have no more talk of *Il Gazzettino* if you please.'

A real smile lit Claudia's face at last. 'Take care of yourself while I'm away. I'll ring when I get back.'

She let herself out of the apartment, leaving Elizabeth with the faint comfort that Jacques' visit might have been for the best after all. It was the first essential step in letting Claudia see him as the man she'd finally outgrown, and no longer as the much-missed lover she'd had only briefly.

Elizabeth walked back into the drawing room to check, she thought, that it had been left exactly as she required. But her heart had a different purpose and led her towards the painting that hung above the fireplace. It was signed simply 'Llewellyn', as he always did, and its subject was a canal-side scene on the little island of Burano out in the lagoon, a row of fishermen's cottages reflected in the still water outside their front doors. The painting spoke of warmth and mellow sunlight and the riotous medley of colour that the Buranesi chose to live with – magenta alongside shocking pink, ochre partnering Prussian blue – because, according to legend, it allowed the men working far out in the lagoon to identify which cottage was theirs.

Elizabeth stared up at the painting, thinking of the volatile, mad, life-enhancing Welshman who soon would be unable to paint such pictures. The colours blurred and tears not shed since Walter's death trickled down her cheeks, but she brushed them away, irritated by the unexpected weakness; she must be getting old after all. Instead she'd do better to think of Llewellyn's daughter, and consider how long it would be before Claudia gave up the fight to convince herself that she could ignore what she now knew and stay in New York.

Three

Marco Polo airport on a late-January morning was pleasantly uncrowded. Leif collected his luggage from the carousel in record time and was debating whether to find a trolley or manhandle it himself when he felt a tap on his shoulder. He turned round to find a tall, thin-faced man looking at him.

'My name is Giancarlo Rasini,' the stranger said, holding out his hand. 'If you're Leif Hansson, welcome to Venice. You did say to look for someone large and fair-haired!'

Leif answered with a slow, pleasant smile. 'Large, fair and untidy, I think I said. I still haven't learned the knack of travelling neatly!' He stood for a moment inspecting the tall Italian, who spoke an English as unaccented as his own. He knew Rasini's reputation and something about the man himself after numerous telephone conversations, but now was the moment to discover whether or not they'd be able to work together. Despite what had just been said, Leif recognized that his welcome remained in doubt, and he thought it not unreasonable – his Italian hosts had problems enough without an alien observer, who might or might not be helpful, imposing upon them.

'Thank you for coming out to meet me,' Leif said next, 'but I'm afraid I'm making your busy working day worse.'

'Not at all,' Rasini insisted politely. 'Shall we go? Our "taxi" is waiting outside.'

With the luggage shared between them he led the way out of the building towards a dark-blue launch tied up at the quayside. At its stern fluttered the pennant of the Magistrato alle Acque, Leif's first reminder of just how old was the lagoon city and its institutions. For how many centuries past had a long succession of magistrates been responsible for keeping Venice safe from its encroaching waters?

When they were settled in the boat and the pilot had been given the signal to leave, Rasini gestured at the bleak seascape ahead.

'It will be a choppy ride, I'm afraid. The wind is strengthening, and it's been raining since dawn, which means another high water later on.' He turned to look at his companion. 'Not quite what you were expecting perhaps?'

Leif smiled at the grave enquiry. 'I was warned about the rain and the need for seaboots – by Claudia Matthias.'

The Italian's expression still didn't change. *Did it ever relax?* his guest wondered. Was this how Venetians were, courteous but not cordial to visitors they'd rather not have had? He thought the mention of Claudia Matthias was going to be left hanging in the air, but finally Rasini spoke again.

'Of course Claudia knew Venice very well. We have a saying here, *"andare per le fodere"*, which means going through the "linings" or the nooks and crannies of the city. She was familiar with them all, I think. It's strange to imagine her living happily somewhere else, but that seems to be the case.'

His cool tone of voice dismissed the subject of Claudia Matthias, prompting Leif perversely to pursue it. 'She mentioned that her home and yours are close together,' he suggested, resisting the temptation to quote the rest of what she'd said.

Giancarlo steadied himself with practised ease as the launch buried its nose in a wave and lifted sharply again. 'We're all close to each other here,' he agreed calmly. 'Venice is a small city. But, yes, her parents and my grandparents are neighbours and good friends.'

He spoke only for his elderly relatives, Leif noticed, not for himself. Even in this day and age did a scion of an ancient aristocratic house still consider himself as being made of different clay from the inmates of a *pensione*? Napoleon might have thought he'd abolished the Golden Book a couple of hundred years ago, but Leif could easily see this man beside him – still indefinably elegant even in his heavy, sea-going clothes – clinging to some innate certainty that he was different from lesser mortals. If his distant air didn't derive from that then there had to be some other reason for the aloofness that he seemed to wear like a second skin.

Leif abandoned the puzzle and stared out instead over the bows of the launch at an unwelcoming silver-grey lagoon stretching to the skyline and there, dimly visible through another squall of rain, a darker grey shadow insisting that the city built so improbably on a submerged forest of wooden piles did in fact still exist.

Suddenly Rasini spoke beside him. 'The Serenissima isn't looking her best, I'm afraid – no sunlit canals reflecting white marble and rose-red brick today! You'll get used to her moods and deceptions, but just remember that at any one moment she's never quite what she seems.' His voice now held a mixture of sadness and pride, and Leif registered the hint of something about Giancarlo Rasini: at least this cool, reserved aristocrat loved what he and his colleagues struggled so continuously to protect, of that Leif could be sure.

'Elizabeth Harrington gave me a slightly different warning,' Leif decided to confess. 'She said I must expect to be changed by coming here. You both make Venice seem more like a living person than an inanimate assembly of brick and stone and water, balanced here precariously between lagoon and sky!'

At last the Italian's austere face relaxed into something approaching a smile. 'Signora Harrington was right, Leif. The sea-witch city ignores the summer day-trippers who swarm here in their millions, and rightly so, but she won't ignore you, I'm sure.' Then he leaned over to direct the pilot as the boat's speed slackened and they turned into the slightly calmer waters of the Bacino that would lead them to the mouth of the Grand Canal.

Leif stared about him, easily able to recognize the Doge's Palace and the tall columns that marked the entrance to the Piazzetta and, opposite them across the water, the massive dome of the Salute Church heaving its silver-grey bulk into the darker grey sky. Even here everything seemed drained of all other colour except for the sooty black hulls of a fleet of gondolas moored along the Riva. But what he now saw through a veil of rain he knew the returning sunlight would sooner or later transform. He could wait for that; for the moment he was content to meet the Serenissima first in this desolate winter mood.

The wash of a passing *vaporetto* made the launch bob up and down, but a moment later they'd turned into a more peaceful side canal. A paved pathway ran along one side of it, and the pilot edged them gently in towards it until they came to a halt in front of wrought-iron gates that led into a garden still bare and leaf-less at this time of the year.

'The Pensione Accademia,' Giancarlo announced. 'It has a good reputation – you'll be comfortable here, I'm sure.' He waited until they were standing on terra firma and the pilot had gone to announce their arrival, then held out his hand.

'We shall see you at the *ufficio* in a week's time, *non è vero*? I'm glad you're going to use this first week to get your bearings and find your way about. But tomorrow evening my grandmother hopes you'll dine with us at home, and as the palazzo's side entrance isn't easy to find in the dark I'd better come and collect you – about seven thirty, if that's convenient?'

A moment later he and the pilot were aboard again and Leif was left to think about that unexpected invitation as he followed the *pensione*'s porter along the path to the front door. At last, if Elizabeth Harrington was right, his Venetian make-over was about to begin. Already he was becoming aware of the truth of what Rasini had said, but it seemed possible that the gap between first impressions and reality applied as much to its people as to the city itself.

The following evening Leif realized that he'd forgotten to ask an important question: how informal would the verbal invitation given by a Venetian countess turn out to be? He had no idea, but his rule in life was always to err on the side of being under-dressed. When Giancarlo arrived at the *pensione* to fetch him, therefore, he was wearing the elderly grey suit that he had worn to Elizabeth Harrington's salon in New York, but he looked anxiously at his host.

'Not quite smart enough for your grandparents?' he suggested, and saw a smile tug at the Italian's mouth.

'My grandfather might just notice if you wore nothing at all; Donna Emilia only draws her line at the Hawaiian shirts and Bermuda shorts beloved of American visitors! Shall we go? It would be quicker to take a boat round to the front of the palazzo, but our water entrance is kept boarded up, like most people's are now.'

Outside he turned away from the direction Leif expected and led him instead to a small bridge across the *rio*.

'The ideal route between two points is never a straight line here,' he explained. 'There's always some water in between.'

'Is that what made you a marine engineer – a Venetian's natural affinity with water?' Leif asked as they walked along.

He had to wait a moment or two before his companion answered. 'Strictly speaking, I'm not a Venetian at all – I was born in Florence where my parents were living. In 1966 I was a small child and was safely at home, but they were drowned in the catastrophic floods that hit there as well as here. Perhaps I grew up wanting to help prevent that happening again, but Venice became my home and I gradually learned as well to realize how precious and irreplaceable it is.'

He turned to look at Leif's apologetic face, lit by the wall-lamp they were passing. 'Don't think it hurts to talk about my parents; it was a long time ago. But now you know why I still

41

share my grandparents' home – it's my turn to look after them.'

'Thank you for telling me,' Leif said simply.

Another small bridged *rio* and another alleyway – a *calle*, Leif now knew it should be called – brought them to a gateway where Giancarlo halted. It led them into a courtyard graced by a splendid antique well-head; against one wall a flight of shallow stone steps climbed to massive doors that now stood open. An elderly maidservant waited there, offering a smiling, *'Buona sera, signori.'*

'Meet Battistina,' Giancarlo said, 'the mainstay of my grandmother's household.'

She nodded at this introduction, obviously accustomed to being presented thus to the Contessa's guests, and prepared to inspect the newcomer in her turn in case he didn't deserve to be let in. But the sheaf of white freesias in Leif's hand received an approving nod, and she closed the door behind them.

A corridor, an anteroom where their outdoor coats were left, and then another flight of beautiful Renaissance stairs brought them to the palazzo's *piano nobile* and the *portego* that formed its heart – an enormous room whose tall lancet windows and balconies at the far end overlooked the Grand Canal. Leif had an impression of old Persian rugs, fragile as silk on the marble floor, and of lamplight catching the gilded frames of dark old portraits on the walls; the faded elegance of it all spoke of wealth that had long since begun to ebb away. An electric fire simulated glowing logs in one of the huge fireplaces, and around it were grouped shabby, comfortable armchairs.

Giancarlo introduced the evening's guest and Leif bowed over the Countess's thin, blue-veined hand, half-afraid that his own strong fingers might hold it too roughly. But she smiled at the flowers he offered her, and he saw strength still in her face and traces of the great beauty she had been.

'How clever of you, Signor Hansson, to guess that I love white flowers best of all.' She touched a bell that brought the housekeeper into the room. 'A simple glass vase, *cara*, please – the plainer the better, don't you think, for these lovely things?'

Battistina's considering nod suggested that she agreed. She would see to the flowers while the Signora Contessa attended to their guest.

Now it was Count Paolo who held out his hand to Leif. Nearer ninety than eighty, but still upright, he smiled the charming, shy smile of a man whose happiest hours were spent in the haven of his library. The outside world had grown too noisy and violent for someone who remembered more gentle times. But Venice, at least, was Venice still, though more threatened than before, and he sincerely pitied those who had the misfortune to live elsewhere.

While their grandson poured white wine Donna Emilia took charge of the conversation. 'Giancarlo mentioned that you know our dear Elizabeth Harrington. If you saw her in New York, perhaps you met her little Venetian protégée as well?'

It took Leif a moment to equate the 'little protégée' with his remembered image of the poised and elegant Claudia Matthias. 'Yes,' he finally agreed, 'I saw them both, very briefly among a crowd of people in Mrs Harrington's apartment.' A rueful smile lit his face. 'The evening came as something of a culture shock after spending the past six months in the emptiness of the Arctic Circle!' He looked round the shadowy room. 'This isn't much like the frozen north either, but in its own way it's just as beautiful and peaceful.'

From then on, Giancarlo realized, he needn't worry about his Norwegian friend. Leif Hansson looked perfectly at home there at least, and Donna Emilia was already smiling kindly at him.

'Maria and Llewellyn will want to hear about their daughter,' she said. Then a gleam of amusement showed him how the Countess had looked as a young woman. 'Did Claudia mention her father?'

'Only to explain the name of Matthias by saying that he was born a Welshman.'

'And still is,' she agreed. 'After nearly forty years of living among Venetians he remains what we are not – talkative, transparent and ebullient, despairing one moment, and joyful the next. He's also a fine artist, of course, and what he sees he paints with love, which makes him remarkable.'

44

In English a little less fluent that his wife's, Count Paolo now put in a tentative suggestion. 'My dear, perhaps you should tell Mr Hansson a little more about our neighbours before he meets them.'

Donna Emilia nodded, took a sip of wine, and went on. 'David Matthias, or Llewellyn as we know him, arrived here a penniless young vagabond. He was thankful to marry Maria, whose father owned the Pensione Alberoni where they still live, and to everyone's surprise it became a very happy marriage. Three children were born – Lorenza, living here again now that her husband is the stage designer for the rebuilt Fenice; Marco, a bachelor still at home with his parents; and Claudia in New York. So far, all quite normal, but now it becomes more interesting!' She sipped her wine again and for a moment Leif wasn't sure whether she'd drifted back into the past, forgetting the people she was with, or whether she was, like any good storyteller, keeping her audience waiting for the dénouement that was to come next.

'One day about six years ago my husband called at the palazzo next door expecting to meet its new owner, an American called Nathan Acheson. Instead, he found an English girl who was redesigning it – very beautifully – before Mr Acheson and his wife arrived.' She smiled across the hearth at the Count. 'Paolo fell in love with her there and then, and after that she walked into our lives as if we'd always known her. But rather more dramatically, by coming to Venice, Jessica also walked into Llewellyn's life – she was the daughter he'd fathered unknowingly before he left London forty years earlier, and had never heard of since.'

'Not normal at all,' Leif murmured inadequately. 'What happened after that – did they all settle down happily together?'

Donna Emilia shook her head. 'Each of the Matthias children, for their own separate reasons, deeply resented Jessica – which was all the more sad because dear Maria didn't – and Llewellyn came to adore the eldest child he hadn't known. Jessica eventually married a charming Frenchman called Jacques Duclos, and settled with him in Paris. She returns regularly to Venice – to work with Marco, as it happens – but Lorenza and Claudia still refuse to accept her as part of their family.' The Countess smiled at her guest. 'There's more to learn, but is that enough information to be going on with?'

He agreed that it was, just as the little tinkle of Battistina's bell informed her mistress that dinner was now ready, and they followed her into a small room leading off the *portego*. The housekeeper was there waiting to serve them with a seafood risotto that Giancarlo explained was a *specialité de la maison*.

'You needn't fear the shrimps, by the way,' he added. 'Battistina makes sure they're caught from the Adriatic, not the lagoon!'

The risotto was delicious, as were the grilled swordfish cutlets that followed it and the delicate white wine that Count Paolo said came from the Trento region to the north of the Veneto – once Austrian but long since part of Italy again. From that he led Leif on to talk about the work he'd been doing in the northern lands, and Donna Emilia wanted to know about his parents' long friendship with the Harringtons. It wasn't until dinner was over, and they were back in the *portego* drinking coffee, that Leif could return to the name he'd heard mentioned in New York.

'I'm sure Mrs Harrington said that Nathan Acheson has a home here. Is he still your neighbour?'

'Not only that,' Donna Emilia replied, 'he and Elvira are our dear friends, but Nathan is also one of this city's great benefactors. Paolo, you explain to Signor Hansson.'

The Count looked across the table at their guest. 'You won't have come here unprepared, I'm sure. You'll know that Venice has been dying for a long time in terms of population – because fewer and fewer of its citizens continue to live here. Nathan decided to tackle the problem by setting up a Trust that would buy up derelict property, renovate it, and then rent or sell it to young Venetians who would otherwise leave us to go to the mainland.'

'Simple but effective all round,' Leif agreed, 'provided you can find a good, wise friend like Mr Acheson.'

'And also when you have a young man like Marco Matthias to run the trust, and a bril-

liant designer like his half-sister, Jessica –
Elizabeth Harrington's granddaughter inci-
dentally – to work alongside him. Together
they show what can be done with old houses
that have been left empty and neglected for
years. It's very heartening,' the Count said
with great contentment.

'I'd like to see some of the work in progress,' Leif suggested, 'but first I'd better
learn my way about – I made a start today.'

'By going straight to the Piazza? Giancarlo
asked.

'No, my simple plan is to get to know one
sestiere at a time, so starting from where I
already was, at the *pensione*, I began in
Dorsoduro. San Marco I'll leave till last – the
icing on the cake!'

'It's the icing to the extent that the *"centro
storico"* is what most people come to see,' the
Count agreed, 'but the real Venice, the flesh
and blood, still-living city is better found
outside St Mark's Square – look at the hidden
campi and *calli* of Cannaregio or Castello, Mr
Hansson, if you want to know Venice properly.'

'Which brings us,' Giancarlo put in, smiling
affectionately at his grandfather, 'to the heart
of our problem and the battle that's been
going on for a long time. In the red corner are
the people who want to keep Venice for the
Venetians, the place where they can work and
shop and sleep at night; in the blue corner we
have the preservationists who see it, rightly, as
a treasure-house, but one that now belongs to

the world – a world, we have to admit, that has contributed generously to the cost of its survival.'

'There doesn't,' Leif ventured after a moment, 'seem much hope of a compromise between them, does there? But if we can't find the means of keeping Venice safely upright and secure, the question of what it survives as surely becomes academic anyway.'

'The problem in a nutshell,' Giancarlo agreed sadly. 'But one we aren't yet close to solving. And to make matters worse, most of us can't even decide which corner to fight in!'

It was a discussion Leif would have liked to go on with, but a glance at the Countess's pale face reminded him that elderly hosts were probably thankful when a guest got up to leave before having to be edged towards the door. He stood up, thanked them charmingly, and shook his head when Giancarlo offered to guide him back to the *pensione*.

'Let me do it alone. With two small bridges to cross, I can't go very far wrong!'

In fact, he regained the now-familiar alley and *pensione* gateway having had to retrace his steps only once. In winter at least, Venice was clearly not a night-time place. No sign or sound of life disturbed the stillness; he could have been walking through a mysterious but totally deserted city, and the thought made him shiver, as though anticipating the Serenissima's final end. He told himself to blame his coldness on the freezing night air, but he was grateful all the same to step into the

Accademia's warm, friendly hall and have the receptionist wish him a cheerful *'buona notte, signore'* that said the end wasn't yet after all; he'd just been misled by another of the old sea-city's illusions.

Four

The first meal of the day at the Pensione Alberoni was always peaceful now. Remembering how it had been years ago, Maria thought it strange to find herself missing the noisy arguments that had turned the breakfast table into a miniature battlefield more often than not. In the end, of course, Llewellyn would lose patience with his children and roar at them, *'Basta* – be quiet; that's enough!' Then peace would return for a little while.

It was usually Claudia who deliberately provoked the other two; she was her father all over again – eager to offer or accept a challenge. No wonder he'd loved her the most, and missed her still, even more than the rest of them did. And she was the one who'd least accepted Llewellyn's English daughter, imagining that if some of his affection now went to Jessica there'd be less left for her. Maria supposed that life in America was teaching her wayward daughter many things, but

50

would she learn there that loving was like every other god-given talent; it didn't diminish but grew by being used? Maria could remember, without pain now, having to discover about the other women in Llewellyn's vagabond years before his wanderings had finally ended in Venice, but they hadn't stopped him learning to love Tommaso Alberoni's plain daughter. Life with her fiery, unpredictable Welshman had taught Maria a lot about the human heart.

'*Mamma ... buon giorno; come stai stamane?*'
The loving enquiry came from Marco as he walked into the room, dark hair still curling damply from his shower, and his formal dark suit indicating a day to be spent wrestling with bureaucrats whose only function seemed to be to obstruct the good that Nathan Acheson's Trust achieved for Venice.

Maria smiled at her son, a gift she still thanked the Blessed Virgin Mary for every day. She loved her daughters, but girls had to detach themselves, in a way that sons never did, when they began to tend families of their own. That was how life went on. But if Marco found a girl to marry one day – and she prayed that he would – she knew the cord binding mother and son wouldn't weaken.

She poured coffee for him now and watched him break open a roll. But instead of beginning to eat it he looked at her instead.

'Mamma, when Jessica was here last week I explained about Llewellyn – she had to be told before she found out for herself.'

Maria thought about this for a moment, then nodded. Yes, perhaps it was better that Jessica should know, and Jacques too, of course. But Marco hadn't finished what he had to say.

'When she was here Jacques was in Africa. I assumed he'd go straight back to Paris, but he had to attend a meeting in New York, and he also saw Claudia there.'

Maria read in her son's face what he was about to say next, and said it for him. 'He told Claudia about her father, and now she's very angry at being kept in the dark.' Maria looked sadly across the table. 'Will she forgive us ... understand why we wanted her not to know?'

Marco gently stilled his mother's hand, which drew agitated patterns on the table-cloth. 'She knows that you and Papa only wish for what seems best for her – to stay where she is and be happy.'

'She mustn't come home,' Maria said. 'That would upset her father more than anything, but ... but...' She stopped, unable to put into words what she was thinking, and it was left to Marco to find the excuse for her daughter that she needed.

'Claudia will have had to go away again, Mamma ... you know what her job is – assignments here, there and everywhere. You'll hear from her when she gets back to New York.'

Maria's face relaxed a little, but one anxiety still remained. 'We won't tell Llewellyn that she knows. We must wait until she telephones, *non è vero, tesoro*?'

52

Marco's nod agreed to this. Then, forgetful of the roll he still hadn't eaten, he stood up to leave. 'Got to go, Mamma – yet another trip to Padua to meet yet another official who will hint that the permit I need can be had at a price! How does this benighted country survive at all?'

'Because of men like you,' she said truthfully. 'How else?'

He smiled at that but, without answering, kissed the top of her head and walked out of the room. Left alone, Maria poured herself more coffee and thought, as she frequently did, about her children. Lorenza, once a worry to her, was now a comfortably married woman, whose youthful anguish over Giancarlo Rasini had probably been all but forgotten; Marco had been a different problem, growing up and getting into trouble along with other rebellious young men who'd wanted to put their little world to rights; but working for Nathan Acheson had shown him how he could best help the city he loved; she thought Marco was content now.

It left only Claudia to fret over; the eager child who'd always wanted to know what lay just over the horizon, who was never going to be content to stay safely here with them in the lagoon. For that adventurous spirit alone she'd been Llewellyn's favourite, but Maria frowned over the thought, wondering whether it was still true. He'd grown to love his English daughter more and more, convinced he could never make up for all the years he hadn't known that she existed. Claudia would have resented that in any case – she needed the people she loved to love her most in return – but far worse had been losing Jacques Duclos to Jess as well. That was why she stayed in New York and wouldn't come home even now – and *mustn't* come home, Maria thought now, at least for as long as work on Marco's buildings brought Jess back to Venice.

With this settled in her mind, Maria felt calm enough to climb the stairs to the studio at the top of the house. Llewellyn would be there already, desperate to catch the best of the light that still enabled him to be sure of the colours he was using. It was becoming harder, she knew, but they didn't talk about a time when even the lagoon's pure light would not be enough to allow him to go on painting. He kept the studio unheated, and the room felt bitterly cold when she walked in; but she knew from long experience that he wouldn't leave it until his mittened fingers grew too cold to hold a brush.

'Marco's on his way to Padua, *amore*,' she said as he turned round to smile at her, 'and I'm going to the fish market, but Lucia's working downstairs. She heard the weather forecast early this morning – snow is promised for this evening.'

Half-listening while he considered adding more delicate flakes of Chinese white to the crest of the waves he was painting, Llewellyn waved his brush extravagantly in the air.

'Global warming, don't you know. Venetians used to expect to see snow once in a lifetime, but we've already had two blizzards so far this winter. I abhor all experts, Maria; I cast anathemas upon them!' Then he looked at his wife more closely. 'Go away, *tesoro*; you look pale – it's too cold for you up here.'

Her smile trembled because it was guilt, she feared, not the freezing air that made her pale. In all their years of living together she'd had no secret from him before, but on her way upstairs she'd decided that she would lie bravely about Claudia. The Blessed Virgin – her friend and dear protectress – would have to help, knowing that she couldn't manage it well enough to convince Llewellyn on her own. But he was anxious to get back to his painting, and she could blow him a hurried kiss and leave before he stared at her again. She asked Lucia to take him hot chocolate in half an hour's time and make sure he drank it before it grew cold. Then, wrapped up against the bitter temperature outside, she set out to walk to the Rialto. Perhaps there'd be the little clams today that Marco loved, and turbot for Llewellyn, because he always made a fuss if he had to pick bones out of the fish he was eating.

Shopping wasn't quickly done in wintertime; without the visitors that crowded the markets later in the year, friends and neighbours were easily spotted and must be talked to. She was crossing the Campo San Vio on her way home when elderly Annunziata, watching over her son's newspaper kiosk as usual, hailed her as she went by.

'Signora ... Signora, *momentito*! *Venite qui, per favore.*'

Surprised by the urgent summons, Maria went over to the kiosk where a stranger stood waiting, map in hand. Annunziata explained, this time in the soft Venetian dialect she preferred to use, that she'd just been asked by the *straniere* where he could find the Pensione Alberoni! Now, was that not *una cosa straordinaria* that the Signora herself should come by at that exact moment?

Maria agreed that it was, but her attention was now fixed on the man himself. He clearly hadn't followed what had been said, and his fairness and his brightly checked anorak convinced her of his likely non-Italian nationality.

'You are American, *signore*?' she asked in English.

'No, but I speak English,' Leif answered, thankful to have found someone he could understand. 'I've worked out how you number houses here, but not using street names as well makes it hard for a stranger!' His smile was pleasantly reassuring, and Maria thought she could now guess the reason for his search.

'Annunziata says you're looking for the Pensione Alberoni, but I'm afraid it's no longer open to visitors; it closed two years ago. The Accademia, not far away, is open – we can direct you there.'

'That's where I'm staying, signora; I don't

56

need accommodation. I'm trying to find Signora Matthias, not her *pensione*.' Wariness, he'd read, was built into the Venetian character, but even so it was disconcerting to be expected, as now he clearly was, to tell this stranger why he needed to find her neighbour. 'I have a message for her from a friend in New York,' he felt obliged to explain. And because he could anticipate the lady's next question, he added the name of the friend. 'The message comes from Mrs Elizabeth Harrington.'

Like sunlight breaking through a cloud, a gentle smile transformed the face of the woman in front of him. 'Then you need only give it to me – my name is Maria Matthias! Welcome to Venice, Signor...?'

'Hansson, Leif Hansson,' he said, holding out his hand and now smiling with relief. 'Norwegian, you might have guessed, but my parents lived in New York when I was a child. I've just come from there, and Mrs Harrington asked me to let you know that your daughter is well despite working very hard. I saw her too, looking very beautiful, but of course you'll have guessed that anyway!'

Maria nodded, pleased with this stranger who appreciated her daughter as he should. 'I'm on my way home. Will you come with me and meet my husband?' she suggested gently. 'He'll want to hear about Claudia, and Elizabeth.'

Leif took the laden basket in one hand and offered her his free arm in what he hoped was a suitably Venetian gesture. Kind as always, Maria relieved Annunziata's anxiety (how would the neighbourhood be kept informed if she didn't know what was going on?) by explaining that the *straniere* knew Signorina Claudia in New York, and then they set off at a stately pace back to the *pensione*. Along the way Leif explained that he was in Venice to work with another of her friends, Giancarlo, at the Magistracy, expecting that Maria would then talk of his elderly grandparents at the Palazzo Rasini. Instead, she gave a wistful sigh.

'Poor man,' she said sadly. 'He devotes his life to trying to keep us all safe, but the sea and the winds and the rains from heaven aren't for human beings to control.' It was as far as she was prepared to go herself, but she knew that Llewellyn's well-aired views on the subject would undoubtedly be heard once again if Leif Hansson claimed to be an expert on the problems of the lagoon.

'We can't "control" the elements, Signora,' he simply said. 'Our job is to make the best use of them we can, and to limit the damage we know they're capable of.'

She nodded, thinking how nice and how sensible he was, and then pointed to the canal they were now crossing. 'This is the Rio della Fornace, which means we're almost home. You'll have to meet my son, Marco, some other time, but Llewellyn will be there – probably still painting in his studio.'

The house she led him to stood back from

a garden bordering the canal, and resembled a smaller version of the Pensione Accademia, but what they now walked into had again become a pleasant family home. They were met in the hall by a middle-aged smiling servant who promised to bring coffee to the *salotto* as soon as she'd dealt with the Signora's fish. Maria herself picked up a telephone and spoke into it.

'Can you come down, *amore*? We have a guest.' She smiled at Leif as she replaced the receiver. 'It keeps us in touch – otherwise there are too many stairs!'

Leif's attention wandered round a room that was pleasant and comfortable rather than grand like Emilia Rasini's *portego*. But the paintings on the plain white walls would have graced any gallery he could think of. The name scrawled at the bottom of each gave him the artist's identity, and he recognized the truth of what the Countess had said – it wasn't some enthusiastic amateur who dabbled with paints upstairs, but rather a very gifted artist. He stared once more at a delicate dawn study of San Giorgio Maggiore emerging from the misty, silvered surface of the lagoon, and wished that he owned it himself. Then he turned to face his hostess.

'Your husband's paintings are very beautiful,' he said simply. 'I feel privileged to have seen them.'

She smiled, but he had no time to wonder why her eyes should still look sad because the door then opened and Llewellyn walked into the room. Leif saw a stocky, bearded man, aged about seventy but still vigorous-looking, with a thick mane of grey hair worn slightly too long, deep-set eyes and a wide, expressive mouth. In short, Donna Emilia had been right about him as well: a very un-Venetian man, surely.

Maria explained how the meeting in the Campo had come about and then asked Leif to tell the rest of the story. He skated over their daughter's advice to avoid Venice if he could and did his best instead to sound awed by the sort of company Claudia was keeping in New York.

Llewellyn smiled kindly on their guest. 'We knew from Elizabeth how brilliantly she's doing,' he said with one of his expansive gestures, 'and of course it was only what we expected; but we're grateful to have it confirmed.' Then he fixed his eyes on Leif again. 'All my children are remarkable, I think I can safely say – nothing ordinary about any of them.'

His still-beautiful Welsh voice, wistful now, suggested that it was more than could be said for him; but the smile that lifted the corners of his mouth warned Leif that here was yet another of the deceptions in which Venice seemed to specialize. Before he could say that there was nothing ordinary about the paintings on the wall, Maria intervened.

'*Amore*, Signor Hansson is a scientist, here to work with Giancarlo. Is it not extraordinary that we should know him twice over, so to speak – through Elizabeth, and through our dear friends here?'

'A pleasant coincidence,' he agreed, wagging a finger at her, 'but I forbid you on pain of death, my dearest, to tell me next that it's a very small world! *Au contraire*, the world is unimaginably large; we just happen to live in a small ingrown corner of it where we all know each other.' That settled, he smiled at them both. 'Mr Hansson must meet the rest of the family, Maria. Jess will be back soon; we could have a sumptuous dinner party before the privations of Lent set in!'

In nearly forty years of life with Llewellyn, Maria had still to discover what her husband ever imagined he gave up in preparation for Easter, but she smiled lovingly at him and agreed to ask Marco about Jessica's next visit. Leif explained that he'd heard about the Acheson Trust, and hoped that Marco would find the time one day to show him a house that was in the process of being worked on. It was surely just the sort of hopeful development Venice needed.

But Llewellyn's mobile face suddenly became a mask of despair. 'The Serenissima needs more than hope, my dear boy; she needs a miracle, nothing less than a whole flock of guardian angels in constant attention on the invalid! Maybe clever men like you and Giancarlo can keep her safe from the rising waters, but that leaves the destructive summer flood of visitors, and the pernicious politicians who, alas, are always with us. I'm afraid you can't save Venice from them.' Then as if aware that he'd given real feelings away, he smiled at them again. 'Take no notice – I'm a fond, foolish old man, my disrespectful children will tell you, who likes the sound of his own voice!'

It was time to leave, Leif thought. He thanked Maria for the coffee, promised to keep in touch, and said that he must return to the task he'd set himself of getting to know the city before he started work. But although by the end of the day he'd walked until he was footsore and weary, his mind still lingered over the visit to the Pensione Alberoni. Gentle, kind Maria Matthias looked sad when she forgot to smile, and her flamboyant Welsh husband played the charming clown to hide whatever it was that troubled him. He probably hadn't exaggerated about his family, but Leif couldn't decide whether he hoped Maria's dinner party would take place or not. He was in Venice to do some much-needed arduous work, not to concern himself with people who he sensed couldn't be got to know lightly. Better on the whole not to get involved, he thought, because he felt strongly that they were likely to prove more than an uncomplicated, scientifically minded Norwegian could cope with.

Five

The morning routine at the Palazzo Rasini followed a time-honoured pattern: Donna Emilia's only concession to age was a leisurely start to the day, waiting in her room for the green tea and toast that Battistina brought her. Paolo preferred his coffee and *panino* in the breakfast room, where the morning's *Il Gazzettino* awaited him together with the previous day's *Daily Telegraph* and *New York Times*; he didn't enjoy the modern world but he felt obliged to keep in touch with it to an extent.

Today he didn't linger there; he'd thought of something he could do for the pleasant newcomer Giancarlo had introduced them to. He walked along the passage to his wife's room, kissed her good morning, and then explained that he had a call to make at the Palazzo Ghisalberti next door. She looked blank for a moment.

'Don't you remember, my dear?' he gently reminded her. 'Signor Hansson wanted to see the work of Nathan's Trust; I thought I would go and ask Marco to get in touch with him.'

She smiled at him then, not pointing out that in this small locality the two men were

63

unlikely to avoid meeting each other. 'Your overcoat and hat then, please, Paolo,' she said instead. 'I expect Battistina's already told you that it's very cold out this morning.'

He agreed and went happily away to find the ancient bowler hat that he saw no reason to change for something a little more up-to-date. She thought it possible that he wouldn't find Marco in his office next door; as the Acheson Trust's administrator he was often out arguing with officials or inspecting property around the city. But Paolo knew Nathan's servants very well; they would take care of him and while he waited for Marco to return, Emilia knew exactly what he would do – go and inspect once more the transformation that had been wrought in a once-beautiful but sadly neglected palazzo. It still gave Paolo pleasure to remember his first accidental meeting there with Jessica, who'd been the magician in charge of the work, but there'd been nothing to tell him then that the graceful, gentle English girl who made him welcome was Llewellyn's natural daughter.

After a stormy start father and daughter had grown to value each other deeply, but the rest of the story had been less happy, Emilia remembered regretfully. Their own grandson had fallen in love with Jess, but she'd chosen a charming Frenchman called Jacques Duclos instead, and now, working with Marco on the Trust's properties meant that she still came back often to Venice, a constant reminder to Giancarlo of what he had lost. And

64

Emilia also knew that not even Llewellyn had yet been able to persuade Lorenza and Claudia to accept Jess as a sister. A combination of Welsh and Italian blood hadn't, understandably, produced Anglo-Saxon moderation in any of the Matthias children. But the odd thing was that she recognized Llewellyn more easily in Jessica than in his Italian children; it was the grey-eyed English daughter who shared the warmth and generosity of spirit that made him lovable. Paolo agreed with this, of course, but she'd never aired the opinion with her grandson. His view of their Welsh friend might have mellowed over the years but, to Emilia's lasting regret, the two men still didn't appreciate each other as they should.

She put the thought aside and got dressed instead but, ready to leave the room, went first to stand at one of the long windows overlooking what the Venetians simply called the Canalazzo – to foreigners the Grand Canal. It was always fascinating to watch its constant traffic, even on a late-January morning, but she shivered at the prospect of another bleak, grey day. Impossible now to imagine living anywhere else, but it took someone Venetian-born – which she was not – to love the city in winter and not lose hope of the return of spring.

She thought of Giancarlo, probably already out somewhere in the lagoon, inspecting the massive *murazzi* that, in theory at least, were supposed to keep Venice safe, or checking the state of the wooden *bricole* marking the deep-water channels between the myriad small islands and sand banks. Perhaps his pleasant Norwegian friend was with him. But then she remembered with a smile what Leif Hansson had said: he'd still be trudging methodically round Venice *sestiere* by *sestiere*, until he came to the Piazza of St Mark.

She turned away from the view at last as a tap came on the door. It was Battistina bringing the morning's mail, and pleased to announce that it contained an envelope with a foreign stamp – *inglese*, she thought, but the Signora Contessa would be able to tell. English it certainly was, Emilia agreed, since it pictured the head of Queen Elizabeth II.

Five minutes later, sitting at her desk, she was reading what the envelope had enclosed when her husband returned from his journey next door.

'Not really a necessary visit, my dear,' he said when she looked up at him. 'They already know about Mr Hansson's arrival at the *pensione*. But it's always a pleasure to talk to Marco. He'd just finished telephoning Jessica. Some ridiculous permit they'd been waiting for has finally been granted, and there's urgent work to do, so she'll be back very soon.'

Emilia picked up her letter and waved it at him. 'Someone else will be here too – Anna Lambertini – the daughter of my god-daughter, Gina,' she reminded him, seeing that he looked blank. 'She's been in London studying new techniques of picture restoration and now she has to put them into practice here. Where else? We must have more dilapidated paintings in Venice than anywhere else on earth.'

'Gina wants her to come here ... to stay?' Paolo asked faintly. 'Won't she want something more ... more lively?' Horror filled his face at the thought of the things Anna Lambertini was likely to want – strange music, noise, and food at odd times of the day – or, more probably, night. Emilia smiled and offered comfort.

'Gina was quite right to ask us to make her daughter welcome, but she will stay for a few days, then thank us – very prettily I expect – and suggest finding accommodation elsewhere!'

Looking more cheerful, Paolo agreed that a brief visit was, of course, unavoidable. Then, about to seek consolation in his library, Emilia's voice halted him at the door.

'You didn't finish telling me about Leif Hansson,' she reminded him.

'Oh, well, Marco is going to meet him, of course, but Llewellyn has also decided that he must be entertained at the *pensione*. There's to be a party as soon as Jessica arrives. I shan't mind going if she'll be there. Marco outgrew his revolutionary phase long ago, but I always imagine that Lorenza still regrets there's no Madame Guillotine left to chop off my poor old aristocratic head!'

His wife gave the little croak of laughter that

had first entranced him sixty ears before, but then she answered seriously. 'Don't blame her, Paolo. She fell in love with Giancarlo at the most painful adolescent stage. He probably didn't handle it very well and Lorenza mistook embarrassment for disdain; it was more bearable to pretend that she wasn't high enough in the social scale for a Rasini to notice that she was beautiful – which she undoubtedly was; much more so than Claudia. Shall we ever see her again, I wonder? Llewellyn especially still misses his youngest daughter.'

Aware of a new book awaiting him in his library, Paolo had no view to offer on the subject and, settling down to write to Gina Lambertini, Emilia allowed him to escape.

Cannaregio, in the north-west of the city – Leif's next area to explore – proved to be exactly where Marco suggested they should meet if the object was to visit a house that was being worked on. Faithful map in hand again, Leif duly arrived outside the church of the Madonna dell'Orto, and found waiting for him a man who had to be Llewellyn's son: he had the same stocky build, but with his mother's gentle smile. But there were none of his father's expansive gestures; he gave a brief handshake and *buon giorno* and then he led his guest towards a house bordering the *rio* of the same name as the church.

'I don't suppose you can imagine what it looked like six months ago – virtually a ruin.

In days gone by it would have been either left to fall to pieces or pulled down.'

Reluctant to say that perhaps a ruin was best pulled down, Leif said nothing at all, waiting for Marco to go on.

'It's taken a long time to wash out the salt that was destroying the brickwork, but it's finished now – which means that we shall have a sound, weatherproof building still here, looking as it did when it was originally built; no modern cement and mortar to jar with its surroundings. The changes are inside – four self-contained apartments that young people will be able to afford to buy, beautifully designed by my sister Jessica – half-sister, I should properly say. Perhaps you haven't discovered yet that ours is a rather complicated family!'

Leif's pleasant smile appeared. 'I was given a brief outline by Elizabeth Harrington in New York, the evening I met Claudia.'

The mention of his youngest sister made Marco's face look strangely grim for a moment, but he waved the subject of her away with a gesture that was reminiscent of Llewellyn, and suggested that they should inspect the inside of the house. Half an hour later, out in the cold air again, Leif congratulated his companion.

'It's marvellous work that you're doing – and if you can do it, so can other people, surely?'

Marco accepted the compliment calmly, and gave credit where he reckoned it was due.

'Other people must find another Nathan Acheson,' he pointed out. 'Someone not only with money to put at risk but with enough proper understanding of what Venice needs as well.' Then he glanced at his watch. 'Lunchtime. If you don't mind a pizzeria there's one in the *campo* round the next corner; the food is good and the wine is reliable.'

He was right on both counts, Leif decided ten minutes later, and the simple little restaurant suited his own tastes perfectly. There'd been time enough already to discover that more pretentious places usually offered dull food at extravagant prices. Marco grinned ruefully at him when he suggested this.

'It's an age-old Venetian custom, I'm afraid, performed with great skill – parting visitors from their money! No wonder the day-trippers who pour in during the summer bring their food with them.'

'And also no wonder most Venetians dislike them,' Leif commented. 'They contribute little or nothing, but do damage to the fabric of this very fragile city all the time.'

Marco nodded, again with the smile that made him look his real age – probably ten years younger, Leif reckoned, than he was himself.

'You sound like our esteemed Mayor – anti-tourist to the extent of commissioning posters deliberately calculated to put visitors off: tacky souvenir stalls, refuse-laden canals, even dead rats!' Sober again, he stared at his companion. 'You won't have had time to

70

discover it yet, but nothing's quite what it seems here. Every argument can be turned on its head, and God alone knows which one is right.'

He signalled for the bill, shook his head at Leif's attempt to pay, and stood up to leave. 'I must get back to work, and you've got more walking to do. Ciao, Leif, and *arrivederci*!'

With that he smiled and walked out, leaving Leif there to order more coffee while he sorted out his impressions of the morning: Fact 1: for better or for worse he wasn't going to be able to avoid getting to know the Matthias family. Fact 2: Marco revered the man he worked for and had learned to love his half-sister even if Llewellyn's other children had not. Fact 3: it might not be long before his own scientific impartiality deserted him and he became just as blindly opinionated as everyone else involved with this illusionist city. But for the moment he still had the *sestieri* of Castello and San Marco to explore, and he was determined to do that and take his first trip out into the lagoon before he reported for work on Monday.

He'd spent most of his evening hours so far poring over maps and charts that indicated islands scattered like small change over the surface of the water, some inhabited, many now deserted or never occupied at all. With reed-beds, shallows, and innumerable sandbanks, they all affected the twice-daily ebb and flow of the tides from the Adriatic into the lagoon, and from there into the network

71

of canals that made the existence of Venice possible. All this an oceanographer must become familiar with before he could be useful to Giancarlo and the Magistrato's other hardworking officials. But, Castello first, he thought, and then San Marco. He thanked the *padrona* for the delicious pizza, promised to return, and then stepped outside to find that the promised whiteness had finally arrived. As a rule he disliked snow in cities – it was meant to lie deeply on hillsides, serene and undisturbed – but here at least it covered up what he'd already seen too much of in Venice: rotting stone and brickwork, refuse floating on deserted canals, the whole worn-out sadness of a place that winter exposed too cruelly.

But the snow barely survived an overnight change of wind direction; the following day, with driving rain blotting out the view of San Giorgio Maggiore that he still remembered from Llewellyn's painting, Leif's first acquaintance with Piazza San Marco suggested that it was merely a continuation of the lagoon. Sirens had warned of another *acqua alta* in time for the wooden *passerelle* to be put up and for Venetians who had to go out of doors to don their wellingtons once again.

It was interesting, to say the least, to see the Campanile and the intricate façade of the Basilica strangely reflected in the water at their feet, but Leif was only too aware of the danger it represented. However much was done to strengthen defences, dredge canals, and raise pavement levels, the unavoidable truth was that rising sea levels threatened the very survival of the lagoon city.

He was anxious to start work with Giancarlo and his band of dedicated but constantly thwarted colleagues, knowing that it wasn't they who were responsible for all the years of futile argument that had taken the place of action. The blame should be put where it really lay, he thought: with the politicians of whatever shade, whose only shared principle seemed to be that if they did nothing at all, at least they couldn't be accused of having done anything wrong.

Leif splashed his way back to Pensione Accademia and hung up his clothes to dry. Another evening spent poring over maps of the lagoon was in store but then his room telephone rang. It was Llewellyn, inviting him to share a family supper. Jessica, his English daughter, had arrived for a very brief visit. It had stopped raining and Leif was required to put on his boots again at once to come and meet her.

Maria's drawing room seemed pleasantly full of people when Leif walked in. Some he already knew: Emilia Rasini, elegant in black, was deep in conversation with her host, and Maria smiled up at Giancarlo, but Marco stood with a couple Leif didn't know until he was introduced to the *pensione*'s elder daughter, Lorenza, and her husband, Filippo Adani. He, much nearer middle-age than his wife, looked touchingly proud of her, and Leif could see why: Lorenza was clearly the beauty of the family judging by her perfect features. His own opinion was that a little irregularity added more in interest than it took away from symmetry. Signora Adani might improve on acquaintance but he suspected that even as a younger, more impressionable man he wouldn't have been bowled over by her.

Still, he smiled and bowed correctly over her hand before being urged forward, by Llewellyn now, to meet the woman talking to Count Paolo. Here, obviously, was the eldest of his children – the English daughter whose existence had so troubled the Matthias family.

Not a beauty, Leif decided at first glance. She was slender to the point of thinness and, dressed with deliberate simplicity, seemed to refuse to stand out in a crowd. But there was no mistaking the pride in Llewellyn's face when he introduced her, nor the pleasure in the face of the gentle old man to whom she'd been talking.

'My father says you're here to work with Giancarlo,' she said in a low-pitched voice. 'He and his colleagues need all the help they can get if this wondrous place is to survive for another few hundred years.'

'It's certainly threatened,' Leif agreed, not commenting on the rest of what she'd said.

But she noted the omission and challenged it with unexpected directness.

'Only you aren't sure yet whether it's worth the effort of saving? You've seen too little sign of confidence in its future, too much dilapidation, too many closed churches full of slowly rotting treasures?'

'All of those things,' he said levelly, 'and something more worrying still – no one has yet got round to deciding what its future ought to be.'

There was a little silence, then Count Paolo joined in. 'Mr Hansson is right, my dear Jess. We prefer to hide from the truth, but a scientist coming fresh to Venice sees our problems more clearly.'

She smiled at her old friend, but spoke seriously again to Leif. 'You're both right, of course, and heaven knows some scientific detachment is needed. But it doesn't last very long – no one seems able to stay temperate about Venice; it must be hated or fallen in love with for ever.' Her grey eyes inspected Leif's face. 'We shall have to see which it is with you.'

He found himself wishing that she would smile at him as she'd done at Paolo Rasini, but he spoke gravely, as she had done. 'Remember I've only seen the "wondrous place" under snow or blinding rain so far; if the sun should ever reappear then scientific detachment might desert me too.'

She nodded, accepting the *amende honorable*, and then Llewellyn returned from refilling his guests' glasses.

'Jess love, there hasn't been time to tell you that Leif knows your grandmother. He saw her recently in New York, and Claudia as well, of course.'

Now Jessica's slow smile did reappear. 'At one of her mammoth Sunday evening parties, I suppose?' she suggested ruefully. 'No concession to advancing age for my magnificent Gran – she simply ignores it!'

'Still, at least Claudia's there to keep an eye on her.' Then Llewellyn added for his guest's benefit, 'With Elizabeth's help my little daughter has found her true *métier* in New York despite fierce local competition. America is rich because its people work hard. With rare exceptions like my children, that can't be said of Europeans – bone idle now, most of them, I'm afraid.'

Jessica looked solemnly at the other two men. 'My father would like to say something especially nasty about the work-shy French, but he remembers his Parisian son-in-law whom he actually likes very much!'

About to insist that family feeling had never yet curbed his tongue on any subject whatsoever, Llewellyn was interrupted by the arrival of his wife's housekeeper come to announce that the Signora's dinner was served.

At table, placed between Maria and her daughter, Leif asked about Filippo Adani's return to the rebuilt Fenice Theatre.

'Of course it took years longer than it should have done,' Lorenza replied, 'but

76

that's the way things are here.' It was stated as a fact, with an Italian's usual calm acceptance of incompetence and bribery at every level of governmental life. 'But at least we're now back in Venice. My husband hated working at La Scala – Milan is like being abroad to a Venetian; we are clannish people, Mr Hansson.'

She was warning him, Leif supposed, until he noticed her glance across the table at Jessica, intent on something her neighbour, Giancarlo, was saying.

'You had to welcome an English sister,' he risked saying with a pleasant smile.

'Half-sister,' she corrected him coolly. 'She lives in Paris. But she seems to enjoy coming here whenever she can. Jacques doesn't seem to mind too much; I'm afraid my husband wouldn't be so forbearing!' It was said with a smile that might have been meant to take the sting out of the words, but Leif understood the message he was meant to receive: for a reason he didn't understand, the English half-sister remained what she had always been to Lorenza, someone to hate.

It was a relief to turn to Maria and be given a smile that offered real kindness instead. He had only to mention his visit to the Trust house with Marco to launch her on a happy stream of reminiscence about her son, and when it was time to return to Lorenza again he firmly asked for information about the forthcoming opera production that Filippo was working on.

77

It wasn't until they were back in the drawing room, drinking coffee, that he found himself near Jessica again.

'Forgive me for not realizing it earlier,' he said, 'but I now remember why the name of Duclos is familiar. Your husband was responsible for the stunning photographic "Portrait of New York" some years ago.'

She nodded. 'There was one of Venice first, done while he was here recovering from an injury. Claudia worked with him on both of them, then stayed on in New York to make a career for herself there. Jacques now runs his father's film company in Paris but he still sometimes gets talked into visiting the world's unhappiest corners to make the rest of us see what's going on.'

Wanting to dispel the sudden sadness in her face, Leif abruptly changed tack. 'I've got one more day of idleness left – I thought I'd venture out on to the Lagoon tomorrow, see Murano, Burano and Torcello on my own. I'll be introduced to the rest of it by Giancarlo soon enough.'

'Leave plenty of time for Torcello,' she suggested quietly, 'and expect a struggle to hang on to scientific detachment there; once seen it's never forgotten. But wrap up – the cathedral will be perishingly cold!'

He smiled at that, suspecting that the combination of practicality and mysticism might be typical of her, but moved aside to let Marco talk to her instead about the work they planned to do together the following day

78

once she and Maria had made a pilgrimage to St Mark's. It was, he thought, a measure of their dedication to Nathan Acheson's dream that she would fly to Venice for a brief weekend, and then spend a Sunday with Marco planning how best to bring a ruined house to life.

With the evening at an end, he thanked Maria warmly for inviting him, but found Llewellyn still beside him as he walked to the door.

'I heard you mention Torcello to Jess. Is that a personal pilgrimage?' the Welshman asked. 'Or would you like a companion if he promised not to talk too much? I'm the only member of my household who doesn't seem to be busy at something tomorrow.'

His wide mouth smiled but Leif's sudden impression was of a man who tried too hard. Joviality, in company, at least, was a habit Llewellyn couldn't shake off, but the sadness of the clown lay underneath its bright surface.

'I've nothing against a companion who talks,' Leif heard himself say. 'I spend quite enough time on my own doing solitary work.'

A different grin transformed Llewellyn's face again. 'A boys' day out – what a lark! I'll pick you up at the Accademia – shall we say half past ten?'

Leif agreed and said goodnight, only certain as he picked his way back to the *pensione* through the puddles that a day spent in the company of the mercurial artist would be anything but dull and therefore not wasted.

79

Six

The expedition got off to a good start because for the first time since he'd arrived Leif stepped out into brightness; there might be no trace of warmth in the day as yet, but suddenly there was colour – and what colour! A duck-egg-blue sky, green canal, softly faded rose-red brick, and cream stone that seemed to absorb the light and gently reflect it back again. He watched Llewellyn walk towards him and smiled at the sight of his velvet-collared cape and wide-brimmed hat – no half measures about the Welshman; let the world recognize him for the artist he was.

He turned out to be an ideal companion – knowledgeable, humorous, perceptive and, best of all in Leif's opinion, everyone they met seemed to like him. He'd walk easily enough with captains and kings if any such appeared, but he was equally happy chatting to the *vaporetto*'s crew or the fishermen mending their nets on the quay at Burano.

There, because it was approaching midday, Leif asked him to suggest a *ristorante* where they could have lunch, but Llewellyn shook his head.

'We'll go on, if you can wait another ten

minutes. An old friend of mine on Torcello will offer us the best *fritto misto* you'll get outside of Harry's Bar – at a quarter of the price!'

Arriving at the neighbouring island, there seemed little to justify Torcello's reputation as an experience not to be missed. Leif knew its history – the first settlement in the lagoon fifteen hundred years earlier, and the beginning, therefore, of the mighty Venetian republic. But silt brought down by the rivers flowing into the lagoon had choked the waterways and reduced the island to a malarial ruin. All that seemed to remain were some neglected, swampy fields bordering a canal, and a few scattered houses. It was at one of these – clearly a kind of café in the summer season – that Llewellyn suddenly stopped.

'It's closed,' Leif pointed out with disappointment, aware that he was hungry.

'Closed, but not to us. Graziella knows we're coming and I can smell the fish cooking already.'

Llewellyn's knock on the door was scarcely needed before the door was opened by a small, smiling woman who greeted him with arms outstretched and a smacking kiss on both cheeks – someone else who liked him, Leif had time to observe before he was warmly welcomed himself, and urged to feel at home.

'*É buono, il fritto misto, cara?*' Llewellyn asked. '*Il mio amico qui è un straniere molto importante, capisci!'*

'*É buonissimo, Signor Davide – come sempre,*' she answered firmly, wagging a finger at him.

A table was already set for them in the friendly little room, with snowy tablecloth and napkins, and sparkling glasses. Leif smiled at them both. 'I don't care whether it's good or not – I like this place!'

'The food will be wonderful – it always is,' Llewellyn said. 'But today I've explained to Graziella that you're a very important visitor to Venice!'

He smiled as she came back into the room with a flagon of wine and a basket of freshly baked bread. '*Cinque minuti, signori,*' she promised, and bustled out again.

As good as her word she was back five minutes later with the *fritto misto*, cooked to perfection and assembled on the plates with the eye of an artist.

'It's a labour of love,' Leif exclaimed, looking at his share of the feast.

'Exactly that,' Llewellyn agreed, pleased with the Norwegian's proper understanding of what he was being offered.

Little was said while they concentrated on the food, but when coffee was on the table, accompanied by the small glasses of grappa Graziella insisted were necessary against the cold outside, Llewellyn suddenly began to talk.

'This is a special place for me – always has been, but more so now because it's where I met Jess for the first time. I'd been told of her

82

existence and the fact that she was coming to Venice, but she had no intention of getting in touch with me; didn't want to know me, which was understandable enough. But in my heart and very bones I knew that somehow, somewhere, we'd meet. Then I walked into Santa Maria Assunta one bitterly cold morning and there she was, reading Ruskin! I recognized at once that she belonged to me.'

He stopped speaking, but Leif didn't interrupt, wanting him to finish what he'd begun.

'You've met Jessica now ... can understand that the waste of not knowing about her for thirty years is a loss I can't make up. Maria and Marco have learned to love her, but my daughters will not – more waste that I can do nothing about.' He tossed back the last of his grappa and smiled at Leif, but there was heart-breaking sadness in his face. 'Life gives and it takes: who are we to expect more than that? Now, let's go to the cathedral before it gets too dark to see it properly.'

They said goodbye to Graziella and stepped out into the cold afternoon. The path led them to a small grassy space, once the island's piazza, Llewellyn explained.

'Ruskin called Torcello and Venice mother and daughter. Hard as it is to believe now, this is where the whole incredible story began. All that's left is what you see – Santa Fosca over there, beautiful but not what we're here for; and what's just in front of us – the oldest, most venerable building in the lagoon.'

He led the way into the austere emptiness

83

of the church, where the cold was intense enough to leave their breath visible on the air when they spoke. But Leif stood rooted by the stupendous mosaics that entirely covered the west wall – the story of the apotheosis of Christ and the Last Judgement, still being told in the pictures that medieval artists had created out of imagination and faith a thousand and more years earlier.

But there was something else as well. Llewellyn gestured to the opposite end of the church where, covering the entire roof of the apse and seeming to lean over them where they stood, was the overwhelming figure of the Madonna and Child, her black cowl and robe starkly severe against the mosaic's background of dim gold, and all the sorrows in the world written in her tear-stained face.

It was Llewellyn who finally spoke. 'Time to go, I think. The verger will be here soon to close up, and we're probably in danger of freezing to death.'

They walked back in silence to the quay, where a small knot of people waited for the *vaporetto*'s arrival. On board ten minutes later, in the comparative warmth of the boat's cabin, Leif finally found something to say.

'I'm glad I saw the church empty ... not noisy with summer visitors.' He hesitated for a moment. 'I upset your daughter last night; she reckoned I was too detached about Venice, seeing it as no more than an acutely difficult technical problem we might or might not be able to solve.'

Llewellyn's withdrawn expression changed to one of sudden interest. 'Did she suggest you should come to Torcello?'

'I said I was coming anyway, but she warned me that it might make a difference to scientific detachment that I wouldn't be able to undo. I don't know yet whether she was right, but at least I'm beginning to understand what would be lost if Venice went the way of Torcello.'

A blinding smile suddenly lit Llewellyn's face. 'Jess would say that will do to be going on with!' Then he tucked his arm in Leif's – a gesture the Norwegian knew he would have resented from any other man, but in Llewellyn he seemed to sense some need for comfort, that asked him not to move away, and so arms linked in friendly companionship, they rode the glistening surface of the water back to a now twilit city.

Jessica and Marco walked slowly home from Campo San Giacomo dell'Orio, work satisfactorily completed for the day. The rescue of a once-beautiful house could now be put in hand, and before the year was out it would be not only beautiful again but fit for several families to live in. It would mean that a dozen or so people could stay where they belonged instead of moving to the mainland. Marco saw the Trust's achievement mainly in those terms; for Jessica it represented beauty restored instead of being allowed to fall into ruin. But they laughed about their different

85

priorities, knowing that each perfectly complemented the other.

Back in the Rio della Fornace, they found the *pensione* empty, Llewellyn still not back from his outing with Leif Hansson, Maria taking tea, as she usually did on Sundays, with her brother and sister-in-law. What had been her office when she was the *pensione's padrona* had become Marco's special den, and he chose it now instead of the drawing room as the place to offer Jessica an *aperitivo*.

With the golden Prosecco poured, he smiled at her over the top of his glass. 'Thanks for coming, Jess – now we can get started on the house without any more delay.'

She stared at him for a moment, still marvelling that their first troubled acquaintance should have led to so deep and satisfying a relationship. In those early days Marco had been part of a rebel group protesting loudly against the very thing she'd come to Venice to do – transform a rundown palazzo for rich American clients. Now the rich American – Nathan Acheson – was his employer as well, and Marco no longer wanted to tear down anything that could be saved and put to use again.

She knew him very well now and suspected that more was on his mind than the building they'd spent the day discussing. Direct as usual, she spoke the question in her mind. 'Have you heard from Claudia since Jacques saw her in New York?'

Marco's black brows drew together in a

frown. 'I've spoken to her, but only because I telephoned her, knowing that Mamma waited every day for her to ring. We didn't want her to come rushing home – just to send her love, and say that she thought of us now and then.'

'What happened when you rang?' Jess asked.

'Well, I got angry of course – told her she was a selfish cow! Being Claudia she shouted back. I was *sciocco, imbecille* – and much more to that effect – if I didn't understand that Llewellyn and Mamma had decided she wasn't to be told, so how could she ring?' Marco's voice was full of sadness now. 'That was an excuse, I think. She's changed, Jess. The lovable, caring, maddening girl we knew is now a smart, successful New Yorker who might just consider paying us a visit when she can fit it into her busy schedule.'

'Shouldn't you blame me and Jacques for that?' Jess asked quietly. 'Between us we caused her great unhappiness.'

Marco waved that away. 'She couldn't have what she wanted six years ago – time to have grown up, I reckon.'

But Jess shook her head. 'There's something else as well. I used to think she didn't come home because there was a chance she might bump into me here. That's still a problem for her, one I understand, but she told Jacques that she'd never live in Venice again – for her it's a dying place, and Claudia is all for living.'

'Then she's stupid as well as selfish,' Marco

almost shouted. 'We aren't going to let our city die.' Then his voice grew quiet again. 'Enough of my little sister; we must manage without her. Has Llewellyn talked to you about the future?'

Jess nodded, remembering a little scene in the studio upstairs that still brought her close to tears. 'He wanted to show me what he was working on, in case he was no longer able to judge whether it was any good. I insisted he must finish it because it was beautiful – the lagoon at dusk, serene and magical. He said he'd call it *Approaching Night*.' Her voice broke on the words, but she cleared her throat and went on. 'I think it will be his last picture, my dear; it's a struggle already to be sure of the colours he's using.'

'What will he do?' Marco asked slowly.

'I've no idea ... "Rage against the dying of the light", I expect, being a good Welshman; then eat his heart out and make life very difficult for Maria and you!'

They sat in silence for a moment, then Marco abruptly changed tack again. 'I haven't told him or Mamma yet, but my Venezia Viva friends want me to stand for Mayor at the next election. No decision needed yet, thank God; I've got a month to decide.'

It was a fresh blow, Jess thought numbly, but one she might have expected. Ever since she'd known him Marco had been involved in the murky and sometimes dangerous waters of local politics. It was Nathan Acheson who'd steered his burning ambition to change the world into something achievable instead.

'I can see why your friends want you to,' she said at last. 'A competent man in charge is treasure enough; an honest, competent man is beyond price. But you'd have to give up your work with the Trust – is that really what you want?'

'I wouldn't give it up altogether – I couldn't; it means too much. If Nathan agreed, I might find someone to help.'

'Then you'd have no life of your own at all ... you have precious little now,' Jess pointed out, trying to smile. 'What your dear Mamma longs for is for you to marry, raise a family, and steer well clear of the sink of iniquity that she rightly believes the world of politics to be!' Then she added in a different tone of voice, 'Talk to Nathan, and ask Llewellyn's advice as well – it would please him to be consulted.'

Marco nodded, and poured more wine into her glass. 'How do you reckon the day with Leif Hansson has gone?'

'Total failure or complete success,' she answered. 'But failure's more likely, I think.

'So do I,' Marco agreed. 'It's not that I didn't like the Norwegian, but I doubt if he's come across Llewellyn's equal before; they won't have known what to make of each other.'

At which point the door opened and the man himself appeared – like a genie conjured out of a bottle, Jess thought, and the genie in question was quite capable of guessing what they'd just been saying.

'Ah, you're back already,' Llewellyn said blandly, 'and I'm just in time to join you in a glass of Prosecco.'

Jess glanced at Marco, but he simply smiled back; he would let her ask the question.

'Did you have a good day with Mr Hansson?' she ventured finally.

Llewellyn looked from one to the other. 'You're waiting to hear that either I tipped him overboard because he was such a bloody bore or he walked out on me!' He grinned at their expectant faces. 'No such thing – as it happened, we had a lovely time. Leif appreciated Graziella's *fritto misto* just as he should, and he paid the Madonna in the cathedral exactly the right tribute – complete and ravished silence.'

'Then he was a good companion,' Jess quietly agreed. 'Marco and I hadn't quite got the measure of Leif Hansson.'

'And what's more,' Llewelln went on, to rub salt into their wound, 'he's not only thinking about our problems here; he's beginning to feel them as well. The man has a heart, in addition to brains.'

Jess smiled ruefully at her father. 'You've made your point! Now, discomfited, I shall retire to the kitchen. Lucia has promised to teach me how to cook guinea fowl the Venetian way.'

She paused on the way to the door to kiss the top of Llewellyn's head, then left father and son alone together, hoping to have given Marco the chance to talk about his own alternative future.

Seven

The following morning Leif presented himself at the Magistrato's offices in San Polo. Giancarlo was already there, in a room whose walls were lined with maps and charts – large-scale replicas of what Leif had spent his evenings studying.

'Measured by size alone,' his host said wryly, 'the lagoon doesn't amount to much compared with the waters you normally survey; but measured by complexity, it's all the challenge we want!'

Before Leif could agree the desk telephone rang and Giancarlo moved to answer it. There was time to stand in front of the huge chart, locating names that were already familiar – San Giorgio Maggiore, of course, and San Michele – the city's cemetery. Then the islands he'd already visited, and half a dozen others that he knew were inhabited. It left dozens more that were empty of anything but bird life, innumerable sand banks, and areas that only the fishermen were allowed to use. All of them affected the coming and going of the tides on which the life of the fragile Serenissima depended. Add to this already complicated equation the effect of rising sea levels worldwide, and the problems that the city's watchdogs faced became an almost insoluble nightmare.

Giancarlo ended his call and waved a hand at the sea world outside the windows. 'Let's begin out there, shall we? Conditions are good today – little wind and excellent visibility – and we have to make the most of them when we can.' He glanced at what Leif had brought with him – sea boots, heavy waterproof jacket and ear-flapped cap – and nodded approvingly; there was obviously no need to worry about his guest as Leif was clearly a man who could look after himself, praise be.

He was also, it appeared as the day wore on, an experienced boat handler who was as familiar as Giancarlo himself and their pilot with the demands of a water-governed existence. They identified for him the islands he didn't recognize – the peaceful, bird-haunted sanctuary of the Franciscan monks on San Francesco del Deserto; Sant' Erasmo, Venice's kitchen garden; San Servolo, now a university; and San Lazzaro, famous for its Armenian monks and their precious library.

'The outlying islands,' Giancarlo explained, 'were where the Republic sent its unwanted citizens – the lepers, the mad, the fallen women. Venice is still full of churches, but when they were being built I'm afraid piety didn't go hand in hand with Christian compassion.'

'Did it anywhere then?' Leif suggested. 'Does it now?' But he decided not to confess his own conviction that the richer and more elaborate the church, the harder it was likely to be to find Christ's message within it.

By the time they moored alongside the quay at Pellestrina it was long past midday. Sheltered from the icy breeze, they ate the ham rolls the pilot produced from his locker, and gratefully drank hot coffee from a thermos. Inevitably the conversation turned to the endlessly debated question: how was Venice to be protected from another abnormal combination of tide, wind and rain like the one that had nearly proved catastrophic in 1966? The weathered face of Giovanni, the pilot, expressed all the frustration he couldn't put into English words. He despised as *sciocci* those who couldn't – wouldn't – see what their bitter opposition to MOSE, the barrage scheme for the lagoon, had meant for Venice.

Giancarlo smiled at the older man. 'It meant too much delay, I'm afraid, and the scheme will now have to take account of what we think we know is happening to sea levels, and what Signor Hansson here probably does know.'

'You almost make it sound hopeless,' Leif suggested, irritated by what seemed to be a calmly aristocratic acceptance of defeat. But he was startled by a sudden flash of anger in Giancarlo's dark eyes.

'Of course it's not hopeless. The barrage will be built, and all the time we're making improvements that we get very little credit for. Venice is no longer sinking because mainland industries are now forbidden to take water out of the lagoon bed; pollution isn't the problem it was – changing from oil to methane gas for heating has seen to that; we continually dredge the lagoon and the canals, deal with sewage, raise pavement levels, strengthen the sea walls; and we send the oil-tankers for Marghera through a special deep-water channel instead of the Giudecca Canal. Does this suggest that we fold our hands and do nothing?'

Leif was silenced for a moment by anger that he knew was real and justified. 'Forgive me,' he apologized. 'My argument should be with the politicians who frustrate you at every turn and do nothing but talk and horse-trade. I know your politicians are bad, but I don't suppose they're worse than anyone else's.'

Giancarlo's smile forgave him another error. 'Any Italian will tell you that they are – much worse! Now, we've finished the coffee, I'm afraid – it's time to move on.'

Warned now to be more careful, Leif said very little on the journey back to Venice. He looked about him instead at the extraordinary seascape through which they travelled – it was a haunting, mysterious place, this lagoon, and he could easily imagine that people born to it would never be able to live anywhere else. At last, with the Bacino in sight again, he said as much to Giancarlo, and saw the Italian nod.

'It's a harsh environment for those who live here, but uproot them and they miss the ghosts and the beauty!'

Back where'd they started, Leif offered the customary farewell handshake to Giovanni, and then to his host who suddenly looked apologetic.

'I'd ask you to share the supper Battistina insists on preparing for me but I'm summoned downstairs this evening. My grandmother has a new house guest – the daughter of her god-daughter who has some work to do in Venice. Donna Emilia hopes that I shall at least be able to understand what the girl says; my grandfather, she fears, will only look at her in silent wonder!'

Leif grinned at the thought, wished him an interesting evening, and then walked back to the Pensione Accademia, aware of a change in the early-evening atmosphere: Carnival was about to begin. Shops had been crammed for days with elaborate fancy dress, and masks that ranged from the grotesque to the exquisite. Coming towards him now was a figure – male or female, he couldn't tell – already wearing the traditional white mask, black gown and tricorne hat. Despite a well-earned reputation for keeping at least one eye firmly fixed on the main chance, there remained in Venetians, it seemed, this almost childlike delight in fantasy and dressing-up – yet another aspect of this hallucinatory place in which nothing was ever quite what it seemed. Even the reticent and self-controlled Giancarlo had let his guard slip in that passionate outburst on the boat earlier in the day. Leif reminded himself that he was among a race of people more wily, more sophisticated, and probably more interesting than he was used to, and he must proceed with care if he was to prove Elizabeth Harrington wrong and leave the sea-witch city unscathed.

Thanks to Battistina at the palazzo and Lucia in the *pensione*, there was an almost daily exchange of news between them, with the balance of information normally in Lucia's favour – more seemed to go on in the Matthiases' *pensione* than Battistina could lay claim to at the Palazzo Rasini. This morning, though, she had something to tell, and she was eager to track down her friend, certain to be found shopping as usual in Campo San Vio.

Since they were also related by marriage – Giovanni, Lucia's husband, being cousin to Battistina – there were family enquiries to be made first, but with these out of the way the serious business of the morning could start. A young woman had come from London to stay at the palazzo. She had some connection with the Signora Contessa that Battistina didn't properly understand but, judging by the quantity of luggage Beppe next door had kindly helped them with, she was there for a long visit.

'Young, you said – very modern, I suppose,' Lucia suggested, alerted by the mention of Londra, which everybody knew to be a violent, sinful, though doubtless very exciting city.

'Young and modern,' Battistina agreed, remembering the signorina's long straight hair and a skirt so short that it hovered, in her opinion, on the very edge of indecency. 'Still,' she continued, determined to be fair, 'she was very polite to Donna Emilia, and she had a nice smile for *il Conte* as well.'

'I dare say she smiled at Count Paolo's handsome grandson too, but she'll soon learn not to waste her time there, poor girl,' Lucia said pityingly.

It was an argument they'd been unable to settle for years: the *pensione*'s housekeeper convinced that a man who'd let Lorenza's beauty go unnoticed was beyond redemption, matrimonially speaking; Battistina clinging to the hope that a wife might still be found for the last of the Rasinis before it was too late.

'Signorina Anna is here to work, cleaning up old pictures,' she said severely, 'not to find herself a husband. But I'll say this, Lucia – it was lovely to hear someone laughing in the palazzo this morning – and Donna Emilia, too – trying to explain that leather boots with heels like stilts might do for London, but they wouldn't keep out the *acqua alta* here.'

Lucia agreed – laughter and rubber boots were both undoubtedly needed for daily life in Venice. Harmony restored, they parted as if it might be years before they met again, Lucia to turn off towards the entrance to the *pensione*, Battistina still with the bridge to cross over the *rio* before she could get home.

She climbed the steps but then, as she quite often did, set down her basket to lean against the parapet and watch what was going on down below. No surprises there; she knew everyone along the canal, recognized the postman fastening letters to the end of a string so that Maricri Fiocca could pull them up to her top-storey apartment; saw, as she expected, a barge stacked with crates making for Enrico's *trattoria* at the far end of the *rio*, and the rubbish barge working its way down towards the Canalazzo. Other places, she knew, didn't live like this, but it was how Venetians lived, and always would do, no matter what nonsense people talked about their city being threatened by this or that or the other disaster. Giancarlo and his helpers were there to keep them safe – and she had no doubt that they would do so.

But with Giancarlo now in her mind, she remembered what she hadn't said to her friend just now. He'd been engaged long ago to a French girl who was killed just before their wedding, which Lucia would probably have forgotten about by now. What she didn't ever know was that he later fell in love with Signor Llewellyn's English daughter, Jessica, when she first came to Venice. Battistina couldn't understand, even now, how the signorina she'd so thoroughly approved of could have chosen someone else in the end; but so it had turned out, and there had been no one since then to boast of to Lucia and make Donna Emilia happy. Their new young guest might have a winning smile and long, long legs, but more was needed than that, Battistina thought sadly, and she had little hope of Anna Lambertini.

It was time to be going home. She picked up her basket, descended the steps on the far side of the water and was nearly back at the side entrance to the palazzo when she was approached by someone else who must be greeted and talked to.

Bianca Bruni and her husband, Beppe, were employed by Nathan Acheson to look after the palazzo next door – better still, they'd been given a flat there to live in, and it meant that Bianca could look her neighbours in the eye again. Marriage with her feckless Neapolitan had survived, despite Beppe's numerous escapades, but now respectability had been achieved and Bianca daily gave thanks to the Blessed Virgin Mary for sending them Signor Acheson.

This morning Bianca also had news to share. Instead of waiting until Easter as usual, her *cari signori Americani* were due to arrive any day. She must begin at once to clean and polish rooms that Battistina knew she never kept in anything less than perfect order, and even now Beppe was at work, planting up the courtyard urns with plants that he expected to burst into bloom overnight.

Glad to have been the giver of good news, Bianca hurried on her way. Battistina went more slowly back to the palazzo, disappointed when she arrived to find Donna Emilia already explaining to her husband the gist of a telephone conversation with Elvira Acheson.

'Nathan has been ordered to rest ... too much work and too many people clamouring for his advice; the poor man is worn out, Elvira says.'

'And he would rather rest here than anywhere else, dear, sensible man that he is,' Paolo Rasini commented with pleasure. 'How nice it will be, my dear, to have our neighbours back again, and to have those lovely rooms being lived in again.'

Emilia smiled, remembering his first bemused acquaintance with Nathan's wife ... his second wife, they'd later discovered. Elvira – his secretary for some years before they'd married – had arrived in Venice first, while Jessica and her team of craftsmen were putting the finishing touches to the rebirth of the palazzo. She hadn't shared, or even understood, her husband's devotion to a city she reckoned had no right to exist at all, and it had taken years of staying there with Nathan afterwards to overcome her fear of being so closely surrounded by water.

In all that time, as far as Emilia knew, Elvira and Paolo had continued to mystify each other, he with exquisite politeness, she with a very kind smile in return. But a conversation with Nathan was a pleasure to look forward to, and Paolo now headed happily towards his library in the expectation of it. There was probably some reference he needed to check, Emelia thought – no doubt a piece of the Serenissima's fifteenth-century financial skullduggery that might have escaped the scholarly American's attention.

It was Marco who took the news of the Achesons' arrival back to the *pensione* that evening, causing Llewellyn to announce happily at the supper table that it never rained but it poured visitors, what with their new Norwegian friend and Emilia's young guest already there, and now Elvira and Nathan expected back. He would certainly want to see Jess, so they must persuade her to return soon, and bring Jacques with her this time.

'Amore,' Maria gently reminded her husband before he could remember that Carnival gave him all the excuse he needed for party, 'Nathan has been unwell. Perhaps he needs quiet and rest, not merry-making.'

'Quiet and rest are for when Nathan's in his grave,' Llewellyn pointed out. 'What the poor man needs is a change from always talking about money with dreary bankers and international economists and shyster heads of state! He needs civilized conversation, and good food and wine shared with people like us.'

She smiled as she always did when Llewellyn wanted her to, and simply said it was time to make sure Lucia was going to serve the fettucine with truffles just as she'd been taught to. Left alone with his father, Marco refilled their wine glasses, wondering how to phrase what he wanted to say; but it was Llewellyn who spoke first, more diffidently than usual.

'Good thing Nathan's coming back early – you need to talk to him about this election business. Be guided by him, please, Marco – he'll give you good, unselfish advice. And don't for God's sake think you can't refuse because that would be letting down your friends. It's the kind of emotional blackmail they're bound to use, and it gets idealists like you into endless trouble.'

Marco smiled, but shook his head. 'I'm thirty-two, Papa, not the infant rebel who got talked into protest marches and painting rude words on walls! In any case we've little chance of winning given the competition I'd be up against. But that isn't to say we shouldn't still try – people are sick to their hearts of chicanery in high places.' He took a sip of wine, then gently broached the other matter on his mind. 'Will you speak to Nathan about yourself while he's here?'

Llewellyn's answer came at once, firm and final. 'Certainly not, and nor are you to discuss me with him. I won't be pitied, and I don't yet need help. Anyway, you know as well as I do – Elvira's always in touch with Elizabeth Harrington. If she gets to hear about me, Claudia will too.'

'You're quite sure about not telling her?' Marco ventured, not looking at his father.

'Of course I'm sure – you know what our bossy little girl is like; she'd be over here in a brace of shakes, convinced that we can't manage without her. I'm not having that; she must stay where she is and get on with her own life.'

Marco stared fixedly at his wine, aware that he wasn't nearly practised enough in the gentle art of not telling the truth. Llewellyn was quicker than most at guessing what he was not supposed to know, but somehow they must sustain the lie that Claudia hadn't been told, because the truth would break his heart. He was saved by the door opening and the fragrance of truffles wafting in, seductive enough to divert his father's attention to the dish Maria was carrying into the room.

After the most unsettling two weeks he could remember, Leif reckoned that he was beginning to get the hang of life in Venice. It was no longer strange to walk outside knowing that locomotion meant a boat-ride or his own two feet. Like any true Venetian, he'd learned not to sit down on the *traghetti*, but to make the public gondola crossing of the Grand Canal standing up. And when the hour of midnight boomed out over the sleeping city he knew what he was listening to – the great bell of St Mark's Basilica. He'd crossed enough refuse-laden canals, seen enough decaying, scabrous buildings and flooded alleys to understand how fragile was the Serenissima's hold on life, but he'd fallen in love with her nonetheless. Fixed by the tides – *'sei ore la cala, sei ore la cresse'* – the rhythm of each day was more gentle here; the lagoon light was like no other he'd ever known, and there still remained the unquenched vitality and colour to be found in every small *campo* around which Venetians still lived.

He put this into words one evening when he was in Giancarlo's flat on the top floor of the Palazzo Rasini, eating the supper that Battistina had brought up to them – *fegato alla veneziana* she called it proudly. Leif pointed to the glistening, golden wedge on his plate, accompaniment to the delicious liver and onions, and smiled broadly at his companion.

'I'm even getting to enjoy polenta – there's devotion for you!'

'There's no escape from it here,' Giancarlo agreed ruefully, 'but I grant you it's an acquired taste.'

Leif speared another chunk, but instead of eating it laid down his fork and spoke more seriously. 'Jessica Duclos was right – she warned me that detachment wouldn't last. But as affection grows, so does anxiety.'

'You can't escape that either here, I'm afraid,' his host admitted. 'The more you learn about our situation, the more precarious it must seem, and the more incredible it becomes that sheer necessity alone doesn't stop us arguing endlessly about what ought to be done.'

'The dead hand of bureaucracy – local, regional, national – is bad enough,' Leif suggested, 'but for every reasonable line of action there seems to be a perfectly valid counter argument. Take the deep-water channel at Malamocco: certainly it keeps oil tankers out of the heart of Venice, but opponents rightly point out that it brings ocean currents in faster and more unpredictably elsewhere.'

He stopped talking, suddenly aware of the tired face of the man opposite him who'd spent his working life grappling with the problems of the lagoon. 'Sorry,' he said quickly. 'Some guest I turn out to be. There's an English saying, I think, about teaching one's grandmother to suck eggs!'

'There's an English saying for almost everything, according to my grandfather,' Giancarlo said with his rare, charming smile. 'Don't apologize for being kind enough to find our difficulties engrossing. But you must enjoy being in Venice as well, not think about our problems all the time.' He hesitated for a moment, then unexpectedly reverted to something else Leif had said. 'My grandparents hoped Jessica would stay here once she'd discovered the city. She seemed to belong so ... so perfectly. It was a grief to them when marriage to Jacques Duclos took her to Paris to live instead.'

There was nothing in the quiet words to tell him so but Leif felt suddenly sure that the grief had been shared by their grandson. And he saw in his mind's eye Lorenza Adani at the *pensione* dinner table, staring fixedly at Jessica. There'd been Claudia Matthias, too, in New York, suggesting – quite wrongly, it seemed – that *pensione* and palazzo inmates didn't meet on the same social level. So which of the two sisters hated Jessica Duclos because Giancarlo had loved her instead of one of them?

The silence in the room grew too long, and Leif hurriedly found something else to say. 'How is Count Paolo getting on with your grandmother's guest, by the way?'

The question dragged Giancarlo back from whatever memory his mind lingered on, and amusement brought his face to life again. 'Much to her surprise, I think, the visit is going rather well and, instead of being in a hurry to move out, Anna seems to like being here. She's discovering, apparently for the first time, that elderly people can be interesting, and my grandfather rightly took that as the compliment she intended when she told him so!' He stared at his guest for a moment, aware that Leif never talked about himself at all. 'Are you part of a large family, without any difficult generation gaps?'

'Scarcely – my widowed mother lives in Oslo, but I've no brothers or sisters, and since my job doesn't fit a settled married life, I've stayed single. I may regret that later on, when I'm too old to do anything about it.' He looked round the shabby, comfortable room that could only have belonged to a man living on his own. 'It becomes a habit, doesn't it –

being alone?'

Giancarlo nodded. 'It even comes to seem natural, which of course it isn't.' But his thin hand brushed aside a confession that might have given too much away to the perceptive man watching him. 'Have you been to our beautiful new Fenice yet? There's a Mozart season on at the moment, highly regarded even though his music isn't what Italian audiences mostly go to enjoy. I think you met the theatre's stage director, Filippo Adani – he's David Matthias's son-in-law.'

Leif nodded at the reminder. 'I haven't heard him called that before – even his children just refer to him as "Llewellyn".'

'It's how he always signs his paintings too, but it took me a long time to use the name. The truth is that I disapproved of him and he quite rightly found me a humourless prig!'

'Am I going to be told why?' Leif asked candidly. 'There must have been a reason.'

'Oh, there was. For years he and my grandmother collaborated – at his instigation – in a scheme I found mildly fraudulent and they simply found funny. Groups of tourists would be brought to the palazzo for tea with Countess Rasini; there they'd just happen to see the painter hard at work in another room. They would clamour to buy, of course, and Llewellyn would make my grandparents take the proceeds – a contribution towards the hideous cost of keeping the palazzo roof over our heads! But the "views" he churned out then blinded me to the artist that he really is.'

That shed some light on all the people concerned, Leif thought, and he found himself enjoying the image in his mind's eye of the serenely elegant Donna Emilia entertaining her guests while Llewellyn conned them into parting with their money. Well, it was a time-honoured Venetian custom, and no doubt the 'views' they took home had been charming. But suspecting that it might still be a faintly sore subject with the stiff-necked aristocrat sitting opposite him, Leif spoke of something else.

'The day we went to Torcello together I sensed some sadness in Llewellyn,' he said slowly, 'even though he told me what the place meant to him. Perhaps it was because of the rift between his Italian daughters and Jessica Duclos ... Or can an artist not help yearning for the masterpiece he may never paint?'

'Both things, I expect, and others besides – he's a complicated man in ways a Venetian probably can't understand. But he's blessed in his wife. According to my grandmother, the Welsh lion has been tamed into submission entirely by love!'

Leif suspected that the lion might occasionally still roar if provoked enough, but he spoke instead of the girl Llewellyn reminded him of. 'I only met Claudia Matthias briefly in New York but I'd say she takes after Llewellyn, not Maria. She put me in my place very briskly!'

'They were very close, she and Llewellyn.

Lorenza always wanted a more conventional father, I think, so it's rather sad that she's the one who's here, while Claudia never comes home. Families are a mixed blessing, it seems, and a sometimes unwelcome fact of Venetian life is that everyone knows what is going on; there's no such thing as big-city anonymity here.'

'Another warning,' Leif said with a smile. 'I've collected quite a few of them.' But Giancarlo's old long-case clock striking eleven made him realize that it was time to leave, instead of lingering to ask what else it would be safer to know about life as it was lived along the *rio*.

Escorted downstairs as far as the palazzo's courtyard gate, he thanked his host and, by extension, Battistina, and then set out on the walk back to the Pensione Accademia. The day's rain had cleared, leaving the night fine and starlit, and as usual he marvelled at the night-time quietness of a city where the only sounds were the slap of water against stone as the incoming tide seeped into the canal, and two church clocks in the neighbourhood insisting, not quite in unison, that it was still only just eleven. There was something else to think about as well – his arrival at Marco Polo airport and the guarded welcome of a man he'd thought he'd never learn to like. He'd been wrong about that, and no doubt there would be no end to the mistakes he was likely to make in this deceptive, sea-witch city.

Eight

Marco knew that everything was ready for the Achesons' arrival: the palazzo lay in perfect, shining order, and Giorgio, Nathan's lagoon boatman whenever he came to Venice, had just set off for Marco Polo, with Beppe in attendance to help with the luggage and to assure his *cara* Signora that *il sole* had only been waiting for her to return to the lagoon; no more rain and *acqua alta* now.

The thought of their likely conversation made Marco grin, carried on as he knew it would be in Elvira's shaky Italian and the Venetian dialect Beppe had acquired over the years grafted on to an undying Neapolitan accent. But, however linguistically challenged they might be, they understood one another – the man whose post-war Naples childhood had only taught him how to survive and the Bronx working girl whose marriage to a rich and powerful financier had transformed her life. What they shared, Marco knew, was complete devotion to Nathan Acheson, the most unassuming and private man who ever told the high and mighty what they ought to do.

It would be an hour or so before Giorgio threaded his way through the lunchtime

110

traffic on the canal and brought the launch back to the palazzo's side entrance. There was time to walk about the house again, checking that all was well.

A marble staircase led up from the mezzanine where the Trust's offices now lay to the *piano nobile*, the heart of the palazzo. It was here in the great *portego* that Jessica had created a room of the utmost beauty, its colours as delicate and subtle as the lagoon itself. The beautiful double doors stood wide open, and Marco expected to see diligent Bianca there, making sure that no speck of dust had fallen on any shining surface since she had last looked. But it was an unknown girl who stood at a table between the tall windows overlooking the canal – a florist, Marco assumed, let in by the housekeeper – who was arranging bowls of cream-coloured narcissus that had already begun to scent the air.

'*Buon giorno,*' he said, slightly surprised that Bianca should have left her there alone.

'You must be Marco Matthias,' she answered unexpectedly in English. 'Donna Emilia said I might bump into you here.'

This was no florist, he realized now, registering not only her voice but her clothes – a soft sweater that was fashionably over-large for her slight figure, brief tartan kilt, and expensive Gucci shoes. A rather beaky nose and decided chin ruled out conventional prettiness, but he doubted if that bothered her; she had the confident poise of a girl who never lacked admirers wherever she went. He struggled to remember a name he'd heard mentioned, because now he thought he knew who she was.

'Anna ... Anna Lambertini, I'm guessing – staying at the Palazzo Rasini,' he suggested, holding out his hand. 'I expect Bianca let you in.'

The girl gestured to the flowers. 'I was instructed to bring these for Signora Acheson ... Donna Emilia wanted them here to welcome her.' Then she glanced slowly round the room. 'It's not what I expected at all, I must say.'

Assuming it to be not what she liked either, he interrupted before she could go on and probably say so. 'Designed by my sister, Jessica Duclos. We and the owners think it's very beautiful. They haven't lived here for five hundred years, so for them time-worn furniture and dim family portraits weren't an option.' He spoke more crisply than he meant to, irritated by what had sounded like criticism in her voice, but that didn't seem to worry her either.

'Myself, I rather enjoy things that are time-worn and dim, but I can see that if they're not part of your family history there's no point in pretending that it's Great-Uncle George in Hussar uniform hanging on the wall, or Great-grandmama Euphemia in crinoline and pearls!'

Marco thought she spoke with the certainty of someone whose family walls were decked with just such bloody portraits; she was altogether the sort of girl he liked least. Over-privileged and over-indulged, they came like starlings every summer to stay at the Cipriani or the Danieli with the sort of equally obnoxious young men who raced about in high-powered boats, oblivious to anything but themselves.

'I'm sure Mrs Acheson will enjoy the flowers,' he said stiffly. 'If you've finished here, Bianca will come and clear up the mess'

But now this annoying creature was shaking her head. 'Weren't you always taught to clear up your own mess? I was; but perhaps it was different for boys – nothing too menial or humdrum for them!'

She was laughing at him, but he realized it just in time to prevent himself answering in kind. Instead, he managed to smile and speak in a friendlier tone of voice. 'I think I heard that you're here to help with restoration work on damaged paintings – it sounds like a job for life.'

'Given the neglect they've suffered, yes, it is,' she agreed with sudden sharpness. 'But unless the buildings they go back to can be made weather- and pollution-proof, the rescue operation will be a complete waste of time and money. You'd think that would be simple enough to be understood by the idiots in charge here.'

She had all the faults of her kind, he thought, and hadn't missed a single one. Opinionated, firmly convinced that hers was the only point of view worth considering, and with priorities very different from his own.

'The "idiots",' he suggested as quietly as he could, 'have other things to worry about than old paintings, of which Venice has far more than her fair share.'

'I know about the problems ... who doesn't?' She dismissed them with a careless wave of her hand. 'But if all the treasures rot into little pieces who will want to come to Venice then? Doesn't it survive on its visitors?'

'Its visitors are helping to kill it – can't you understand that?' Despite himself, he'd shouted at her and he feared it was exactly what she'd wanted. He took a deep breath and tried to sound the rational, unemotional man he knew himself to be. 'Perhaps you've not been here in the summer months – haven't tried to make your way across a *piazza* or get on a water bus, or buy some small necessity of life that can't be found any more because the shops are all selling tourist trash instead.'

She stared at him for a moment, taken aback by the depth of feeling she'd unsuspectingly stirred up. What had Donna Emilia said about him? Mixed parentage, Venetian and Welsh – perhaps that accounted for something unpredictable in a man who looked Italian, but perhaps wasn't quite what he seemed.

'I do see the problem,' she was kind enough to admit, 'but I don't quite understand how Venetians can hope to go on living here if they turn up their noses at the visitors who provide their bread and butter.'

That was at least one of their problems in a nutshell, and he would have had the grace to admit it if she hadn't sounded so much like a school teacher instructing a half-witted child.

'We could stay here arguing all day and still not agree,' he said instead. 'More useful perhaps if we both got on with what we have to do.'

'Me saving paintings you don't want, you shoring up another decrepit building – I think that's what Donna Emilia said you do.' She smiled at him and waved the bundle of flower-wrapping paper and string in her hand. 'See – not a scrap of mess for Bianca to clear up!' Then she walked past him to the door, tartan kilt swinging, and he caught a faint scent of her perfume on the air. The provocation was deliberate, he felt sure; she wanted him to be aware of her.

His voice halted her at the door and made her turn round to look at him. 'If you really want to know about Venice, the man you should talk to is Giancarlo Rasini – I assume your paths cross from time to time in the palazzo.'

'Frequently ... I make sure they do!'

Another sweet smile and this time she was gone, leaving him to reflect that it had been about the least friendly opening conversation with a girl that he could ever remember. He could still recall meeting Jessica for the first time; that had been fraught with emotion too, but there had been none of the teasing

115

challenge that Anna Lambertini had offered just now. He wondered for a moment how Giancarlo coped with her, and then decided that under the benign eye of Count Paolo and Donna Emilia's more critical one she probably behaved more sedately.

There was time to return to the floor below and have the first of the day's tussles with bureaucracy before Giorgio brought the Achesons home to the palazzo. It wasn't the word Elvira would have used even now, he knew – she remained the New Yorker she'd been born. Still Marco had no doubt that Nathan Acheson understood what he was returning to: the home Jess had created for him. That was the certainty that allowed the three of them to work together so happily. But back in his office, Marco didn't immediately begin to work; the 'idiots' in the Commune, as Anna Lambertini would surely call them, could wait while he sorted through the worries in his mind. There were secrets to be hidden: no talk of Claudia to Llewellyn, or talk of him to Nathan or anyone else. But his own future had to be discussed with his employer, and last but not least, there was anxiety about Nathan himself. Was he simply overworked and tired, or did something more than that ail the man they all depended on in different ways?

Jolted out of these thoughts by a tap on the door, Marco's frown faded at the sight of Bianca with the tray of coffee she insisted on bringing down to him when he was

116

working there.

'The rain has stopped, Signor Marco. Beppe promised it would for the Signora Acheson,' she announced proudly.

'And Beppe's never wrong,' he agreed, smiling at her. It was doubtful that her husband's information network extended quite as far as the weather from on high, but the fact remained that, with his Neapolitan ear close to the ground, the palazzo's general factotum had an uncanny grasp of everything that was going on.

'I think everything is ready except the new shrubs Beppe planted – they aren't quite blooming yet,' said Bianca, anxious they shouldn't avoid the blame for anything that might be thought their fault.

'They'll bloom in their own good time,' Marco pointed out. 'Meanwhile there are lovely flowers waiting for the signora in her drawing room.'

The housekeeper's worried face relaxed into a smile. 'Sent by Contessa Rasini,' she explained in the slightly hushed voice she used when referring to their neighbours; it was still hard to believe that she and Beppe now lived among such exalted company. 'A very pleasant young lady brought them, and even took the trouble to arrange them herself.'

'I know – I met her,' Marco admitted. 'She's staying with Donna Emilia at the moment.' It was as much as he was prepared to say, so he busied himself instead pouring the coffee

Bianca had delivered. Then his telephone rang and she very properly went away.

Ten minutes later he went out into the courtyard garden where Beppe's planted pots and urns did indeed show only greenery. In the early days of his employment at the palazzo the Neapolitan would have embellished them with plastic flowers, if need be, or stolen real blooms from whichever neighbour's garden happened to have them, but over the intervening years Elvira had taught her handyman how he must behave and Nathan could now more or less confidently hope that anything found on the premises did belong to them.

Marco was still enjoying that thought when, through the iron gate, he saw Giorgio's launch pull up outside. Already Beppe was on the pathway with the mooring-rope and by the time he got there, the Achesons were standing on terra firma again, where Elvira certainly preferred to be.

She smiled as he went forward to stoop and kiss her on both cheeks. Fifty now to her husband's sixty-eight, she was a small, neat woman with small, neat features that didn't seem to alter with age. As usual she was elegantly dressed, but Nathan's great wealth had never gone to her head, and Marco had heard her bargaining in the Rialto markets with a shrewdness no true-born Venetian housewife would have been ashamed of. Nathan himself certainly looked bone-tired but his smile was as kind as ever for a young

118

man he greatly valued.

'Ciao, Marco, it's good to be back,' he said. 'What sort of winter have you had?'

'An occasional fine day but mostly cold wind and a lot of rain, even a little snow! My father will be pleased to explain that it's the result of global warming. The so-called experts, he says, are just like politicians – either fools or liars!'

'Should I remind him that I'm supposed to be some sort of expert myself?' Nathan enquired, tongue in cheek.

'Please do; it will take the wind out of his sails. Mamma says you're to ignore any suggestion he makes for throwing a party – he won't believe that you might prefer just to rest.'

Elvira, walking ahead of them, overheard this and turned round. 'Of course he's got to rest – bronchitis nearly turned to pneumonia, and Nathan's been very ill, Marco, so no parties, and no Trust business either. An old house or two will just have to be allowed to fall down for the time being.'

'Then as soon as I've seen you upstairs I'll take myself off to Cannaregio,' he promised. 'No business discussion until you give permission.'

'Before Elvira hustles you away, am I allowed to ask if all is well at the *pensione*?' Nathan asked casually. 'It sounds as if Llewellyn at least is his usual self.'

Unprepared for the question, it took Marco a moment to frame the necessary lie. 'Things are as normal as they ever are when he's around. And your neighbours next door are well, though not quite as usual. Donna Emilia has a young guest staying with her – working on damaged pictures at San Gregorio – and Giancarlo is collaborating with a Norwegian oceanographer called Leif Hansson, a nice man everybody seems to like. By a strange coincidence he knows Jessica's grandmother in New York.'

Nathan nodded. 'Elizabeth Harrington mentioned him to me just before we left; she'd seen Jessica's husband too, she said.'

Again wrong-footed by something he had not expected, Marco reminded himself that it didn't matter; Jacques had only spoken of Llewellyn to Claudia. There was no reason for Elizabeth Harrington to have any information to pass on.

'Jacques's brief visit was to make a report to the UN, I believe,' he explained after a small pause. 'Jess wasn't with him, so he didn't hang around in New York.' Then he saw with relief that Bianca had the door open at the top of the courtyard staircase; he would hand her *cari signori* over and leave before Nathan thought up some fresh question to ask.

Half an hour later, while Elvira busied herself with unpacking in her palatial bedroom next door, Nathan stood at the windows of the *portego*; it wasn't warm enough yet to open them and stand on the balcony overlooking the canal, but it soon would be. When spring came to Venice it came suddenly, and then there was nowhere else he wanted to be.

The view never failed to enchant him – the curved bow of the Rialto Bridge upstream, and across the shining stretch of water a lovely medley of old palaces stretching down towards the Campanile and the Piazzetta, but for once his mind refused to relinquish a problem he knew would need to be dealt with. Marco's hesitations hadn't been lost on him just now, and they made it clear that the shocking news Elizabeth had given him about his Welsh friend was something he was still supposed not to have been told. It was entirely in keeping with the man he knew that misfortune was to be ignored – even if condemned to death, Llewellyn would have defied grief and called for a party instead. Knowing the truth, Nathan had acted in a way that had seemed right in New York. Elvira, of course, would refuse to believe that anything he decided to do was less than perfect, but Nathan knew that the certainty of being right was the trap that men like himself easily fell into. Playing God was a role they felt sure they could manage, forgetting that the pieces they shuffled about the chessboard were other human beings with hearts and minds of their own.

He'd meant well, but good intentions were what paved the road to hell. The person he needed to talk to was Jessica; she would know whether he'd been right or wrong to interfere, and she would gently tell him so.

Nine

The days just before Lent brought early visitors, but Leif couldn't help feeling that if they came expecting the licentious revelry of eighteenth-century Venice, they'd leave asking for their money back. Groups of masked and costumed would-be courtesans and Casanovas didn't quite make a Carnival; some truly roistering spirit was needed. Without it, the enterprise of bringing it back into the city's calendar seemed not much more than a municipal ploy to kick-start the tourist season. Still, Carnival or not, it was joyful to stroll along the Zattere on a fine morning that promised the return of spring, and since he'd agreed with Giancarlo that for once they'd take a weekend off he was free to enjoy himself.

Coming towards him now was someone he thought he couldn't mistake, even though Llewellyn was sheltering behind dark glasses and not wearing his showy cape and hat. It seemed to Leif as if the Welshman hesitated for a moment, uncertain that he wanted to stop. Then he changed his mind and held out his hand with a boisterous, 'Well met; my Torcello friend! Why don't we see anything of you? It's Giancarlo, I suppose, keeping your nose to the grindstone. I'd swear he was a Puritan if I didn't know the Rasinis have been Holy Romans for centuries.'

'We work hard,' Leif agreed, smiling at him, 'but today's a holiday.'

'Then we've got time to sit in the sun and drink a glass of wine together. My friend Tommaso will have his tables out a little further along, and there we can sit and sneer at Palladio's monstrous church across the canal! Ruskin said some silly things about Renaissance architecture, but he was quite right about the Redentore.'

Borne on this flow of conversation, Leif was steered back the way he'd come, to where a young waiter was indeed polishing the tables that had been brought out of winter storage. With wine ordered, Llewellyn sat back in his chair with a quiet little sigh, gaiety apparently forgotten because some train of thought he wasn't inclined to share now occupied his mind. Leif would have been content with the friendly silence but he was remembering the journey back from Torcello, and his feeling then that some unspoken sadness Llewellyn couldn't always control welled up and left him isolated from the rest of them.

'I was thinking about the Carnival just now,' Leif began tentatively, not sure that his companion was prepared to listen. 'I know it's fantasy but it ought to seem real. Somehow it doesn't, so it can't be made to work, and that's all the more odd because Venice is full of illusions that do seem real – it's a very confusing, contradictory place altogether for a straightforward Scandinavian like me!'

Attention now held, Llewellyn removed his dark glasses and smiled at him. 'For a sensible Norseman, I think you understand it very well. Fantasy is like light dancing off water into some old room where ancient mirrors reflect it back again – double illusion in fact – not a gaudy reproduction of what properly died a long time ago.' He sipped some wine, and then went on, aware of how easy it was to talk to this chance-met man, who didn't insist that people should confide in him. 'Ever since I arrived here years ago I've been trying unsuccessfully to paint light on water; I believe it's even harder to paint snow, but there's not a lot of call for that in Venice!'

Leif smiled at that but shook his head. 'Your paintings are beautiful, but I can understand that you're never satisfied ... don't artists always want to try again?'

'Sometimes not,' the Welshman answered after a little silence. 'Sometimes we lose heart and then we give up.' But he brushed the thought aside with one of his sweeping gestures. 'Have you been here long enough to judge whether Venice can survive or not? Can it keep its head above the flood without another Mount Ararat to perch on?'

'I think so,' Leif replied, 'always provided we convince the opposition that the barrage that is being built must be allowed to operate when needed, and that recalculations can be made regarding the type of ocean surges it will have to withstand in future. These are problems that men like Giancarlo and his team are trained to deal with; what they can't do is decide what Venice survives *as*.'

'Living city, dead museum, or some miraculous compromise that the fools who govern us will be quite unable to devise.' Llewellyn delivered himself of this pronouncement and then remembered someone else. 'Marco met a girl the other day who shares my opinion about the bureaucrats – she's staying with the Rasinis at the moment. My son didn't take to her at all but to me she sounds worth knowing.' He stared across the table at Leif. 'If you're not one of those strange people who go to sleep at the opera or don't go at all, we'll invite Anna Lambertini and you can meet her too.'

Leif promised to stay awake and, when given a choice, chose *La Bohème* instead of *Così Fan Tutte*.

'Quite right,' Llewellyn said approvingly. 'Italian sopranos don't suit Mozart – they will wobble!' He consulted his watch, not inclined to believe that a nearby church clock striking noon could be right. 'Just time to call on Donna Emilia on my way home; she might like to come with us, in which case we'll rope in Marco as well. Paolo rarely goes out at night now.'

He stood up, threw some notes on the table, and smiled a farewell. '*A bientôt*, Leif.' Then he walked away with the purposeful air of a man who knew that he had something to do.

Left alone without anything pressing to do, Leif stayed where he was, trying to work out why the tall, classical building facing him across the width of the wide canal should have earned not only Ruskin's disapproval but Llewellyn's as well. All he knew about it was that it was built in thanksgiving for relief from a sixteenth-century plague. With the Venetians' long memory for their past, it might have happened yesterday, and it was still commemorated on the third Sunday of every July, when a pontoon bridge carried huge crowds across the canal to attend Mass in Palladio's 'Redeemer' church.

Belonging to a country in which – in the world's opinion at least – not a lot had ever happened, Leif liked the daily reminders of history that he kept stumbling across in Venice. They confirmed his own view that life was a continuing procession which everyone joined for a while and in due time left to make room for generations coming along behind.

He half expected to hear no more about the opera outing, but got back to the Accademia after lunch to find a message waiting for him. The last performance of *La Bohème* was scheduled for that very evening so would he please meet the Matthiases in the foyer of the Fenice at seven thirty? Evening dress was not required, and the entertainment would be rounded off by supper at home after the performance.

He discovered that evening how beautifully the theatre had finally been reconstructed, despite the long saga of muddle and delay. Claimed to be the most beautiful opera house in the world before its disastrous fire, it didn't belie its name now: the phoenix had risen splendidly from the flames.

With the help of his useful son-in-law, Llewellyn had even inveigled a box out of the management, and to this he proudly led his guests. While he escorted Donna Emilia, Leif expected to look after Maria, but Marco made it clear that this was his job. Leif was there to attend to Anna Lambertini, the girl Llewellyn had reckoned might be worth knowing.

Leif's first glance took in her charming outfit – black velvet skirt and silk tunic of old gold. A second look discovered the intelligence and humour in her face. What, he wondered, was there not to like? Marco must be hard to please if a girl as attractive as this one failed to satisfy him. She even shared Leif's own view of the performance when they came to discuss it over supper at the *pensione*, and put it into vivid words. Puccini's music demanded to be listened to, got entirely lost in, and who cared if it might or might not have been performed better at La Scala or Covent Garden?

She stated the opinion with her usual certainty that she was right, Marco thought. There were no doubts or maybes for Anna Lambertini. He also suspected that she was well aware of the impression she'd made on Llewellyn and Leif. Impelled by irritation that he couldn't conceal, Marco now flatly disagreed with her.

'Opera hovers on the edge of being absurd at the best of times,' he insisted to the astonishment of his parents, who'd never heard him voice such an opinion before. 'If the performance isn't absolutely first class – and it certainly wasn't tonight – then instead of hovering on the edge, it falls clean over.'

'Rubbish – utter balderdash!' shouted Llewellyn, well known for listening entranced to operatic melodies churned out by the Café Florian musicians in the *piazza* every summer. 'How can any son of mine say such a thing?'

The evening suddenly seemed in danger of turning sour, and it felt to Leif as if emotions had been aroused that had little to do with what they were supposed to be discussing. He had no idea what to do about it himself, but Donna Emilia apparently did. With her irresistible smile, she suddenly entered the debate on Marco's side.

'I think your son is quite right, my dear,' she said to Llewellyn calmly. 'How can it not be absurd when the heroine, dying of consumption, is required to sit up and sing an aria of the utmost complexity? Marco is only saying that if she sings it exquisitely we forgive the absurdity, and if she doesn't, we can't!'

Llewellyn was forced to smile at his old friend; even if she didn't quite believe what she was saying, she'd understood that Marco had needed help, and he loved her for her kindness.

'Then let us drink to the Fenice itself,' he suggested. 'Still an opera house to stand comparison with any in the world. I think we can all agree on that.'

Whatever had threatened the success of the evening, the danger was over, Leif decided. Maria was smiling at her husband again, and Anna Lambertini was clearly enchanted with him even if she'd given up on his surly son. All went well now until Maria asked Leif how he spent his Sundays in Venice – not working, she hoped.

'Sometimes,' he admitted, 'but tomorrow I'm going to take the water bus to an island I haven't seen yet – Chioggia. Well, it's not quite an island, I know, but it seems to have its own distinct personality, nevertheless, as well as the best fish in the lagoon, Giancarlo says.'

Anna's mouth sketched a charming pout. 'He's forgotten to mention that to me.' Then she smiled at Leif. 'I'd come with you tomorrow if you'd let me; I don't restore paintings on Sundays!'

'Of course, Anna ... Anyone else? Marco?' Leif enquired, trying to sound enthusiastic about enlarging the party to that extent.

'Thanks, but I'm busy tomorrow.' It wasn't quite rude, but it wasn't cordial either, and as if aware of the fact Marco offered his mother an apologetic smile. 'Excuse me, Mamma, while I see if Beppe has arrived outside for Donna Emilia.'

He left a small silence behind that Maria hurried to fill. 'Sunday is practise day for the rowers in the annual race down the Canalazzo – it's a great charity event,' she explained to Anna and Leif. 'Marco couldn't let his team down by not being there.'

'All rowed fast but none rowed faster that Marco,' Llewellyn misquoted with a grin and ended the evening for them on a laughing note. But later, when their guests had said goodnight and left, and he and Maria were in their bedroom together, she looked sadly at her husband.

'Marco is unhappy, *amore*; he was almost rude to Anna this evening, and that isn't like him. I pray every day that he won't go on with this wretched political business. He must make up his own mind – I know that – but it's just that the uncertainty is so bad for him on top of his anxiety for you.'

Llewellyn came up behind her to enfold her in a hug. 'You're anxious about me, sweetheart, but it doesn't make you irritable with everybody else. And Marco should know by now that the only way to end uncertainty is to make up his mind.' He kissed the top of her head and released her, then thought of something else. 'Leif's a nice man, and Anna Lambertini is a charming girl, and they're already on the way to liking each other. I think I shall go into the match-making business when I can no longer see to paint.'

130

That was too much for Maria; blinded by sudden tears, she knocked over a little perfume bottle on her dressing table, and then buried her face in her hands. Llewellyn raised her to her feet and kissed her tear-stained face.

'You'll have to get used to me joking about it, *amore* – I can't manage it in any other way,' he said gently. 'Now, come to bed and be comforted.'

Ten

Very infrequently Easter Sunday occurred early enough to coincide with Llewellyn's birthday. Maria saw that it was going to happen this year, and she had no doubt that he would have noticed it as well. His birthdays were always mentioned well in advance, just in case his family should carelessly overlook them and, matching Easter Day as it was going to, this one would normally have received special publicity. But he was making no reference to it at all, and it was behaviour so unlike him that she was forced to consult her son one morning as soon as Llewellyn had left the breakfast table.

'What do you think, *tesoro*?' she asked anxiously. 'Are we not to notice the date because he refuses to believe that he's going to be seventy? Or is he so sad and so frightened about the future that he can't celebrate his birthday, or Easter, or anything at all?'

Marco considered the questions seriously, aware that if he did so she would be content to accept whatever he said. Then his grave expression relaxed in the smile that was so like her own.

'Papa would rather not be seventy, of course – he wants to be young forever!' The smile faded as Marco went on. 'But it's also true that he can scarcely bear to think of a time when he won't be able to paint. For him, especially, blindness is going to be a kind of death. So he occupies his mind with other things – playing games with us, for example, leaving us to guess what we're meant to do about his birthday.'

'So what shall we do?' Maria wanted to know. 'Dine out at Harry's Bar or Cipriani? Lorenza and Filippo would come, of course, and if Jessica and Jacques could fly down and spend Easter with us, that would make him happy.'

Marco nodded. 'We need them, it's true, but I think he's hoping for something more than that. Could you manage it, Mamma, if Lucia got in extra help? We'd have to invite his dearest friends – the Rasinis and the Achesons – but also some of his cronies at the Ateneo, and his favourite students from Ca' Foscari and San Servolo. I think he'll see this as a sort of goodbye to them, so we need to make it a splendid one – don't you agree?'

132

He was right, as always, and she nodded, aware that neither of them had mentioned the one other person Llewellyn would grieve not to see. They couldn't – shouldn't have to – beg Claudia to come home for her father's birthday; if other things in her life seemed more important, they must manage without her. And at least, thank God, as far as he knew nothing had changed between them. Maria wrote long, loving letters to New York as usual about what went on along the *rio*, pretending to believe that it was still of interest to her daughter, and Claudia occasionally telephoned them, to speak mainly to Llewellyn. In conversations that Maria now felt to be unreal, he went on playing the role of masterful but adoring father to the girl he still thought of as 'little Claudia'. But even to her he'd said nothing about his birthday this time.

Maria pushed the pain of it away and tried to smile at her son. 'We keep it a secret if we can – the party I mean?'

'We try,' Marco agreed. 'He's normally like a ferret at a rabbit hole if he thinks things are going on that he knows nothing about, but I think he'll pretend not to guess what's happening.' A glance at his watch brought Marco to his feet. 'Time I went, Mamma. Elvira has agreed that Nathan's well enough now to inspect the house at Cannaregio. He hasn't seen it since we were still washing salt out of the brickwork. I think he'll be pleased with what Guido Moro and Jess have done.'

She smiled wholeheartedly now, knowing that his own contribution wouldn't be mentioned; the credit would go to their architect and Jessica. But she relied on Nathan Acheson to understand that he could search the length and breadth of Italy and not find another steward like her son.

She also needed Nathan to convince him that the work he did for the Trust was far more real and useful than trying to become the next Mayor of Venice. If he should succeed, 'they' would only end by breaking his heart. Like most Italians, Maria had no doubt that those in authority above them must be numbered among the powers of darkness; they observed none of the laws they passed, dispensed usually with truth, and knew nothing of kindness – the only virtue she absolutely insisted on. Her prayer was that Marco could be kept from having to join and, inevitably, fight them, but she didn't say so now; whatever he decided she would have to accept – that was what was required of mothers in her view.

'I'll go and talk to Lucia,' she said instead. 'If Llewellyn asks why we're so busy, I shall say that we have to discuss Easter.'

'Bravo, Mamma – and it's only half a lie!' He stooped to kiss her cheek, then turned round on his way to the door. She wondered if he was about to speak about Claudia at last, but all he said was, 'We forgot Leif Hansson – Papa would like him to come.'

She nodded and added his name to the list

she was already making in her head. With thirty or more people to cater for, one extra would make no difference – two extra in fact because Emilia's young guest, Anna Lambertini, would have to be invited as well. Marco would agree to that even if he couldn't be persuaded to like her.

Maria thought she knew the reason behind his dislike. He'd argued and fought with two opinionated sisters while they were all growing up together – that was a natural part of normal family life. But Anna couldn't be handled in that way and Marco, not knowing how else to deal with her, preferred not to have to deal with her at all. There had been other girls, Maria remembered, more docile and biddable than this one – prettier too – but they hadn't appealed to her son either. Or perhaps, she now thought, it had been the other way round? Did today's young women only want the sort of man who kept a car expensively garaged on the mainland and waited for the first opportunity to leave Venice behind for the wealth to be made in Milan and the power to be had in Rome? She put the thought away with a sigh, and began the more soothing task of making lists in preparation for Llewellyn's birthday party – lists would be needed if Lucia was to remain calm and unflustered.

Marco enjoyed the walk to Palazzo Ghisalberti – so named still because Nathan had seen no need to erase the name of its long-previous ancestry. Beppe was already outside, wearing the nautical rig he always insisted on when he was going to be in charge of the signor's motor launch. Given the fineness of the morning, it was a pity they were only voyaging as far as Cannaregio. Despite not being qualified to venture out into the lagoon, he'd hinted that a trip across to Pellestrina or Chioggia would do the boat's engine good, but it seemed that the Signora had decided to come with them and he knew that the shorter a boat journey, the better she liked it.

Carefully handed in and settled a few minutes later, Elvira actually smiled for once at the prospect of being afloat. Who could resist it, Marco wondered. Who, seeing the Canalazzo sparkling in the sunlight and the sheer beauty of what lined its banks, could want to be anywhere else? For the moment, at least, Nathan's wife seemed to agree, and her pleasure was reflected in his smiling face. He'd waited long enough, Marco knew, for Elvira to learn to share his own delight in the lagoon city.

Alongside the Rio Madonna dell' Orto their rescued house looked resplendent in the morning sunshine, although he frowned over an adjective that didn't seem to fit a building that had no garish newness about it – what they looked at perfectly fitted its surroundings, with nothing to indicate the transformation inside. Half an hour later, with the inspection over, Marco felt Nathan's hand rest on his shoulder for a moment, which was all the comment he needed on the work that had been done.

Marco walked with them to where Beppe waited beside the launch, but explained that he would go on foot now to the Campo Giacomo dell'Orio as the architect, Guido Moro, would be waiting for him there to discuss their next project. Nathan smiled at his wife and she lifted her hands in a little gesture of resignation.

'I know, you're not an invalid any longer. You want to walk with Marco, and you can't wait to look at another crumbling house! I shall go home and persuade Emilia and Paolo to let me take them out to lunch.'

In a rare public gesture of affection, Nathan kissed her hand, and then Beppe was instructed to take the Signora and her guests wherever she wished them to go. Beppe's bow in reply assured *il Capo* that he, Guiseppe Bruni, would of course do this, but moreover he would return the Signora to the palazzo safely no matter what peril might stand in the way. Then, with a show of boatmanship that he knew was being watched, he swept the launch round and took Elvira back towards the Grand Canal.

Still smiling at the exuberance of it, Nathan fell into step with Marco. 'You'll have to lead the way,' he confessed. 'It's my ambition never to get lost in Venice, but I don't know this area yet at all.'

Marco explained their route: a little wriggling through the *fodere* would bring them to the San Marcuola/San Stae *traghetto* and, once across the Canalazzo, they'd be almost at the Campo Giacomo dell' Orio. They talked as they walked, *capo* and steward content to be starting on the rescue of another derelict house that could be brought back to useful life again.

It was past noon when Marco finished explaining the renovation he and Jess had planned and, outside in the *campo* again, Nathan suggested lunch in the nearby *trattoria* he could see in a corner of the square. Settled at a table there a few minutes later, he seemed wholly at ease, a man whose life would be lived, given the choice, in just such simple surroundings – despite the fact that Nathan Acheson lived in one of the city's most beautiful palaces, Marco thought it might well be true; that too had been a work of loving preservation, not a sign to the rest of the world that he was such a rich and influential man.

They followed the *padrone*'s recommendation – the red mullet that had been bought in the *pescheria* that very morning – and the house white to go with it, which was cheap but good. While the fish was being grilled they nibbled grissini and sipped the wine. Then, after a moment or two, Marco broke the friendly silence.

'May I talk to you about the future?' he asked abruptly. 'My friends at Venezia Viva want me to stand for Mayor in the next election. I have to decide, I know, but of course it affects the Trust.'

'You want to give up the work we do?' It was a simple question that brought no pressure to bear, either way.

'I don't want to at all,' Marco said slowly. 'In fact it hardly bears thinking about. But I wondered if you'd agree to my sharing my salary with a part-time assistant – that way I could still be involved.' Nathan's impassive face gave him no help and he was obliged to soldier on. 'You'd probably prefer me to leave altogether, I expect. I could say no to my friends, but it feels wrong somehow, as if I'd be letting them down; Llewellyn calls it emotional blackmail, but it isn't quite that ... They desperately want a change in the way our affairs are run. I probably shan't win, of course, but that doesn't affect whether or not I ought to try.' He was talking too much, he knew, rambling as would-be politicians always did, and it was a relief when Nathan took charge of the conversation.

'There's no question of sharing your salary with an assistant,' he said gravely, but at the sight of Marco's suddenly desolate face his own rare smile appeared. 'Let us find the assistant anyway, and pay him properly, whether you decide to stand and get to be Mayor or not – you've been overworking on my behalf for years.'

Marco stared at him, bereft of words for a moment. 'Thank you ... thank you very much,' he finally managed to mumble, but it

139

was left to Nathan to go on talking.

'I know what Venezia Viva campaign for, of course. Apart from anything else, like the present Mayor they'd discourage tourists – if not ban them altogether if they could!'

'Only it's not that simple, is it?' Marco confessed. 'I used to think it was. I met a girl the other day who made me face reality – after I'd finished shouting at her! In truth, how can we survive without the flood of summer visitors? Close down the hotels and restaurants and tourist shops and there'd be precious few jobs left to keep our own people living here.'

'There are alternatives,' Nathan suggested, 'but we must discuss them another time. Here comes the *padrone* with our fish, and he'll expect us to give it proper attention.'

While they ate it was Nathan who went back to what Marco had said earlier. 'My guess is that the girl you spoke to is Emilia's young guest – opinionated, I'm afraid my wife thought her, but Elvira's since learned to take a different view of Anna Lambertini. The palazzo now houses a stray kitten that was being tormented by two youths in the lane outside, until Anna caught sight of them. She descended on them like the wrath of God, Elvira said, threatened them with several large elder brothers – imaginary of course – and then made a present of the kitten to Battistina! Our impression is that Anna's arrival has been good for our friends at the palazzo. The girl they really wanted for Giancarlo was Jessica, of course, but she is out of reach and Anna Lambertini now seems the next best thing.'

Marco was saved from having to answer this by the return of the *padrone*, anxious to know their opinion of the red mullet. Assured that it had been excellent, he bustled away to bring the coffee they had ordered, while Marco shared the last of the wine between their glasses. Then Nathan suddenly decided to mention what else was on his mind.

'Telling Maria that you're going back into the political arena will be like confessing to some life-threatening disease, but there's another problem as well, isn't there?' Marco shot him a questioning glance. 'I spoke to Elizabeth before we left New York,' Nathan went on to explain. 'She gave me the news about your father.'

Feeling suddenly winded by the unexpectedness of this remark, Marco struggled to find his voice. 'Jacques was only going to tell Claudia – she must have passed it on.' He hesitated, searching for the right words. 'It's bound to seem odd, hurtful probably, that we haven't told you ourselves. But Llewellyn didn't even want Claudia to know, in case she decided to give up New York and come rushing home.' Marco was deeply angry with his sister, but he wasn't prepared to admit, even to Nathan, that she showed no sign of doing anything at all. Instead, he went on talking about his father. 'His eyesight is slowly fading but when he can no longer see to paint he's going to pretend that he's giving up because

141

he's bored with being an artist – anything rather than have his friends feel pity for him. So Mamma had to promise not to tell; but I refused not to tell Jess and she insisted that Claudia ought to know as well.'

Nathan nodded, not commenting on Llewellyn's way of dealing with the tragedy that was slowly overtaking him – it was how he was, even though it put an unfair burden of silence on his wife. The thought of Maria made Nathan revert to how the conversation had begun. 'Does your mother know about the Mayor thing, or is that something else we are not to mention?'

'She knows it's in the wind, and I think she's relying on you to talk me out of it! She has great faith in you.'

'Shall I try to talk you out of it?' Nathan enquired gravely. 'I will if you want me to.'

Marco shook his head. 'Thank you; it would be very easy to say "yes, please", but I've spouted enough hot air with my friends about what we think Venice needs. Now it's time to nail our colours to the mast, I reckon.'

'I reckon so too,' Nathan agreed. 'Perhaps Maria will let me persuade her instead!'

Marco's smile reappeared at that, enough in itself to win at least the vote of every right-minded Venetian woman, Nathan thought. But there the conversation ended – Marco to go to the Municipio, to discuss with officials there which families most urgently needed re-housing; Nathan to test his skill in navigating himself back to the palazzo. But his mind

142

kept wandering from the route he ought to take. It wasn't often that he felt obliged to query a decision that he'd made – such waverings weren't appreciated in the high-risk negotiations that he was usually involved in. But the Matthias family was dear to him, and affection had persuaded him to interfere – wrongly, it now seemed. His only comfort was that Claudia was still in New York and so nothing had come of it after all. He hoped one day to be able to tell that to Llewellyn, and then they might be able to laugh together about the illusions that so-called 'important men' cherished of themselves.

Eleven

Leif was pleased to see that the doleful season of Lent was coming to an end. He'd made it a habit to drop into any church he passed that happened to be open – too many of them seemed to be resolutely closed – but he disliked the Lenten shrouding of every statue in a purple veil; it was an unnecessarily morbid reminder of the road to Calvary, he reckoned.

He said this to Giancarlo one day when they were out in the lagoon, taking soundings and measurements as usual. Their lunchtime break while they were moored to a *bricole*, munching on ham rolls, allowed for conversation.

'What else have you had time to decide you don't like about the way we do things here?' his companion asked. 'I haven't visited your country, so I've nothing to compare, but much of what goes on here must strike you as bizarre.'

'Sometimes bizarre,' Leif agreed, 'but more often beautiful, in unexpected ways.' Not the least of these, he could have explained, was his surprising friendship with the man beside him – the last thing he'd expected when they met for the first time at the airport. But he'd got to know Giancarlo Rasini better now – he understood what made him the reticent, private man he certainly was, and could see behind the facade of courteous detachment to the grace and warmth that Giancarlo so successfully kept hidden from the world.

But this couldn't be said aloud, and so Leif spoke of generalities instead. 'I suppose what I enjoy most isn't just that over the centuries Venetians have so ingeniously adapted their lives to the strange demands of being here; it's also the sheer style with which they've managed it!'

'Expand, please,' Giancarlo asked with a smile. 'I'm interested, and of course we love hearing ourselves being talked about!'

Leif thought for a moment. 'Well, for example, the artistry of a gondolier maneuvering his boat; the housewife elegantly cleaning her marble floor with damp sawdust before she sweeps it; the fishmongers in the market making a work of art out of their displays ... And I'll be damned if even the children playing football in some hidden *campo* don't do it with the same inborn sense of style!'

Giancarlo threw a hunk of crust to a hovering gull, and then turned to smile at Leif. 'It's a generous compliment. You could more easily have pointed out our failings – too many scabrous buildings and unscoured canals, not to mention the lagoon itself, probably irremediably damaged by what's been done to it. The industries at Mestre and Marghera get most of the blame – unfairly now, I think. We've upset what Nature – or the Creator if you like – intended here; allowed developers to reclaim what should still be water, or wetland at least; done nothing to check the intensive farming which has poured chemicals into the rivers and thence into the lagoon.'

'But still you don't lose heart, and nor would I if I lived here,' Leif said. He stared at what lay around them – the island-studded, silver-grey water, today at least lying peacefully beneath an immense and slightly paler sky, the deep-water channels marked by wooden posts that leant together in clumps of two or three, like old men exchanging gossip. 'It's a very addictive place, I find,' he finished wistfully.

Giancarlo nodded by way of answer. 'No wonder painters can't stop trying to capture it – it's never the same, even from one moment to the next.' He hesitated before going on. 'My grandmother's guest enjoyed her visit with you to Chioggia.'

Leif smiled at the memory of it. 'Kind of Anna to say so, considering that it rained for most of the day, but she didn't complain once – rare in my experience of young women. I like her very much, even if she does think she knows more about Ibsen's plays than I do! She, by the way, is not very complimentary about Venice – all she can see, I think, are the signs of neglect and no great hope for its future.'

'I know. We aren't spared her opinions at home; there's no question of Anna Lambertini wanting to spend her life here even though she'd never be out of a job!' It was enough, he hoped, to show Leif that she hadn't been earmarked as the next Countess Rasini; if his own interest in her was real, as Giancarlo suspected it was, then he was free to spend all the spare time with her that he could.

The lunch break was over, but Leif remembered something else as he untied their mooring rope. 'Maria Matthias has been kind enough to invite me to Llewellyn's birthday party – I assume you're all going too?'

'Of course – Anna as well. And if you haven't met our neighbours, the Achesons, that will be a pleasure in store ... they're enough in themselves to give Americans a very good name in Venice.'

146

'Strangely enough I heard about Nathan Acheson in New York,' Leif commented. 'He's one of the city's great benefactors, Elizabeth Harrington said.'

'And her grand-daughter Jessica designed the interior of the palazzo Nathan now owns. I hope you begin to see how compact and interrelated our world is here!'

'Cosy, but dangerous if you want to keep secrets hidden,' Leif agreed. 'Now, it's my turn to steer, I think, if you're prepared for us to go aground on all the sand or mud banks I can't yet identify!'

The cold and mostly sodden weather relented just in time for Easter. Instead of scurrying along submerged under umbrellas, people looked up and smiled again. 'The winter is past, the rain is over and gone,' as the Song of Solomon rightly said; God was in his heaven after all, and the sun was shining again on Venice.

Birthday or not, Llewellyn always went with Maria to the Basilica on Easter Day – not so much, she suspected, for devotional reasons as to relish the almost oriental splendour of the church when it was celebrating its greatest festival of the year. He loved it all – the Patriarch being escorted to the High Altar under a canopy of cloth of gold, the rest of the clergy, gorgeously robed, carrying between them the treasures that Venetians had systematically looted over the centuries from less happy lands; candlelight gleaming on gold mosaics, the swirling fragrance of incense, and the glory of organ and choir – Christianity hadn't seemed much like this in the Welsh mining village chapel of his childhood.

This Easter Day, because it was his birthday, the Matthias family were out in force. Afterwards, by careful prearrangement, Llewellyn was taken to lunch with Lorenza and Filippo and their children while the rest of them hurried home to prepare the party he still gave no sign of knowing anything about. By the time he returned the stage was set for a celebration that was clearly more than just a family dinner party.

He went about the room counting the small, flower-decked tables, set with gleaming glass and silver and candles waiting to be lit. 'I was about to suggest going out to dinner,' he remarked blandly to Maria, 'but we seem to be expecting quite a lot of guests here instead.'

'A few friends, *amore*,' she answered with a blameless smile. 'Just the people you like most.'

He clutched his head theatrically. 'A rough idea of numbers, please. After all, I might have to make a little speech of welcome and one does like to be prepared.'

Trying hard not to smile, Jess came to her stepmother's rescue. 'Only thirty-five at the last count ... and don't pretend you haven't guessed what's been going on. Maria and Lucia have toiled over the preparation for days, and Jacques has bet me good money that your welcome speech is already written!'

'Vipers all,' Llewellyn said sadly, 'but being a man of exceptional forbearance and angelic sweetness of nature, I dare say I shall forgive you. Am I allowed to say a few words or do I merely sit enthroned in a corner and let people approach and kiss my hand?'

Seeing that his wife was now helpless with laughter as well, Jacques came to the rescue this time, and did his best to sound severe. 'You act the part of a forbearing and sweet-natured man who remembers his age and his reputation as a distinguished artist – no libelous comments about the people who run this city, no character assassinations of fellow painters you don't like, and no calumnies about your long-suffering family. How does that sound?'

'Extremely dull,' Llewellyn said truthfully, 'but I shall do my best. Now, unless I can be of help in any way, I shall retire for an hour or two ... I may even meditate a little.' He gave them a sweet parting smile, kissed his hand to Maria, and climbed the staircase to his bedroom.

'Very above himself,' Marco remarked anxiously when his father was out of earshot, 'but he won't get too outrageous if Donna Emilia is here.'

Maria tried to smile but her eyes were suddenly full of tears. 'He explained it to me the other day, and you must understand too, my dears – the only way he can deal with what's happening to him is to play the clown. He'll be full of fun and laughter in front of other people and save his weeping for when he's alone.'

Jess went to put her arms round her step-mother. 'You rest too, please ... you've been working so hard. Marco, Jacques and I can see to anything that still needs doing, and this evening all we have to remember is that it's Easter Day and Llewellyn's birthday, and no one else will know anything more than that.'

Marco hesitated, then confessed. 'Not quite true, Jess – Nathan does know. He was given the news by your grandmother in New York, but he won't have passed it on – not even to Elvira.'

Jacques considered this for a moment, then gave a little shrug. 'So Claudia spoke to her; perhaps we should have guessed that would happen, but it's unlike Elizabeth to have told anyone else. I still don't think it matters as long as Llewellyn doesn't know.' He glanced at his watch, and then at Jess. 'Now, my dear one, you persuade Maria upstairs while Marco and I start opening wine; after that we need only climb into our gladrags and await the first arrivals – they'll be the ever-hungry students, I expect!'

Two hours later Maria felt able finally to relax, as Llewellyn's party was going with a swing. He'd made a charming little speech of welcome, and then asked his guests simply to enjoy themselves; but he was a good host, watchful for anyone looking lonely or left out. Then, with supper served, Marco stood up to propose a toast to his father. The room fell silent, waiting for him to speak, but in the small silence a commotion outside in the hall could suddenly be heard. Seconds later, obviously feeling that his moment had come, Giovanni – Lucia's husband – appeared in the doorway, unable to contain his good news.

'*Signore, signora ... la signorina Claudia è acqui!*'

And there she was, Marco thought numbly, standing large as life behind Giovanni, still wearing the hat and coat she'd travelled in. How like her – how bloody well like his maddening little sister to turn up now, just when Llewellyn had recovered from the sadness of not hearing from her.

Leif watched with interest, remembering their brief meeting in Elizabeth Harrington's drawing room. Even tired after the long flight she still looked as she had then, poised, elegant and self-aware. She wasn't at all disturbed to have this audience for the reunion with her family; perhaps she'd even planned it that way. But he had to retract the thought immediately as she explained that the flight had been badly delayed; she'd expected to reach Venice by midday.

With Maria openly weeping, and Llewellyn for once almost bereft of words, it was left to Marco to get the party under control again. Watching him, Jess realized that she hadn't fully understood what years of working for Nathan Acheson had done; the young, gauche, earnest rebel of her first acquaintance had become this assured but charmingly modest man. When a seat for Claudia had been found he stood up and the buzz of conversation died down.

'For any of you who don't know her – or no longer recognize her at least – my little sister, Claudia, has just arrived – a trifle late, but much better late than never.' A hubbub of welcome broke out, which Marco allowed for a moment or two and then quelled with a lifted hand.

'He's more like Llewellyn than I realized,' Jacques murmured in his wife's ear. 'Can't you just see him swaying the voters?'

'Alas, yes I can; but hush – he's still talking.'

Marco had now picked up his glass. 'When Claudia burst in on us so dramatically I was about to propose a toast to my father, whose birthday today is the reason you – family and dear friends – are all here. He was born a Welshman but I know of no Venetian who has loved Venice more, or recreated it in paintings more beautifully. May we drink his health, please?'

When the shouts of 'to Llewellyn' had died down the man himself got slowly to his feet. Trembling hands had to be jammed into the pockets of his jacket, but he managed a ghost of his old grin.

'Before you arrived,' he explained in his lilting voice, 'I was told by my dear family that if I made a speech I was forbidden to mention politicians or any of my fellow artists – for obvious reasons!' He waited for the laughter to die down, and went on more seriously. 'But there is no speech, my friends; I only want to thank my dear Maria for taking pity on the vagabond who arrived here forty years ago. She and my children have had much to bear since then, but at least I can claim to have truly loved them, and I shall do until I die.' Then he kissed his tearfully smiling wife, and went in turn to embrace his children before going back to his seat.

Jess smiled unsteadily at Marco beside her. 'Not a dry eye in the house now,' she murmured. 'And you did very well too, little brother. Jacques thinks you'll make a politician yet!' Then she looked across at Claudia, deep in conversation with Count Paolo. 'I'm glad she came, even if you had to goad her into it – she's what Llewellyn needed to make the day complete.'

'And we have to admit as well that she's cleaned up a treat,' he said reluctantly. 'No trace now of the untidy, scruffy student who never knew which colours she could safely wear together – I expect we have your grandmother to thank for that.'

'Elizabeth will have enjoyed helping,' Jess agreed. 'I wasn't nearly such good material for her to work on.'

Marco grinned but shook his head. 'You haven't heard her telling people what a piece of perfection you are – I have!' He glanced at his watch and then back at Jess. 'Time to ask Mamma to lead her guests back to the drawing room. It seems to have been a long evening but it isn't over yet – I expect Llewellyn will insist on singing, don't you?'

'When have you known him not?' she asked, trying not to laugh. 'His dear, piano-playing friend is here, so I can't see him missing an audience of this size – usually it's just us!'

But later on, when the brief recital was over, she agreed with Donna Emilia that the songs had rounded off a memorable evening.

'He's an extraordinary man, your father,' the Countess said with great affection in her voice. 'What we should have missed if the "vagabond" had never come to Venice!'

'And I should have missed knowing my natural father,' Jess commented gravely. 'I had the best of stepfathers in my lovely Gerald, but blood calls to blood in the end.' Then she looked across the room to where Anna Lambertini sat talking to Leif Hansson. 'Those two are getting on well together.'

Donna Emilia nodded, sadly Jess thought. There, she probably feared, went one more chance of a girl who might have made her grandson a good wife. Loving when all hope was gone was something Jane Austen had ascribed to women, but Giancarlo's heart seemed just as stubbornly fixed on the past, and Jess could share Donna Emilia's anxiety for him. When his grandparents were dead who would there be to love him as he deserved? Even as the thought was in her mind she turned to find him beside her.

'Dear Jess, I wish Llewellyn had a birthday every week to bring you back to Venice!' he said with his rare smile. 'Am I right to think you didn't expect this one to bring Claudia back?'

'Total surprise,' she confessed, 'but thank goodness it came off – she might have been delayed enough to miss the party altogether.'

'What now – a few days here, then back to New York?'

'I'm sure so, but that doesn't matter; she came when she was needed.' It had sounded too vehement, Jess realized from the puzzlement in Giancarlo's face, for someone who didn't know what his family knew about Llewellyn. 'They still miss Claudia very much,' she tried to explain. 'I don't say it to Maria, of course, but I doubt if she'll ever come back here to live. Venice is too small now, for Claudia, and too unchallenging.'

'She makes a serious mistake if she only equates challenge with size; Venice makes quite enough demands on its citizens.' He'd sounded too sharp, he realized, and brushed the comment aside. Then he turned to his grandmother with his usual gentle concern for her. 'Time I took you and Grandpapa home, and our hosts must be wanting to be rid of us.'

But when the last guest had gone the evening yielded one more surprise, again provided by Claudia.

'My old room, Mamma?' she asked of Maria with a smile.

'Of course, dearest – it's always ready for you. We hope you can stay, *tesoro*, just for a little while at least. You look tired out and much too thin.'

Claudia kept them waiting for a moment before she replied. 'I'm here to stay, period. I've been commissioned to write a report on the state of Venice for UNESCO – months of work if the job is to be done properly. So I've said goodbye to New York for the time being. I hope the Serenissima and I will learn to get on with each other again!' She blew them a smiling kiss, reminiscent at last of the girl she'd once been, and then walked up the staircase to her room.

She left a little silence behind her that Maria was the first to break. 'Can it be true that our daughter has come home, *amore*?' she asked of Llewellyn unsteadily. 'I'd begun to think she never would.'

His own smile wavered on the edge of tears. 'It's true, but for the right reason, my love – nothing to do with me, and that's how it had to be. You're worn out; let us go to bed.' With an arm about her shoulders, he led the way up the stairs, leaving Jess, Jacques and Marco still gaping at each other in shock.

'Now, thank God, we can at least stop pretending about Llewellyn,' Jess finally murmured. 'He won't mind her knowing now.'

'And also, thank God, we can all go to bed,' said Jacques. There seemed no point in mentioning what Jess and Marco must be well aware of – that Claudia hadn't even greeted them. Perhaps it hadn't been a deliberate omission on her part, but he couldn't help feeling sad that the troubled past wasn't done with yet. The ongoing drama of the Matthias family was still alive and well.

Twelve

Jess was still asleep when Jacques went downstairs the following morning, to find Lucia and Giovanni putting everything to rights after the party, and Marco, having already breakfasted, on the point of leaving the house. He was on his way to a meeting on the mainland, he explained – more bloody-minded bureaucrats to wrestle with or bribe over this or that new permit they'd dreamed up.

'The wheels of government must be oiled,' Jacques pointed out with a smile. 'Still, rather you than me; I hate officialdom. I shall break my fast alone because no one else seems to be up, and then take a bracing walk along the Riva. *Ciao, amico!*'

He'd no sooner helped himself to grapefruit and a croissant in the breakfast room than the door opened and Claudia walked in, dressed more formally than he would have expected.

'What it is to be young,' he said with his pleasant grin. 'You look in good shape for someone who crossed the Atlantic yesterday – no jet-lag?'

'It's easier coming eastward.' She poured herself coffee and sat down at the table. 'Now, what shall we talk about – the weather?'

He was warned by the coolness in her voice, but soldiered on. 'Why don't we talk about you? Was it true what you said last night – is there really a UNESCO job, or is that a way of disguising the fact that you just decided to come back for the sake of Llewellyn – who still hasn't been told, by the way, that you know about his failing eyesight?'

She stared at him across the table, and he could see in her face no trace of the boundless affection she'd once offered him. It was his fault, he reminded himself; so now it was up to him to establish a different kind of relationship that she would accept. At last she answered his question.

'The job is certainly conveniently timed, but it's real. Other people wanted it but Nathan Acheson swung it my way – rightly so because I shall do it very well.' She sipped her coffee before going on. 'Not being supposed to know about Llewellyn, I couldn't come until I had a reason for leaving New York.'

'Very true,' Jacques agreed. 'I also remember that you said you hated Venice. Was that for real as well? You loved it once.'

The faint smile on her mouth reminded

158

him of what she didn't need to say – that she'd loved him once as well, but how fortunate it was that one grew out of childish habits. 'I expect I shall get used to being here again,' she remarked instead, and then decided that it was her turn to ask a question. 'Are you and Jessica staying long? I thought you only dragged yourselves away from Paris for brief visits.'

'An extra day or two this time – we thought Llewellyn might feel flat after his birthday. We didn't know, of course, that you would be here.' He thought she waited for him to say that since she was there, he and Jess could now go home; instead he knew that he must somehow try to dismantle the barrier of hostility she'd erected between them.

'Claudia, listen to me, please,' he gently begged her. 'Really listen to what I'm trying to say, I mean. I can't undo the past – and I even doubt whether you would want me to in any case; you've moved on since then and left me behind. But whatever blame you reckon attaches to me, it is all mine, not Jess's. She has to come here from time to time to work with Marco. Don't, please, try to punish me by hurting her.'

Claudia's eyes skimmed his face, then looked away again. He was older, a little more lined, and the cap of thick, wiry hair was more silvered now. He hadn't grown any better-looking with age as some unhandsome men did. There was no reason why she shouldn't learn to stop loving him and hating Jessica, but those emotions had become habitual – she didn't know if she could manage without them.

'It makes no difference to me whether your wife is here or not,' she said slowly. 'She won't add to my enjoyment or I to hers, but we shall be very polite to each other, I promise you.' Then, with a gesture borrowed from Llewellyn, she brushed the subject of Jessica aside. 'I noticed that the Norwegian I met in New York was here last night, talking to a girl I didn't know.'

'She's Anna Lambertini, staying with the Rasinis while she works at San Gregorio, restoring damaged pictures. You'll meet her, I'm sure – she's well liked by everyone except Marco, apparently!'

Claudia's old smile briefly reappeared. 'Too modern, too opinionated, for my dear brother, I expect that means. When will he catch up with the real world, I wonder?'

Jacques tried to remember that most sisters liked to patronize their brothers, but still he couldn't resist trimming Claudia's sails a little. 'He'll be in what you call the real world soon enough, I imagine – his colleagues at Venezia Viva want him to run for Mayor.'

Claudia blinked a little at that but didn't comment. Instead she spoke in a different tone of voice. 'Before we end this not-very-friendly conversation, you could tell me how things are here, in case I'm still to be kept in the dark.' She winced at the phrase and Jacques was suddenly reminded of the extent to which she'd adored her father – that probably hadn't changed, no matter what else had.

'Llewellyn's sight is deteriorating slowly but surely,' he said gently. 'The problem is macular degeneration, and there's nothing to be done about it. He might not become completely blind – that depends on how long he lives – but even now it's hard for him to distinguish colours; Jess believes that he's working on his last painting.'

Claudia nodded, but didn't answer for a moment. 'I suppose Mamma will say it's God's purpose for him – I hope she doesn't try to tell him that.'

'I expect she just tells him how much she loves him,' Jacques replied, 'because that's the sort of woman she is.'

'And my sort has just been put very firmly in her place!'

The wry acknowledgement asked for forgiveness and Jacques offered it in his smile. It was how she'd always been, he remembered – maddening and lovable by turns, just as her father was. Perhaps not too much had changed after all.

'You look as if you're about to start work, are you?' he asked, and saw her nod.

'I've to begin by meeting people at the UNESCO office this morning; there's a lot to learn before I can even know what questions to ask, or where to ask them.'

'Why not have given the job to someone here?' he asked curiously. 'Wouldn't that have made more sense?'

'Local passions run high, and Venetians are well known for not saying what they mean, or not meaning what they say. I'm reckoned to have been away long enough to remain impartial ... I shall report it as it is, warts and all.'

'But report it with returning affection, I hope – the frail old lady of the lagoon surely deserves that?'

She smiled but made no promise and, with an airy wave, left the room. Jacques poured more coffee and thought about the conversation she'd described as 'unfriendly'. Then he was suddenly aware of the presence of his wife entering the room, and his frown faded at the sight of her.

'You were looking very grim just now,' she commented. 'Nothing worse, I hope, than too much partying last night, which you don't like!'

'I was talking to Claudia – she left a few minutes ago to start work. I wish I could say that I understood her, but I don't. I can't even be sure whether she jumped at this job because it gave her an excuse to come home or whether it simply represents another step up her professional ladder.'

'Why can't it be both? Jess asked. 'In which case perhaps it doesn't matter.'

'True, oh wise one!' he agreed, smiling at her. 'Now, if you don't take too long over breakfast, you can share my morning walk with me.'

If Jess came to Venice when the Achesons happened to be there it was understood that she, and Jacques too if he was with her, would dine at the Palazzo Ghisalberti. But this time it seemed especially important to Nathan that he should talk to her without Maria and Llewellyn being present. First, though, there was their reunion to enjoy. In the years since he'd first met Jess – when she was still putting the finishing touches to his new home – she'd come to take the place of the daughter Nathan had lost to drugs and suicide; her marriage to Jacques Duclos had only cemented their friendship, not disturbed it.

There was plenty of catching-up to do while they sipped their Bellinis, a delicious mixture of Prosecco and peach juice invented by the owner of Harry's Bar. This was not only the chic aperitif to have, it was exactly the right introduction to the sort of Venetian food that Beppe's wife, Bianca, had learned to cook so well for her Signori – this evening it was baby artichokes, small and tender enough to be eaten whole, scallops grilled with olive oil and white wine, and afterwards a perfect risotto flavoured with shavings of truffle.

Jacques finished the last mouthful on his plate with a contented sigh, and then smiled at his hostess. '"Fate cannot harm me, I have dined today". *Chère* Elvira, the Reverend Sydney Smith and I are at one on this.'

'And, dear Elvira, to thank you and Bianca in the kitchen for a delicious supper, he also can't resist showing off his acquaintance with the lesser-known byways of English literature,' Jess pointed out ruthlessly.

'My wife has a wicked tongue,' Jacques retorted. 'Ignore her, please.' Then he turned to look at Nathan and spoke with the note of banter now missing from his voice. 'But I can't help feeling that food isn't at the forefront of our kind host's mind. Is there a small problem, Nathan, that Jess and I could help with, or are all the world's stock markets about to crash?'

'The stock markets are beyond my control,' Nathan admitted regretfully, 'but something much nearer home is on my mind. Since coming back to Venice I've discovered I know something that I wasn't meant to know.'

He hesitated and Jess spoke instead. 'My grandmother told you about Llewellyn after Claudia told her.'

'Exactly, and mostly because she also confessed to being very worried. Claudia was being torn every which way, feeling sure that she'd be needed here, that Llewellyn would not be able to manage without her, but also aware that she couldn't come without a reason that seemed to have nothing to do with him, or indeed come without some real work to do.'

'It was our fault – that she was torn, I mean,' Jess put in again quietly. 'She wouldn't have known if I hadn't asked Jacques to speak to her in New York. But I thought she'd never forgive us, when the truth finally had to come out, for not telling her.' Jess's grey eyes were on Nathan's face, and she thought she could guess his anxiety. 'You were instrumental in getting Claudia the UNESCO assignment, and you're worried about it? Don't be, please – she'll do you great credit and will make a wonderful job of the report.'

But Nathan shook his head. 'My credit rating doesn't bother me, Jess – and you're right anyway; her professionalism isn't the problem.' He hesitated before going on. 'For a while nothing seemed to be happening – either she hadn't got the job after all or she'd decided she didn't want it; and the truth is that I was relieved. I've probably seen much more of Claudia than you have in the last few years, and I'm very aware of what New York has done to her. The surface changes have been very attractive, but success there comes at a cost, especially for someone not born and bred in the city.' Nathan looked at his wife. 'Am I right about this, my dear? You've seen as much of Claudia as I have.'

'Of course,' said Elvira. 'It's like Protestants converting to the Catholic Church – holier than thou isn't in it. Long ago Claudia forbade herself to feel homesick for her family and Venice; she was going to become the most converted New Yorker there ever was. She certainly made herself successful, but she couldn't quite make herself happy. Nathan's worry is what happens now – if she can't go back to being what she was before she left Venice.'

165

Jacques thought of his conversation with her at the breakfast table, aware that there was more to worry about than even the Achesons realized, but equally aware that it would be unfair to leave Nathan to blame himself if the experiment of uprooting Claudia failed. Jess, knowing what her husband was thinking, decided to help by putting it into words.

'There's another complication,' she admitted. 'For several reasons we needn't go into, Claudia would be likely to blame me for her unhappiness, not anything she hasn't found in New York. She'd settle down here again more easily if I was never around, but even if it seemed right to give up working with Marco – and it doesn't – I can't help feeling that we now have to face up to what we've been avoiding for years. Whatever happens, though, you've been kindness itself in bringing her back here; Maria and Llewellyn needed that – and probably Claudia, Jacques and I did too!' She looked at her husband and seemed now to be speaking only to him. 'It is time we got our family sorted out, and at last we have a chance to do it.' Then she deliberately put the subject of Claudia aside, and the conversation turned to what Nathan thought about Marco's chances of becoming Mayor.

Giancarlo didn't make a habit of dining with his grandparents, but he was downstairs with them tonight at Donna Emilia's insistence that Anna Lambertini sometimes needed livelier company than octogenarians could supply. It was also she who at the dinner table raised the subject then being debated at the Palazzo Ghisalberti next door.

'Poor Maria,' the Countess said sadly. 'She's torn between wanting her son to win, as any mother would, and fearing what will happen if he does.'

'But what *will* happen?' Anna wanted to know. 'Won't everything go on just as before? Surely the Mayor's a sort of figurehead, rather like the Doge used to be, but without the gorgeous costume and the funny little hat!'

There was silence for a moment, and then Count Paolo answered for the other two. 'Not quite, my dear. It's true that the Mayor's hands are often tied – by the regional council on the mainland and the government in Rome – but they only represent faceless authority to most Venetians. For them the Mayor is the man in charge, and when things go wrong they blame him.'

'Then who would want such a thankless job?' Anna asked reasonably.

Now it was Giancarlo's turn to answer. 'A politician who saw personal gain in it; or an idealist like Marco Matthias who simply wanted to try to solve some of our problems. That's why my grandmother says Maria is afraid – Marco will be up against the "system" if he gets elected, and we doubt if the system can be beaten.'

Anna considered this for a moment, aware that the disillusionment Giancarlo had just put into words seemed to be shared by just about every Italian she had talked to. But she returned to a subject that interested her more. 'Marco was at least polite last night at the party. When I met him the day I took flowers to the palazzo for Signora Acheson, he nearly bit my head off! I only suggested that Venice couldn't survive without the tourist industry. Was it such a stupid thing to say?'

'Not stupid at all,' Giancarlo replied, 'and I expect that's why Marco got angry – something will have to replace the tourists if Venetians are to go on living here ... but what? The wealth of the past can't be recreated; the world has changed since then. The old "market place between the morning and the evening lands" no longer exists.'

'But while that problem is being solved people like you and Leif Hansson must still try to keep the market place safe; you are between a rock and a hard place, aren't you?' Anna said with genuine sympathy in her voice.

He smiled ruefully at the phrase. 'That is what it sometimes feels like,' he agreed.

But Donna Emilia had been following her own train of thought. 'I thought Marco did very well last night – it couldn't have been easy for him to cope with his sister's last-minute arrival. She always was an impulsive child and perhaps that hasn't changed; though in other ways, of course, she clearly has.' It was as much as she would say of her friends' daughter, but Count Paolo was too familiar with his wife's voice not to detect the faint tone of disapproval.

'Claudia will be here for some time – she told me that last night,' he explained. 'UNESCO require an up-to-date, exhaustive report of the city and she has the job of writing it.'

Disapproval was written more clearly now in Giancarlo's face. 'They might have done better to give it to someone who isn't already prejudiced against what she must investigate,' he said sharply. 'Claudia seems to think she's outgrown Venice.'

Donna Emilia gave him an understanding smile, but shook her head. 'Give her time to settle down here again, my dear. At the moment, measured against New York, how can it not seem provincial, in poor health, and distinctly *passée*? But I defy even Claudia to be here for a while and not slow down to our tempo ... not rediscover the unique, magical beauty of this place.'

'Donna Emilia is right,' Anna said kindly. 'Look at me, already sold on lagoon life and I've only been here a few weeks!' Then she looked across at Giancarlo. 'Claudia won't take any notice of you – she knows you're prejudiced in favour of Venice. We must introduce her to an unimpressionable, reasonable outsider who can't be suspected of *campanilismo* – dear Leif, in other words! He's been won over already, and even reckons that my job is worth doing because Venice does have a future after all.'

169

Her entrancing smile seemed to promise that if his view could be changed, there should be no difficulty in persuading someone who'd been born and bred a Venetian. But Giancarlo refused to spoil her argument by saying that the 'unimpressionable' Norwegian was more probably captivated by her than by whatever else he'd found in Venice. His own fervent hope was that Claudia's investigation wouldn't stray in the Magistrato's direction, because if it did the job of dealing with her would almost certainly be handed to him. He hadn't liked her as a child and the chances were that he'd like even less the woman she'd become.

Thirteen

On their walk back to the *pensione* after saying goodnight to the Achesons, Jess was only half-aware for once of the magical effect of moonlight on the sleeping city. But as usual, she and Jacques wandered off the route home to climb the steps of the Accademia Bridge; it was their chosen spot to stand and stare at the perfect combination of water and buildings around them, for the moment rendered simply in black and silver instead of the gaudier colours painted by the sun.

Jess pointed down at the glinting waters of the canal, broadening now as it quietly flowed to merge with the sea in the Basin of St Mark. 'Imagine anybody thinking this could be filled in and made into a hellish highway for cars and lorries.'

Jacques glanced down and saw sadness in her moonlit face. 'Don't fret, sweetheart; it will never happen.' He waited a moment and then went on. 'Now tell me what else is bothering you.'

She turned towards him and smiled, comforted by the knowledge that he never failed to sense when she was troubled. 'I think we should go home to Paris tomorrow. I talked bravely this evening about getting our dysfunctional family sorted out, but the truth is that I have no idea how to set about it. The moment will come, I think, when Claudia and I finally settle whatever differences we have, but I'd rather give her time to settle her differences with Venice first.' Jess's hand touched his cheek in a fleeting caress. 'It is between her and me,' she insisted gently. 'She knows that what was between the two of you was over a long time ago.'

Jacques caught her hand in his and kissed it, then tucked it inside the pocket of his coat because it felt cold. 'We'll leave whenever you like, my love, but what will you say to Maria and Llewellyn? They aren't expecting us to go so soon.'

'A white lie, I suppose – perhaps a call from Paris about work needing to be done. It's better than confessing that Claudia can't bear to be in the same room with me; Lorenza isn't much better, but she doesn't worry me so much.'

'More fool them,' Jacques said brutally. 'Lorenza hadn't the slightest chance of capturing Giancarlo – she'd had more than enough time to succeed long before you ever came to Venice. As for Claudia, she and I had gone our separate ways well before you decided you could bear life with me in Paris. They're demented, both of them, to still blame you.'

Jess shook her head. 'Lorenza has a very kind but slightly boring middle-aged husband, and hating me adds a little spice to her life. Claudia is still angry with herself; she knows that if she hadn't made it so plain that she thought I'd never find the courage to follow you to Paris, I would have gone back to London instead. She hates to have made a mistake that I must for the rest of my life be grateful to her for.'

Jacques squeezed her hand, but simply said that she was getting cold, and that it was time they left the city to the visiting moon and went home.

In the morning, while Jacques phoned the airport about changing their flight, Jess climbed the stairs to the studio. Llewellyn was already there, but he was staring at the view out of one of the wide windows, not working at his easel. She went to stand beside

172

him, and slipped her hand in his.

'If you looked at it for a hundred years you couldn't get tired of it, could you?' she asked quietly. 'Jacques assures me it won't be allowed to change too much – I pray he's right.' Llewellyn didn't answer, and when she turned to look at him his face was wet with tears.

'What will I do, Jess, when I can't see it any longer?' he asked hoarsely. 'I try to tell myself how lucky I've been, and I pretend I don't care if I never paint that bloody Rialto Bridge again, or the sunset behind San Giorgio Maggiore, but if I believed in God Almighty I'd go down on my knees and beg him to let me go on painting them until I die.'

She blinked away her own tears and tried to steady her voice enough to answer him. 'I know it isn't nearly comfort enough, but you have painted marvellous pictures, and because you've spent years really looking at it you'll always be able to see in your mind's eye exactly what is here. A compassionate God will surely erase from your memory the ugly things you'd rather not remember – those things that the rest of us must go on looking at.'

He said nothing for a moment, then led her by the hand towards his easel and the painting propped up on it. 'Tell me if this is finished or not; I can't decide.'

She stared at the pictured night sky over the lagoon – a subtle, haunting study in shades of grey and silver. 'It's finished, I think,' she said slowly. 'And it's beautiful.'

'Good – then I'll leave it alone.' His hands brushed the subject away as he tried to smile at her. 'It's a treat to have Claudia home for a while. She mustn't stay too long, though; New York is where her work properly is now.'

Jess hesitated for a moment, then did her best to sound casual. 'Will Maria mind, do you think, if we change our plans and go today? There's work I ought to be getting on with ... I hoped it could wait, but apparently it's urgent. Jacques is trying to change our flight.'

Llewellyn's expression told her she hadn't sounded casual enough. 'Dear Jess, you're the world's worst liar,' he said with amusement and sadness mingled in his voice. 'I suppose the truth is that it's still awkward for the three of you to be here together. It's tiresome of Claudia not to have fallen in love with someone else after all this time.'

'That would only solve part of the problem,' Jess agreed wryly. 'It still leaves me in the role of a half-sister she's never wanted, I'm afraid. But while she's living here again and I'm only an occasional visitor, things might become easier. If not, I could stay with Elvira and Nathan when Marco needs me here.'

It was a doomed suggestion, she could see that at once, and Llewellyn's sudden bellow of rage made it doubly clear. *'Non, nein, nyet!* Jess, you stay here whenever you need to – nowhere else! Is that clear? This is your home as much as it is Claudia's.' But she knew that

174

for all his brave noise he still didn't know, any more than she did herself, how to make a real family of them.

'I'll go and find Jacques,' she said. 'You might have to put up with us for another night.'

But in fact he had been able to change their reservations, and now it was a scramble to make farewell telephone calls to Donna Emilia and Elvira Acheson, then pack, and get ready to leave for the airport. Maria was tearful, as she was at any departure, but Jess was thankful she didn't question the reason for their change of plan – work was work; she understood that.

It was Marco who guessed the real reason at dinner that evening, but all he said was, 'Pity ... I wanted Jess to come with me to meet someone tomorrow.' He looked from one to the other of his parents. 'I think I've found the new assistant Nathan told me to look for.'

There was a brief, shocked silence, which Maria broke. 'Because you need help, *tesoro* – because you work too hard?' she ventured hopefully. But his apologetic smile told her what he was going to say.

'Because I shall have to work a little less hard for the Trust, Mamma, for a while at least. I've made up my mind to stand at the election. Nathan knows, and he even seems to approve, if that's any comfort to you!' His hand covered Maria's trembling one as it fidgeted with some crumbs on the table. 'There's nothing to worry about; I'm almost certain to lose.'

'Everyone we know will vote for you,' she said sadly, 'and they will tell everyone they know.'

Llewellyn now chimed in. 'Sweetheart, it only leaves another fifty thousand or so people we don't know. Why not look on the bright side?'

But she could see the influence of his friends travelling out, like ripples spreading in a lake, until it reached every corner of the city. 'You won't lose,' she said with certainty.

Finally it was Claudia's turn. 'Mamma, the voters will be asked to choose a party – Venezia Viva in Marco's case. "Venice for the Venetians" used to be their slogan and I suppose it still is – down with tourists, and money spent on patching up old treasures and preserving buildings that ought to be allowed to fall down! A lot of people here won't vote for a Mayor with a programme like that tied round his neck.'

But the oddity in all that, she realized even as she said it, was that keeping old buildings from falling down was exactly what Marco did these days, and it was one more thing to lay at Jessica's door. Nathan Acheson employed him to work for the Trust, but it was Llewellyn's English daughter who'd initially converted the youthful firebrand he'd once been into the devoted steward that he now was. So quietly spoken, so damnably gentle, Jessica always was, but how successful she'd been at infiltrating the Matthias family.

Claudia emerged from this train of thought just in time to hear Marco's question. 'Will it make things difficult for your work? Everyone is bound to know sooner or later that we're related.'

She thought about it for a moment, then smiled at him. 'Quite the opposite, I'd say – people will be more anxious to talk to me, I think; after all, you might get elected, and a friend at court is always useful!'

His grin agreed with that and, watching them, Maria felt some of the tension inside her relax. As children the two of them had always fought, of course, but never with any real ill-will. But since Claudia arrived home they'd been stiff with each other, hostile almost, in a way that Maria had sensed but not been able to understand. Now they seemed to be friends again, and because it was one less thing to worry about she was able to smile at them both.

Not one to let the grass grow under her feet or do anything by halves, Anna Lambertini set about her campaign to win over Claudia Matthias to their pro-Venice side at once. She explained to Giancarlo that, being the only one of them who worked with Leif Hansson, he it was who must introduce their charming, Venice-loving Norwegian to Claudia. And who better than her old friend to welcome her back with a delightful dinner party?

But the suggestion seemed to fall on such stony ground that Anna had to draw on unaccustomed wistfulness. 'You don't like the idea – think I'm interfering too much?'

Knowing as well as the next man when he was being manipulated, Giancarlo was kind enough not to say so. 'The first thing to get straight,' he pointed out instead, 'is that Claudia and I are not old friends; we're nearly fifteen years apart in age and have nothing in common except that her parents and my grandparents do happen to be close friends.'

Anna pounced on this. 'There you are then – it's a courtesy to them to show her a little kindness; she's been away a long time, probably lost contact with people of her own age.'

She'd scored with both points, Giancarlo's smile acknowledged, but he knew something she didn't. 'Leif has already met Claudia in New York, and my impression is that they didn't take to each other. We'll have the dinner party if you insist, provided you accept the risk that it might be anything but "delightful".'

Anna considered this for a moment, looking shaken; it was inconsiderate of people not to try to like one another, she reckoned, but she had great faith in Giancarlo's charm as a host, and her own social *savoir-faire* had never been known to fail. 'We must still do it, I think,' she decided, 'but we'll invite Claudia's sister and her brother-in-law as well – safety in numbers!'

In Giancarlo's private view the inclusion of Lorenza was all the evening needed to ensure total failure, but he knew Anna Lambertini well enough by now to realize that beneath her frequent attempts to meddle in other people's lives lay genuine kindness; snubbing her was out of the question.

The dinner party was therefore arranged, and was only slightly altered at the last minute when Lorenza's husband was summoned to Milan and Marco had to be press-ganged into taking his place. Giancarlo's guests met in Donna Emilia's drawing room first and she privately regretted not being able to follow them unseen to the Locanda Montin, a short walk away from the palazzo, and still one of the nicest restaurants in the city.

On the face of it there was no reason why the evening shouldn't be a success – three highly attractive young women escorted by their very presentable companions; but the Countess was keenly aware of stresses beneath the surface. Etiquette demanded that Marco should squire the girl who wasn't his sister – Anna, to whom he could only manage to be warily polite. Leif had to convince Claudia that she wasn't still wishing herself back in New York, and Giancarlo's thankless task was to persuade Lorenza to forget whatever grievance currently occupied her mind.

'Pray that the Locanda is on top form,' the Countess besought her husband when the guests had left. 'Giancarlo's dinner party needs all the help it can get.'

Paolo blinked in surprise. 'Why do you say that, my dear? I thought they made a charming group. Anna isn't pretty exactly, but she's

179

very attractive, which is better. Claudia is both, and Lorenza has always been the neighbourhood's beauty.' He smiled at his wife. 'I must leave you to judge the men, but they looked very adequate to me!'

She agreed with this, and murmured that 'better is a dinner of herbs where love is', which puzzled him still further. But she was curious enough to forgo her usual tea and toast in bed the following morning, and go downstairs to share breakfast with her guest.

'I couldn't wait until this evening,' she explained with a smile. 'Tell me how the dinner party went.'

Anna still seemed to be asking herself the same question. 'I could say that it was awful, but it wouldn't be quite true, because in an odd sort of way everyone enjoyed it! But it certainly didn't go according to plan, and when I plan things they usually do.'

The Countess accepted this, believing it to be true. 'So what went wrong?'

Anna bit into a croissant with gusto, then began to explain. 'Well, Leif was supposed to charm Claudia into rediscovering how lovely Venice is; instead, Lorenza came out of her shell like a hedgehog emerging from winter hibernation and monopolized him completely. So Claudia decided to dazzle your grandson – to show us how it's done in New York, I expect! That left poor Marco listening to me, telling him how to save Venice single-handed.'

Donna Emilia struggled to look serious. 'So

180

where does your campaign to sell Venice to Claudia go now?'

'I don't know; I shall have to think about that, and I can see that Marco's going to need some help as well.' Anna's transforming grin lit her face – Paolo was right, the Countess thought; she was better than pretty. She grew serious again. 'I never dreamed I was going to be so busy here – to think I nearly went to Florence instead!' Then her hand reached out to touch Donna Emilia's. 'I love staying with you, but Mamma says I'm not to make a nuisance of myself. I can find somewhere else to live if you and dear Count Paolo have had enough of me.'

The Countess shook her head. 'You can't possibly leave – we haven't enjoyed life so much for ages. Even Battistina smiles all the time!' She had no hope, as Battistina still did, that her grandson had found in Anna the companion he needed, but a friend was better than nothing, and friends they had certainly become.

'You said Marco needed help,' she remembered. 'Don't you think he and his friends can win?'

Anna considered this for a moment. 'Well, I don't know his friends yet, and I haven't quite got him weighed up either. We got off to a bad start, and it confuses me that he's so unlike his father. He's also much too modest to be a successful politician. But I'm on his side, whether he likes it or not.'

'Then I shall warn him that he's probably

our next Mayor,' Donna Emilia said with a perfectly straight face. She took a sip of tea, then thought of one more question to ask. 'Did Claudia dazzle my grandson in the end?'

This, it seemed, required longer reflection. 'I don't think so,' Anna slowly answered. 'But he certainly paid attention to her and I think that was all she wanted – that he should be very aware that she was there.'

It was exactly what she would want, the Countess realized – to wipe out of Giancarlo's memory the image of Jessica would avenge Lorenza's failure with him, and it would lessen her own failure with Jacques Duclos; a perfect settling of old scores. But it wasn't something the Countess felt justified in explaining now. 'You don't like her?' she ventured instead.

'Mostly not ... but just occasionally there's a glimpse of a different girl, and when she is likeable she's almost irresistible, I'd say, as well as very beautiful.'

'You're generous to a fellow female. I hope she's as generous about you.'

But Anna shook her head. 'I doubt it – she doesn't like me at all. I don't know why, because although I make mistakes I don't do any harm that I know of.'

There was a trace of aching sadness in the remark, reminding Donna Emilia of the ruin that Anna's parents had made of their married life. For all her outward gaiety this girl had known the misery of being used by each of them in turn against the other; family security wasn't something she was familiar with, nor the comfort of unselfish parental love.

'Don't think of leaving here unless you decide you want to,' the Countess insisted. Then she smiled her seriousness away. 'How else can we keep abreast of what is going on?'

Anna got up from the table, and deposited a kiss on her companion's cheek. 'Thank you,' she said gently. 'Now I must run all the way to San Gregorio or I'll be late.'

Then she was gone, and the room seemed too quiet and empty without her.

Fourteen

With Easter a memory already, the Serenissima was coming back to life, like an ageing beauty keeping lines and wrinkles at bay by getting out her make-up box again. A new sparkle in the lagoon light and the first hint of warmth in the air had told the boatmen it was time to start polishing the brasswork on their gondolas. In palazzo apartments, housemaids were drawing back the shutters in readiness for the return of absent owners; and every flower shop and stall repeated the same glad message – spring had arrived.

It was the perfect season, Leif realized, to be in Venice. Braving still unpredictable weather, intoxicated lovers of the place were already there, wandering in *campi* and *calli* that had previously seemed too empty. But these were considerate visitors who knew that a fragile city needed to be treated with care. According to Giancarlo, the nightmare tourist season was still a month away. Then, along with package tours and day-trippers would come the heat, the sense of suffocation, and the relentless business of relieving the holiday-makers of as much money as possible while the season lasted.

Aware of his promise to reintroduce Venice to Claudia in the most favourable light he could, Leif couldn't decide which she would find worse – a city forlorn and rain-soaked as he'd seen it first, or as it soon would be, overheated and swollen with crowds whose only purpose in crossing the causeway was to be photographed in St. Mark's square amid a flock of verminous pigeons. The ideal moment to work on her was obviously now, but he had no heart for the task Anna had set him, and little hope of making any headway with it.

'Worse still, Claudia's bound to think I'm pursuing her,' he remarked sadly to Giancarlo one morning. 'The truth is that New York gloss on top of Venetian guile foxes me completely. I can't cope with her at all.'

'Forget Claudia,' his friend suggested. 'She's an expert reporter, trained to spot partiality a mile off! Venice itself must tell her how to write her report.' He stared at the

184

Norwegian, aware that he would miss him when their work together was finished. 'If you'd rather pursue Anna, as I suspect, why not do that instead?'

Leif smiled ruefully. 'Now that would be a pleasure, but at the moment she's hell-bent on "helping" Marco. She dragged me to one of his meetings last night – not quite my idea of an evening together!'

Giancarlo grinned but couldn't help remembering what his grandmother had said about Anna's family history – it would be sad but not surprising if she shied away from becoming too involved with anyone, even a man as reliable and genuine as Leif. But it was a problem the Norwegian would have to solve by himself.

Unaware of having been talked about, Anna was on her way to the Palazzo Ghisalberti, on an errand for Count Paolo, but when she met Beppe on the path outside the courtyard entrance he announced cheerfully that the Signori weren't there.

'Roma, Signorina, that's where they are; not a good place to go if you ask me – it's full of Romans for a start!'

Anna agreed that this was true, but said she'd deliver to Bianca anyway the book Count Paolo wished to lend Signor Acheson. Inside the palazzo, however, it was Marco she bumped into first, in the doorway of his office on the mezzanine floor.

'Good morning. Do you make a habit of

working on a Saturday?' she enquired.

'Not a habit, only when I need to,' he answered calmly. 'Is there something I can do for you?'

'Only give Nathan this book from Count Paolo,' she said, following Marco into the room. 'Beppe says he and Elvira aren't here.'

'They're in Rome – essential shopping for Elvira, according to Nathan; a summons to the Quirinale for Nathan, if you want the truth!' A smile lit Marco's face for a moment, making him look less tired and less severe. 'He'd rather not have the world know how important he is.'

'He's a lovely man,' Anna agreed, and although it wasn't an adjective Marco would have used, it seemed appropriate. 'Leif and I attended your meeting last night,' she announced next. 'We both thought you spoke very well...' Her voice trailed away.

'But? I'm sure there's a but,' Marco suggested. 'Don't spare my feelings, if by any chance you were going to.'

Anna stared at him, too intent on what she was about to say to be warned by the irritation in his face. 'You talk about Venice all the time, but it seems to me that people want to know about *you*. You have to tell them what you do, the sort of things you value, the reasons why they must vote for you instead of the other candidates. You have to get personal!'

Marco's expression was now appalled, not merely irritated. 'Thanks for the advice,

186

although I can't think of anything I'm less likely to do.' Because he recognized the failing that had just been pointed out to him, he spoke more sharply than he intended. A moment later, to his utter consternation, large tears gathered in Anna's eyes and slowly trickled down her face. The gentlest of men in his normal dealings with women, he was torn between a strong desire that she would just go away and leave him in peace, and horror that he'd hurt her feelings.

'Anna, don't cry, please,' he pleaded. 'I know you're trying to help and I'm sorry if I shouted at you, but I can only do things my way'.

Between one blink and the next her weeping eased and, with her face still tear-wet, she was suddenly smiling instead.

'You shouldn't apologize,' she explained. 'This is my one party-piece – tears on demand – but I can't do it if you stop being nasty!'

Bereft of words altogether now, Marco reached her in a couple of strides, grabbed her shoulders and shook her hard. Then, shamed at having laid violent hands on a girl, he released her so suddenly that she stumbled and almost fell. There was silence for a moment while each of them considered what had just happened, and how they could regain safe ground.

'If I hurt you I'm sorry,' he finally managed to mutter, 'but you're the most maddening, provoking creature it's been my misfortune ever to meet. I hope it won't be me, but some infuriated man is bound to strangle you one of these days.'

Anna smeared her face dry but didn't answer; she was too busy thinking that he was Llewellyn's true son after all, with quite fire enough to earn him election as Mayor. She felt pleased with herself to have got that much established at least.

'If you're ready to leave,' he suggested quietly, now in control of himself again, 'I'm about to lock up and go.'

'Then I'll take myself off,' Anna said. 'I'm glad you're not going to stay here working – you look tired, if I'm allowed to mention it without irritating you all over again.'

The gentle comment was disarming instead and surprised him into a confession. 'I'm playing hookey, as a matter of fact – it's too good a day not to be out on the lagoon.'

She spoke diffidently this time, expecting another rebuff. 'I've nothing special to do; could I come too if I promise not to try to tell you how to steer the boat?'

Caution, strong in him because he was as much Maria's son as Llewellyn's, urged him to refuse, but she'd suddenly sounded forlorn and he'd treated her roughly. 'There's a stiff breeze blowing and the water will be choppy,' he heard himself say instead; 'if you look like being seasick I'll heave you overboard. You can have ten minutes to fetch a warm jacket and some non-slip shoes; after that I'm leaving.'

'Fifteen,' she cried, already making for the door. But she was back on the pathway by the gate in less time than that, having exchanged her skirt for a pair of navy trousers, and carrying a thick crimson sweater to match the scarf tucked into the collar of her shirt.

'You'll need the sweater on – it will be cold when we leave the shelter of the *rio*,' he said as she climbed down into the boat. He could have added, he realized, that he was suddenly glad to see her there, but it was too late now, and he simply turned the ignition key instead and set them moving.

She didn't talk while he negotiated the turn into the Grand Canal and threaded his way through the busy Saturday morning traffic. It was something in her favour, at least, that she knew when not to chatter, and even more pleasantly surprising was his glimpse of her face as she stood beside him with the wind blowing her dark hair – she looked as content to be out on the water as he always was.

Once across the Bacino, with the traffic left behind, she thought she could ask where they were going, since it was now obvious that he had a destination in mind.

'We're heading for a little island east of Burano,' he answered. 'It's called San Francesco del Deserto, the home of the Franciscan monks. Legend has it that the saint was once shipwrecked there, but personally I don't care if it's true or not – the island just happens to be the greenest, loveliest, most peaceful place in the entire lagoon; it's full of trees and birdsong.'

Anna decided to risk another question. 'You work all the time in Venice itself, and I assume that someone who doesn't know these waters could all too easily get lost. How are you so familiar with them?'

Steering one-handed now, and looking entirely at his ease, Marco turned his head to look at her. 'Before Nathan took me on I helped to run my uncle's wholesale fruit and vegetable business. He organized the growing end on San Erasmo, where he still lives. My job was to handle the rest of it, supplying Venice itself and the other islands, so I got to know the lagoon very well. The only thing I regret in my present work is that it doesn't leave much time to come out here occasionally.'

Anna wondered fleetingly how much time he would have if his supporters succeeded in making him Mayor; but, anxious not to stir up another political storm, she asked a safer question. 'What happens on San Francesco?'

'The monks grow flowers and food, tend their livestock, train their novices, and say the Offices that divide up the day and night – in other words they lead the busy, gentle life required of them.'

'Lucky monks,' Anna said quietly, and did not speak again until they reached the island's landing stage and the elderly brother who happened to be there smilingly helped her off the boat.

It was, as Marco had said, a lovely place,

190

and serenity seemed to be in the very air. Watching him greet the monks they came across as old friends, she saw a different man; here Marco was relaxed and happy.

They inspected the beautiful cloisters, visited the church that was less beautiful but just as peaceful, and wandered through gardens where peacocks, geese and chickens roamed at will. Back in the boat later, Marco brought out a picnic basket.

'One of the lagoon's cardinal rules rammed into us as children,' he said with a smile. 'Never come out here without food; likewise a compass and warm clothes!'

They ate Lucia's stuffed rolls in friendly silence but, with mugs of thermos coffee in their hands, Anna decided it was time to talk.

'Tell me about Claudia,' she suddenly suggested. 'She's beautiful and successful – what makes her so angry inside?'

Taken unawares, Marco wondered how to deal with the question. He could snub the girl beside him easily enough – pretend she was vulgarly inquisitive, or simply wrong – but he knew she wasn't either of those things.

'You've met Jacques Duclos,' he heard himself say, 'so perhaps you can understand why Claudia fell headlong in love with him years ago. Being Claudia, she not only did that but also commandeered him as her property. Rather than hurt her, Jacques went along with it, believing she would eventually grow out of what he believed was a girlish infatuation ... Only she never did, even when he eventually married our English half-sister, Jessica. Claudia still believes that he should have belonged to her, which means of course that she hates Jess.'

'Difficult all round,' Anna remarked neutrally.

'Made worse by the fact that when we learned of Jess's existence six years ago, Llewellyn soon learned to adore her as well – another black mark against her, because Claudia always reckoned she was his favourite child. Last but not least, she knew Lorenza had always wanted Giancarlo, and neither of them seemed able to accept that it was hopeless long before he even caught sight of Jess.' He looked at Anna, wanting to make sure that she didn't misunderstand. 'It's not as if Jess sets out to bewitch people into loving her; Claudia would see that as a fair fight. What still maddens her is that Jess just does it without trying at all.'

'Poor Claudia,' Anna said unexpectedly. 'Thank you for telling me.' She relapsed into silence again, thinking how much simpler Matthias family life would have been if the English daughter had remained someone they never knew about.

Marco watched her, trying to remember his first impression of a girl it had seemed easy to dislike. 'I owe you an apology,' he said suddenly. 'That morning you brought Donna Emilia's flowers to the palazzo I decided that you were the spoilt daughter of indulgent, wealthy parents – nothing ever lacking, heartache unknown; not, I reckoned, much like life at the *pensione*!'

'Not much,' she agreed evenly. 'But I think I'd have chosen the *pensione* any day. My parents systematically tried to destroy one another, even though they couldn't be happy living apart either. I escaped when I could, and without me as the battering-ram I think they manage a little better than they did. But I grew up thinking of marriage as a battlefield and hid behind a show of carefree confidence to conceal all the fear and uncertainty underneath. Coming here to live with Emilia and Paolo – so contented to be together – I know what a donkey feels like when it's suddenly turned loose in a lovely green meadow!'

There was a little silence before Marco spoke again. 'What happens to the donkey when it has to leave the meadow?'

'I suppose it has to join the real world again,' she said slowly, 'but at least it will know that the meadow exists.'

After a moment or two he repacked the picnic basket and then turned them in the direction of Venice again. Nothing else was on his mind, he would have insisted, but the task of negotiating them out of the shallow channel they were in and finding their way back across the lagoon. But beneath surface concentration lay something much more important waiting to be acknowledged. Nothing was said, however, until they were outside the palazzo's side gate again, and Marco was still forming the words that would thank her for coming with him when she leaned forward and he felt her feather-light kiss on his cheek.

'It's nice when days that start badly turn out so happily,' she commented. 'Like this one did.'

He didn't answer at once and, as if she feared he might deny what she'd just said, she climbed quickly out of the boat and disappeared through the gate.

Now, he knew, it was time to face his own 'green meadow' moment: he didn't dislike Anna Lambertini at all. In fact he could, with the smallest encouragement, fall in love with her – something to be very happy about, if only Leif Hansson hadn't staked his claim first.

Fifteen

Did children ever cease to worry their parents? Maria asked herself sadly. Could they not at least try to become calm, contented adults once the agonies of adolescence were over? But when she put this question to Llewellyn at the breakfast table, although he smiled at the wording, he shook his head.

'If the child you're thinking of is Claudia then calm contentment was never on the cards! Adventure is what she's always wanted, and that brings anxiety for parents.'

'I know about Claudia; it was Marco I was thinking of,' Maria admitted. 'After a visit to San Francesco he always comes back at peace with the world, but that's not how he was last night. He barely said a word at supper, then shouted at his sister because she said that Emilia and Paolo must be getting tired of having Anna Lambertini foisted on them. As it happens, they love having her, but Claudia wasn't to know that.'

Llewellyn hesitated for a moment before answering. 'Anna went with him to visit the monks,' he finally decided to say. 'I saw them coming back along the *rio*.'

Maria looked relieved. 'Then that explains it. Marco doesn't like her, I know; he should have said no if she asked to go with him. I expect they had another disagreement.'

Llewellyn saw in his mind's eye Marco left alone in the boat – not angry at all. It had even seemed kinder not to call out to him and have him know that the desolation in his face had been noticed. For once, Claudia seemed a safer subject to talk about.

'She won't stay, my love – Claudia, I mean,' he said gently. 'I hope you aren't expecting her to.'

'I don't "expect" anything,' Maria answered with unaccustomed sharpness, 'because I no longer understand my own daughter. I can't blame Jacques – he did his best to laugh her out of loving him – and Elizabeth has been kindness itself in New York. But the girl who

195

went there – untidy, laughing, loving all of us as well as Jacques – has disappeared.'

'That girl won't come back,' Llewellyn agreed. 'The scruffy, pretty, impulsive young-ster had to grow up. But somewhere under-neath today's thin, elegant creature there'll be the same warm and loving heart. She's still our Claudia, yours and mine!'

Maria acknowledged this with a smile be-cause he wanted to cheer her up, but her eyes were sad. 'You're right about her leaving as soon as the report is finished. The only thing that would make her stay is...'

But Llewellyn didn't wait for the rest of what his wife was going to say. 'Isn't going to happen, my love,' he insisted quietly. 'If she'd come back happy to be here, because this is where she properly belongs, I would tell her my news. But I absolutely refuse to have her think she's got to be a comfort to me in my blind old age. If it means spending my days until she leaves sitting upstairs pretending to paint, then that is what I shall do.'

It was said with such gentle firmness that Maria didn't even try to go on arguing. Noisy and full of bluster, he could be reasoned into submission, but she knew when she must give in.

He passed his coffee cup across the table to be refilled and spoke in a different tone of voice. 'Where are they, our troublesome brood, by the way?'

'Marco left early – practise day for the race. I asked Claudia to come to Mass with me,

196

but she said she had to walk around Venice counting how many churches are closed! I suppose it was an achievement, getting this assignment, but either it isn't going very well or she doesn't enjoy doing it. She used to love meeting people and asking questions – do you remember when she first began helping Jacques with his Venetian photographs? He said that everyone they met talked to her because she was just naturally interested in them – loved hearing what they had to say.'

'That won't have changed,' Llewellyn said confidently. 'Look at Elizabeth Harrington, as keen as she ever was to ferret out a story; it's an instinct that she and Claudia have, and one of the reasons they get on so well together.'

But Claudia, sitting at a table under Florian's arcade in the Piazza, could have explained that instincts sometimes got lost. She'd ordered coffee she didn't want as an excuse to rest her weary ankles – regular work-outs at a gym in New York hadn't prepared her for the localized fatigues of tramping Venetian alleyways and climbing the city's innumerable bridges.

But more than physical tiredness showed in her drawn face and, watching her for a moment from inside the café, Elvira Acheson picked up her own coffee cup and walked outside.

'Nathan's out with Paolo Rasini, and I've been to church,' she said, sitting down at

Claudia's table. 'Let's enjoy the square together while we may, shall we? In another
month it will be a heaving mass of ill-dressed,
overheated tourists! Perhaps you won't still
be here by then, but we shall, unfortunately.'

Not sure whether she wanted company or
not, Claudia offered Nathan's wife a smile
she struggled to make friendly. 'I seem to
remember that you used not to enjoy coming
here. Why do you if it's somewhere you'd
rather avoid?'

'Because I'm married to Nathan Acheson,
and have been long enough to know that he'd
rather be here than anywhere else on earth. I
still haven't quite figured out why, but maybe
I shall one day.'

Interested enough to put her own wretch-
edness aside for a moment, Claudia stared
across the table at her companion. Beautifully
dressed, as always, in soft tweeds the colour
of a pigeon's breast, Elvira looked what she
was – a rich man's wife – but either years of
living with Nathan had had their effect, or
she'd always been the shrewd, forthright
woman she undoubtedly was.

'Maybe one day,' Claudia repeated her
words with another faint smile, 'the pessi-
mists will be proved right – Venice, submerged by some freak combination of wind and
tide, will end as she began beneath the waters
of the lagoon! Then Nathan's love affair with
the Serenissima will end, and so will your
duty visits!'

She spoke half-jokingly, but Elvira's delicately made-up face looked suddenly displeased. 'He doesn't believe that and nor, I hope, do you. You must report the facts you find, of course, but all the facts, please, not just those that fit some preconceived idea you might have brought with you from New York.'

It wasn't entirely unfair; even angry as she now felt, Claudia struggled to remember that. Hadn't she spoken to Jacques of the decaying city in a dying lagoon that she had no intention of living in again? But still Elvira's reprimand had felt like a slap across the face, and she had to summon all her grace to answer with at least minimal politeness. 'I've undertaken to report exactly what I find – as investigative journalists are trained and paid to do.'

It was Elvira's turn to stare at her, looking for some trace of the young, would-be reporter Jacques Duclos had brought to New York six or more years ago. 'Then promise me one more thing, Claudia,' she asked in a kinder tone of voice. 'Remember that the way you colour your questions will colour the answers you get, in one way or another. In any case, Nathan won't allow Venice to sink beneath the waves. He hasn't quite come out with it yet, but I know he's planning on retiring here the moment he's allowed to.'

Claudia expected another snub but decided to ask the question anyway, coloured however it might be. 'If not submerged, Venice will still be surrounded by the lagoon, with the hungry sea waiting outside the *murazzi*. Will you have got used to it by then?'

It was a question Elvira had often asked herself, especially on long winter nights when the wind brought the sound of the Adriatic waves into the city, or the desolate moan of a fog horn out in the lagoon. But she could answer the question now truthfully. 'With Nathan I can get used to anything – even streets full of water and Venetian rain!' She got up to leave, but hesitated, struck by some lingering hint of sadness in the face opposite her. 'Shall we walk back together?' she suggested with a smile, but Claudia shook her head.

'I've still got too many churches to visit, I'm afraid.' She spoke cheerfully, determined that Elvira shouldn't leave feeling that she'd been in control of the conversation. But, left alone a moment later, she made no attempt to get up and start walking again. It would have been easier, she felt, to burst into tears.

Marco's anger of the previous night was still uncomfortably vivid in her mind, and even now Llewellyn hadn't seen fit to entrust her with a secret that everyone else seemed to know. But there was another grief as well and it was what had been troubling her most when Elvira Acheson appeared and touched it with a perceptive finger a moment ago. Answers were coloured by the way questions were put and Claudia was too honest with herself not to admit that she'd been approaching people wrongly. Full of some inner distress of her own – angst, the Germans

200

would have called it – she'd made them uncommunicative, and probably sometimes untruthful. The famous dictum of the seventeenth-century Friar Paolo Scarpi came to mind: 'I never, never tell a lie, but the truth not to everyone'. The Venetians had had centuries to practise that. Perhaps nothing of what she'd gleaned till now had been reliable at all, and that wouldn't change unless she sorted out the mess she felt inside.

The thought stung her to her feet, but not to go on looking at churches. Instead, she followed the route Elvira would have taken across the Accademia Bridge, but then branched off the usual way home to wander along the Zattere bordering the Guidecca Canal. It was the sort of spring day that showed the city at its best – crystalline air, sunlight on silver domes and gilded angels, opalescent lagoon, and just across the Bacino, to make the picture complete, the little island of San Giorgio Maggiore with its perfectly composed cluster of buildings – monastery, church and bell tower. Impossible to deny any longer that it was all heartbreakingly beautiful or pretend that she'd stayed away for reasons that had anything to do with Venice itself. Unhappiness, resentment, anger were what had fuelled her determination to stay in New York, but these were the same destructive emotions that she'd brought back here. Despair washed over her in a drowning wave and suddenly she was aware of hot tears beginning to stream down her cheeks. Blinded by them, she turned sharply away from the view in front of her only to collide with one of the metal stanchions intended to stop people falling into the water. She lost her balance and fell, aware of sickening pain in the leg that had hit the post. Dizziness kept her lying still for a moment, but she'd got as far as sitting upright, staring at the bleeding gash on her leg, when someone who could only have arrived by boat knelt down beside her. It was Giancarlo Rasini, not seen since the evening of his dinner party at the Locanda Montin, and probably the last person she would have chosen to see her as she was now, laid low and helpless.

'We were just coming alongside and saw you fall,' he said. 'You did it very thoroughly, too.' He calmly pulled a folded handkerchief from his pocket, made it into a pad over the wound, and then tied it in place with his scarf. Small emergencies like this, apparently, were handled every day.

'Very expertly done,' she managed to mutter. 'Now I'm sure I can totter home.'

'You can totter as far as the boat, otherwise I'll carry you, but you're going to the hospital, not home. Your leg needs stitching, and they'll probably want to give you a tetanus injection as well.'

She thought she was about to argue, but the dizziness returned, and she had to duck her head to prevent herself from fainting. A moment later she was lifted to her feet and found

Leif Hansson waiting to receive her in the boat that idled by the steps leading down to the water. When she'd been made comfortable, with her leg propped up on the seat, Giancarlo took over the wheel, and steered the boat round the point into the Grand Canal.

'No flashing blue light?' she asked Leif, trying to smile.

'Not this time; if you'd fallen in and swallowed some of the canal we might have thought more speed was needed!' He didn't ask how she'd failed to see the stanchion, just held her hand instead so that she could feel the comfort he offered.

An hour later, with her leg stitched and the injection Giancarlo had predicted duly received, she was told she could go home. She walked shakily back to the waiting room only to find him still there, leafing through a magazine as if he had nothing better to do with what was probably his only free afternoon of the week. He wasn't aware of her and there was a moment in which to register what she'd deliberately ignored in the past – the austere, male beauty of a face that didn't smile easily or invite small-talk. There was no trace in it of the effete, self-indulgent, useless aristocrat she'd always pretended to believe he was, and it was one more thing to have been proved wrong about. She might soon have to think that Fate had brought her back to Venice for the express purpose of learning some truths about herself before it was too late.

He'd caught sight of her now, laid aside the magazine, and got to his feet. It was time, she knew, to thank him, and apologize for having wrecked his afternoon, but it seemed beyond her now to behave naturally with him. Instead, some core of anger inside her that wouldn't go away made it an effort to speak without shouting at him.

'You shouldn't have waited ... I was going to ring Marco and ask him to come and fetch me.'

Her sheet-white face told him that the session with the doctor had been painful, but she would have been stoical about that, he thought. It was only in matters emotional that she hadn't yet learned how to handle pain.

'No need to trouble Marco,' he said quietly. 'The boat is still outside. Leif walked back to the *pensione* to tell Maria what happened. She'll know not to worry – that I would be bringing you home.' He looked down at the dressing on her leg, surprised to find it now covered by clean, untorn tights.

A wry smile touched Claudia's mouth. 'Elizabeth Harrington's training,' she explained. 'The well-equipped journalist is never without a spare pair in case of ladders or mud splashes; Elizabeth, of course, didn't bargain for a close encounter with a metal bollard!'

'Less common, perhaps, in New York than Venice,' he commented solemnly. 'Now, do you feel up to walking outside, or shall I find a wheelchair?'

She chose to walk, but when he took her by the hand didn't free herself, because her knees still trembled, and for the moment she felt like a damaged child in need of comfort. It was probably how he saw her, she thought, and that prompted her when they were back in the boat to say what was suddenly in her mind.

'I owe you an apology for behaving like a spoilt teenager the evening you took us out to dinner. Llewellyn would have said that I was showing off again – my besetting sin as a child, but I ought to have grown out of it by now.'

She didn't know how she expected him to reply – by agreeing, if he was honest, or more probably looking embarrassed at yet another social faux-pas by a girl whose family hadn't rated an entry in the Golden Book. Instead, to her astonishment, he began to laugh.

'You could at least share the joke,' she said crossly, afraid that she might begin to weep again.

'All right, I will.' Giancarlo wiped the grin from his mouth, trusting that the truth about the evening would strike her as he meant it to. 'We had the idea that New York had spoiled you for the rather time-worn splendours of the Serenissima, so the whole point of the evening – planned by Anna, I have to say – was to get you to change your mind before you wrote your UNESCO report. Leif, as the level-headed outsider, was given the job of re-awakening your old affection for Venice by telling you how wonderful he thought it was. But, for the reasons you already know, the evening didn't go according to plan!'

He looked at his silent, unsmiling passenger and realized too late the extent of his error, but before he could even try to retrieve it, Claudia spoke again herself.

'The reasons being that my dear, bored sister threw herself at Leif Hansson, and I stupidly decided to compete with Anna Lambertini for the attention of the only other man present who wasn't my own brother.'

The words wouldn't have mattered if the tone of voice had been right, or a smile had warmed her face. But voice and expression were anything but right and he was suddenly angry himself.

'There was no need to point out the lack of choice,' he said crisply. 'Any other man, I realize, would have been more welcome. You'll have to stand my company a little longer, I'm afraid, but I'll get you home as soon as I can.'

She was given no chance to reply, because the engine roared into life and he swept the boat round to face back towards the Grand Canal. Ten minutes later they were outside the *pensione*'s garden gate and it was time to bring the whole humiliating episode to an end. Standing on dry land again, she turned to look at him.

'I'm sorry I spoiled your afternoon,' she said stiffly. 'You should have left me to manage on my own.'

'I'll try to remember next time. Signorina Matthias needs no help of any kind.' But her white, strained face made him add something else in a more gentle voice. 'Ask Maria to make you English tea with lots of sugar in it – that's what my all-knowing grandmother would say you need right now.'

With that he jumped back on board and she was left to face the walk up the path alone. But she couldn't complain about that; it was what she knew she deserved. So far it had been one of the most disagreeable days she could remember, and she wondered what else it had in store. Perhaps Llewellyn was finally going to tell her that he was going blind, in which case she would have to manage to look shocked, and pretend that it wasn't what had brought her back to this imperilled, mouldering but still achingly beautiful place.

Sixteen

She was still trying to decide whether the relief of being indoors would be worth the effort of getting there when the door opened and Leif Hansson appeared. His urgent call brought Llewellyn out as well, and between them they carried her into the house and settled her on a sofa in the hall.

'*Poveretta*, why didn't Giancarlo come in with you?' Llewellyn wanted to know. 'Why leave you standing at the gate?'

'Because I refused any more help,' Claudia admitted unsteadily. She tried to smile at Maria, now kneeling beside her. 'I'm all right, truly, apart from a rather sore leg. Before he drove away my rescuer recommended tea with sugar in it, but I'd rather have a bowl of Lucia's soup – I'd forgotten about lunch before I walked into the metal post!'

'Dearest, of course, some soup,' Maria agreed at once. 'But when you've drunk it you must rest on your bed ... you look so pale and tired.'

She felt better for the soup, but didn't argue when Maria urged her upstairs; it was a blessed relief, in fact, to lie down and close her eyes. But although the pills the hospital doctor had given her made her drowsy, she didn't sleep for long. When Maria knocked on the door a couple of hours later and then walked in, she was wide awake, reliving the events of the day.

Maria pulled an armchair close to the bed and sat down beside her daughter. 'I know your leg hurts, but I don't think that's what makes you look so sad, my love. Was it a mistake to come home ... do you want to go back to New York?'

Surprised because it wasn't the question she'd expected, Claudia tried to grab the lifeline she'd just been thrown. 'Well, I do miss my friends there, and of course I love the pace and excitement of New York – Venice seems half-asleep by comparison.' But even as the words left her mouth she knew them for a lie, and for the second time that day her eyes filled with tears. 'Now shall I tell you the truth?' she asked unevenly. 'I think I'm being slowly poisoned inside – by anger and bitterness. I was spiteful about Anna Lambertini, who's never done me any harm; I was rude to Elvira Acheson today because she rightly suggested I wasn't doing my work properly; and I threw Giancarlo's kindness in his face when he tried to help me. I pretend it's all because I want to be somewhere else, but it isn't that at all – the truth is that I still think Jacques should belong to me ... I feel cheated out of happiness by Jessica.'

There was silence in the room for a while before Maria spoke again. 'If being here makes your unhappiness worse, I think you should give up the work and leave,' she said slowly. 'But before you make up your mind I'm going to have to break a solemn promise I gave to your father, and tell you something I think you have a right to know.' She closed her eyes for a moment, praying for forgiveness, but felt Claudia's hand laid lightly across her mouth to stop her speaking.

'No need to break the promise, Mamma – I know already that Llewellyn is going blind. Jacques told me in New York. It's another reason to be angry – that something so dreadfully unfair should be allowed to happen – but it hurt even more that you and Llewellyn refused to tell me about it ... that I had to find a different reason for coming home.'

'*Tesoro*, it wasn't to hurt you,' Maria insisted brokenly. 'Only to stop you thinking that you *ought* to come back. It was more than your father could bear, the thought of your life being ruined. He doesn't want you to know even now, in case you feel you can't go back to New York.'

Claudia smiled shakily at her mother. 'Then we shan't tell him that I know. I shall have to find something else to do when the UNESCO report is finished, but it will be something here, not in New York. I've come home for good, Mamma.' The decision hadn't just been taken, she now realized; it had been there in her mind all the time, and the relief of admitting it was very great.

Maria picked up her hand from where it lay on the coverlet and held it between her own warm ones. 'Dearest, what I'm going to say now will hurt you, but it must be said. You've scarcely ever seen Jessica and Jacques together, but even so you must realize how perfectly they fit. Perhaps you do still love Jacques yourself; if so, you should try to be glad that he found the woman who could make him completely happy. And you must be glad that Llewellyn found the daughter he didn't know – that's what love is, you see: not wanting something for yourself; only wanting the people you hold dear to be happy.'

Claudia was silent for a moment, reflecting that if she was still being taught a much-needed lesson, it was at least being given to her by someone who had learned about love the hard way in her life with Llewellyn.

'"Love is patient, love is kind",' she then quoted unsteadily, '"it does not insist on its own way ... it endures all things." St Paul could have had you in mind, my dearest Mamma, when he wrote that!'

Maria blushed at the thought and waved it away. *Tesoro*, I know it's been a horrible day, but at least one lovely thing has happened. Lorenza was at Mass this morning and she gave me her news. She's certain now of being pregnant, and she looks a different woman – after six years of marriage she'd been losing hope, I think, of a child of her own. She's been a wonderful stepmother to Filippo's two boys, but now she's content at last.'

For the second time that day Claudia thought back to the evening of Giancarlo's dinner party. Lorenza had probably been on a knife-edge of uncertainty at the time, which accounted for her very untypical behaviour. She wished she could have explained that, at least, to Giancarlo. But Maria was talking again, and she was obviously thinking about him too.

'You know, my dear, what a good, kind husband Filippo is, but I've always feared that Lorenza felt cheated by Jessica, just as you did – quite unfairly, of course, because Giancarlo never so much as glanced her way. But that resentment is forgotten now – Filippo is the father of her child, and the only man

211

who matters.' She stopped talking for a moment, then more hesitantly went back to something Claudia had confessed to earlier.

'You said you threw Giancarlo's kindness in his face – what made you do that? He's such a good man, and there's been so much sadness in his life.'

Claudia accepted the gentle rebuke; but reluctantly. 'Maybe, Mamma. But I'm sure he used to despise us children for the rabble he thought we were compared with his own noble family, and you can't deny that he turned up his aristocratic nose at Llewellyn when all he was doing was helping Donna Emilia out of sheer love.'

Maria knew there was some truth in that but she still bravely fought Giancarlo's corner. 'He thought their scheme was dishonest, and in his heart of hearts your father thought so too! I like Emilia's grandson very much. I couldn't blame him for loving Jess instead of Lorenza, and I've never felt that he despised me or my family.'

'No one could despise you, not even the Pope or the Great Panjandrum himself!' Claudia insisted, giving her mother a hug.

Maria smiled but grew serious again. 'Dearest, of course we want you to stay now that you're here, but what will you do? We can't pretend that Venice offers the opportunities you've found in New York.'

'I know, but what did that Dickens character Llewellyn used to read to us about always say? "Something will turn up"!' She looked at

212

her watch, then at Maria. 'Aren't you and Papa dining with the Achesons this evening? Shouldn't you be getting ready?'

Maria nodded, looking doubtful. 'Perhaps I should have told Elvira we wouldn't come?'

Claudia solemnly repeated a maxim often quoted to them as children – an invitation accepted was a promise to attend – so her dear Mamma must go and enjoy herself, knowing how dearly Llewellyn loved a party. Maria finally agreed and went away, and when Claudia heard them leave she got up and went downstairs to ask Lucia for supper on a tray in Marco's snug rather than in the drawing room.

She was still there when he came in an hour later. 'You look tired,' she said.

'And you, poor girl, look rather the worse for wear,' he answered, smiling at her. 'You were asleep, Mamma said, when I came back from rowing practice. Feeling any better now?'

She merely nodded, more intent on what she wanted to say next. 'You were right to shout at me about Anna. I'd no reason to snipe at her as I did; malice was prompted by a nasty suspicion that she manages her life better than I manage mine.'

He hesitated before speaking again. 'It's not the trouble-free life you probably imagine, either. I don't know why we always reckon that other people have an easier time than we do ourselves.' He watched his sister's face, then risked another question. 'Something else

213

on your mind?'

Claudia nodded again. 'I'm not going back to New York – I told Mamma that this evening. She was about to break her promise to Llewellyn, but I told her I knew about him already, so she didn't have to. I don't know what I'll do when I've finished the UNESCO job – I shall have to think about that.'

Marco was still looking at her, but the change in her was something he could sense rather than see. 'We've been at odds ever since you arrived, and I didn't know why, but now I think I do. You haven't just decided to stay; you came knowing you wouldn't be able to go back, but you were angry about it. You don't seem angry any more – so welcome home, little sister!'

She answered by blowing him a little kiss, not quite able to agree yet that she'd struggled against anger and won. But again he read her mind.

'You're remembering that Jess will sometimes be here, Jacques as well maybe. Is that going to be a problem?'

'Probably, but I shall have to deal with it.' A rueful smile suddenly gave him a glimpse of the endearingly honest girl she'd once been. 'I'm on a learning curve altogether at the moment – painful but long overdue!'

He grinned back at her, but then grew serious once more. 'You mentioned Anna a moment ago. I know she doesn't look or sound like Jess, but sometimes she reminds me of her.' He thought he'd said that casually enough, but he'd forgotten Claudia's trained ear, and now it was her turn to stare at him.

'You don't have to tell me what you feel about Jessica, but are you by any chance learning to love Anna Lambertini as well – in a different, un-sisterly sort of way, of course?'

'It begins to feel like that,' he admitted, 'but nothing will come of it. She won't stay in Venice, and when she leaves it will most likely be with Leif Hansson.' Marco managed to smile at his sister. 'He even allows himself to be dragged to my meetings, because Anna is convinced that I need help. She tells anyone who'll listen that Marco Matthias would make a wonderful Mayor, and Leif is required to pretend that Norway needs politicians just like me!'

Claudia's old smile reappeared. 'Good for Anna! I'll have to come along too and help spread the word – at least, I will if you really want to get elected. Do you?'

'There's so little chance of it that I don't bother to ask myself the question; I'll just do the best I can and wait to see what happens.'

She rubbed her nose in a gesture he remembered from the puzzled days of childhood. 'Nothing is quite as simple as we thought it was, is it? You and your hell-raising friends wanted to take from the rich foreigners here and give to the Venetian poor – all very praiseworthy. But I'm learning enough about Venice to know that it's men like Nathan Acheson who do the most to keep the city going, and you even work for Nathan yourself – poacher turned gamekeeper indeed!'

'None of it seems to make much sense,' Marco agreed ruefully, 'but at least we know what we're campaigning for – to make Venice a better place for Venetians to live in. I doubt if the other parties involved can claim as much.' He looked at his watch, and then came to stand beside her. 'You've had a bad day and Mamma would say you ought to be back in bed. Can you manage the stairs on your own?'

'My leg is sore, but serviceable! It has to be – my appointment tomorrow is with the Magistrato alle Acque, who will almost certainly hand me on to one of his underlings as soon as I ask questions he doesn't want to answer.' She struggled to her feet, and leaned forward to kiss her brother's cheek. 'I'm sorry about Anna,' she said gently. 'You deserve happiness more than most of the men I know.' Then she limped out of the room, leaving him to wonder how long it would be before Llewellyn knew the truth about why she was there.

In the Magistrato's office the following morning Giancarlo was discussing the week ahead as he usually did with the man into whose shoes he would one day have to step. They were colleagues, but friends of long standing as well. Both of them were sometimes disheartened by the opposing sides they stood between, but never inclined to believe that they must stop trying to keep Venice safe –

not only from rising waters, but also from the more lunatic environmentalists, diehard preservationists and greedy entrepreneurs. Within these extremes were most of the people who actually lived in Venice, who didn't want to fill in the Grand Canal and drive cars along it any more than they wanted to see the city condemned to being a petrified museum.

'Time to count our blessings,' the Magistrato said. 'We've got through another winter. There'll be other problems of course, but at least we can forget about *acque alte* and flooding for a few months, thank God.' He smiled at Giancarlo. 'Now for the bad news – a journalist wants to ask us questions! She comes under the auspices of UNESCO, so I couldn't refuse. I've got the Minister of Works arriving from Rome, so I'm afraid I must leave her to you ... her name is...'

But Giancarlo answered while the Magistrato hunted for it on his overcrowded desk. 'Her name is Claudia Matthias,' he contributed grimly. 'She's only recently back from New York, but I've known her since she was a child.'

'Excellent!' said the Magistrato, heroically ignoring his companion's tone of voice. 'You'll be able to make sure she doesn't misinterpret anything you say.'

'I shall be unable to *make* her do anything at all; she's never been what my childhood nurse used to call "biddable".' His face relaxed into a faint smile. 'Between Claudia and the minister from Rome I'm not sure which of us has the more trying morning ahead!'

But when she was shown into his office half an hour later he acknowledged to himself that he at least had the more decorative visitor. Her tweed skirt and suede jacket reminded him of the heather he'd once seen aglow on Scottish hillsides. He glanced down at her bandaged leg, but before he could ask the question she answered it for him.

'Mending, thank you – at least, I hope so.'

He waited for her to sit down, then propped himself against his desk, unaware, she felt sure, that the light from the window made a halo round his dark head. Nothing more was said for a moment while they measured one another – each looking for the other's point of weakness, it seemed. But at last Giancarlo spoke.

'The Magistrato had very little time this morning to explain why you're here – perhaps you could tell me.'

It was asked politely, but it pointedly ignored the fact that her report had already figured in their previous conversation. She reckoned it to be a clever but irritating opening gambit in the game they seemed to be playing, and her voice was cool when she answered.

'I'm compiling a report on the present state of Venice for UNESCO in New York. They channel large sums of money here from private committees around the world, and they need to know that this is still worth doing. The Magistrato's department is an obvious area to investigate, wouldn't you say?'

With the ball thrown back in his court, she relaxed in her chair and offered him a faint smile. But tired of the game, if that was what it was, he came swiftly to the point.

'We can, of course, take you through a mass of technicalities, show you computer models of the lagoon, explain how it's been behaving for years past and how we think it will behave in future, and much more besides. But beyond wasting time that our staff could use more profitably, I'm not sure what you would achieve. What, alas, we cannot do is promise UNESCO and its generous committees that we can always keep Venice safe from damage or destruction – there are too many things we can't control, the Adriatic Sea and the government in Rome being only two of them!'

She was silenced for a moment by the note of authority in his voice, but finally found something to say. 'You sound like my poor Mamma – the fate of Venice, she would say, lies in the hands of God, not of fallible human beings!' But again the tone of her voice was wrong, and she was immediately punished for it.

'Your "poor" Mamma may well be right – she usually is,' he said sharply, and misread the astonishment in Claudia's face. 'You think because Maria is content to stay here, quietly taking care of everyone she comes across, that she's someone to be ignored – laughed at?'

'Not laughed at – loved,' Claudia managed

219

to insist. Then she dragged her mind back to the reason she was there. 'I came looking for information, not promises.'

Giancarlo stared at her solemn face, and spoke more gently now. 'You can have all the information you need, but it would help if your UNESCO employers could try to remember that, however precious the treasures of Venice are, what concerns us most is to keep its people safe, and the city fit for them to live in.'

There was no doubting the passionate sincerity in his voice and it was another reminder of how wrong she'd been about him. She wanted him to know that she loved Venice, just as he did, but he probably wouldn't believe her if she said so. 'My employers are concerned about people,' she insisted instead, 'and about a living city.'

Giancarlo's expression suddenly relaxed into a charming smile. 'Seeing that we've found something to agree on, I'll pass you on to one of my colleagues before we have time to fall out again! Daniele will give you all the facts you need, and probably more besides – he's very enthusiastic about his job, like all the people who work here.'

He opened the door as he spoke, led her along a corridor and ushered her into what resembled the control room of an immensely complicated piece of machinery. There she was introduced to the young Daniele, whose deferential manner seemed to suggest that Giancarlo was only one degree lower than

God. He was instructed to guide the signorina through as many of their activities as she wanted to hear about, and then, with a brief farewell smile, Giancarlo bowed and walked away.

She'd been thoroughly out-marshalled, she realized, but if Elvira Acheson was right it was no more than she deserved – she was still asking her questions wrongly. An effort was needed to smile at the young man standing beside her, but she managed it, and just asked to be shown something of what he and his colleagues did to take care of Venice. It was all the effort that was needed; Daniele happily began to talk.

She stemmed the flood of information at last and, punctiliously escorted to the door, asked him to thank Signor Rasini for giving her such an eloquent instructor. He modestly altered the message when he delivered it, but Giancarlo then surprised him with a question.

'Did you enjoy your morning's work with the signorina?'

Daniele's bemused expression was an answer in itself, but he found words as well. She had been the perfect audience, it seemed – so intelligent and quick to grasp what they did, so appreciative and ... and...

'Perhaps a pleasure to look at as well?' Giancarlo suggested with a smile.

'Lovely to look at, but that isn't what I liked about her most,' Daniele insisted gently. 'She was just so ... so *simpatica*!'

He closed the door behind him and went away, leaving Giancarlo to consider what he'd said. He could tell himself that Claudia Matthias was a professional journalist, trained to manipulate an impressionable young man. But Daniele was intelligent and perceptive as well, so who was Giancarlo Rasini – a tired, nearly middle-aged and probably cynical observer of life – to say that he was right about Llewellyn's daughter and Daniele was wrong? The truth was, of course, that his view of her was coloured by all that had happened in the past. He couldn't help remembering the tiresome, over-confident teenager who'd blamed him for not choosing Lorenza, and for not appreciating her father. Maria and Llewellyn might be hoping that, having remembered she had a home in Venice, Claudia would now stay in it, but his own view was that the sooner she returned to New York, the better; she didn't belong in Venice any more. It was time to put the thought of her aside and go back to his own work, but an image remained in his mind of a girl in a soft-coloured jacket and skirt whose face had looked stricken when he accused her – probably unfairly – of laughing at her mother.

Seventeen

It was still only late April but sudden warmth
had descended on the city, blotting out memories of rain-soaked journeys and flooded
squares. Now, sitting at a café table on the
Zattere, Leif told himself to learn to be content. The view in front of him, bathed in
matchless lagoon light, was as lovely as anywhere on earth; his work there was complex
and rewarding; and in Giancarlo Rasini he'd
found a true friend. Life was very good ...
except for one thing.

He'd pretended at first that Anna Lambertini was like any other charming girl he'd met
– delightful company, but not a serious
challenge to the way of life that suited a confirmed wanderer like himself. He'd even, he
remembered, told Giancarlo that they were
two of a kind – wedded to self-sufficiency.
Shakespeare had been right as usual: those
the gods were about to destroy, they first sent
mad!

Anna hadn't just challenged him, she'd won
hands down, and the carefree bachelor of old
was achingly aware of the treasure he was
missing. He'd got as far as trying to explain to
her how serious he was, but she'd sweetly,

gently edged him away from going on, and he believed he understood why: he wasn't the man her heart was fixed upon.

The irony of it – enough to make those same wicked old gods die laughing, he hoped – was that her choice seemed to be Giancarlo, another loner like himself. He was certain of this even though she seldom mentioned his name when they were out together. She spoke of his grandparents instead and, eyes aglow, of the men who devoted their lives to serving Venice. Even loving Anna as he did, he could see the perfect neatness of her staying at the palazzo, married to his friend. But whether Giancarlo could forsake the past where his heart seemed to be buried was a question Leif couldn't answer.

This was as far as his thoughts had got when a cheerful voice spoke beside him, and he turned to see Claudia Mathias smiling at him. 'Sailors need sea legs; Venetians need ankles made of iron – mine have grown soft in New York, I think.'

'Nothing grows soft in New York; it's a hard city,' he said, smiling in his turn. 'Still, they're very pretty ankles, and they don't seem to have suffered from your fall the other day.' He pulled out a chair for her, asked for more coffee from a hovering waiter, and then observed that she was looking much better altogether than when he'd seen her last.

'I was very grateful for your help, and it was kind of you to take the trouble to visit my parents.' She hesitated a moment before

224

going on. 'You were looking rather downcast when I arrived just now ... was that because you can't feel very optimistic about this place?' Her arm sketched a gesture that reminded him whose daughter she was, but when he didn't immediately answer she went on. 'That wasn't the UNESCO reporter asking – only me, Claudia Matthias, off-duty for the moment, the same as you.'

He acknowledged this with a little nod, then tried to answer her question. 'If you're asking do I think Venice will still be here in another thousand years, no, I don't; but for our lifetimes and beyond, yes, of course it will, which is about as much as we can say for the rest of the planet as well.'

'Definitely downcast!' Claudia commented curiously. She thought back to their first meeting in Elizabeth Harrington's drawing room and her impression of him then as a man who could scarcely tolerate city life. 'Is this all too artificial for you – a place that really has no right to be here at all?'

He smiled at the question but answered her seriously. 'A city built on forests of wooden piles is certainly artificial enough – although I don't expect the green party likes to dwell on that thought – but I want it to survive as much as the rest of you do. What does worry me is the use that Venice is put to. I think it worries your brother, too.'

'And you've been to enough of his meetings to be sure of that,' Claudia pointed out. 'I gather that you and Anna Lambertini often go along to act as cheerleaders – that's another kindness on your part.'

'Kindness on Anna's part,' he felt obliged to confess. 'I'm there to keep an eye on her – she's the sort of girl who could get herself into tight corners!'

He didn't mean to, Claudia felt sure, but he couldn't help giving himself away – even his voice changed when he spoke her name. So why his sadness – unless Marco was mistaken in thinking that she'd leave Venice when he did?

'How much longer are you likely to be here?' she asked next.

'A month or two more should see my work finished. For Giancarlo and the others in the department it's never-ending, of course.'

Claudia had her next question ready. 'What comes then, or don't you know?'

Leif turned away to stare at the sunlit vista in front of them. 'I shall go back to Oslo and a fresh assignment,' he said quietly. 'But I'll be haunted by this place for the rest of my life. Elizabeth Harrington warned me of that, but I didn't believe her at the time.'

Silenced by the ache in his voice, Claudia was now sure she understood the reason for it: he'd be going back to Oslo alone. She was about to risk asking him who would keep Anna out of tight corners when he wasn't there but, as if he guessed what was on her mind, he deliberately turned the conversation to herself. 'When are you going back to New York? I got the impression when we first met that it's where you now belong.'

Claudia found herself wrong-footed by the unexpected question, unable to explain about Llewellyn but not ready with any other reason instead for what she was doing. 'I'm not thinking about the future yet,' she answered untruthfully. 'There's still too much work to be done here.' Then she smiled, and he was aware of the change in her – she hadn't smiled like that in New York. 'If Marco gets to be Mayor he might need a good PR assistant, in which case I'd have to stay!'

'For the sake of this city I hope he does get elected,' Leif said seriously, 'but on his own account I'm not so sure. I don't detect in him the killer instinct that all successful politicians seem to have, but if Anna has anything to do with it he will be first past the post!'

This gave Claudia the chance she'd been looking for to lead the conversation back to Anna Lambertini. 'Llewellyn's seen some of her work at San Gregorio, which he says is brilliant. There must be enough damaged pictures and frescoes here to keep her busy for years ... if she wants to stay, that is.'

'I think she'll want to stay,' Leif suggested slowly. 'But she'll be safe here; the Rasinis will take care of her.' Then, as if there was no more to be said, he asked if he could escort Claudia home before he called in at the Accademia, where he'd made a habit of going to look at one roomful of paintings at a time.

She agreed that this was the only way to avoid artistic indigestion, but insisted that she could find her own way. Then, when they parted company, she went on walking along the *fondamenta* that bordered the Guidecca Canal; she wasn't ready to go home yet – she had too much thinking to do.

As she passed the Stazione Marittima one of the first cruise liners of the season was disgorging its passengers for their obligatory dash round Venice – a visit to the Basilica, of course, to see the famous 'bronze' horses (they weren't bronze at all but an amalgam of copper, silver and gold); a lift ride to the top of the Campanile, probably, for a bird's-eye view of the city and the lagoon; then maybe an ice-cream at Florian's or a drink at Harry's Bar before they were herded back on board again – Venice 'done' in a day. They weren't the worst of the Serenissima's visitors by any means, but they brought to mind Leif's question of a little while ago – assuming that the city could be kept upright and adequately dry, what would she be kept as?

The question surely needed to be put to every Venetian, as well as all the people around the world who contributed to safeguarding the city's treasures, but for the moment her concentration was on matters nearer home. There was Anna Lambertini to be thought about – obviously not destined for Leif Hansson, as Marco supposed – and even more pressingly there was her own future to consider. The germ of an idea that she'd begun by dismissing as impossible was taking stubborn root in her mind, and the knowledge that it would seem wildly out of the question to anyone else only added to its attraction. She hadn't lost her appetite for a challenge and what she was toying with would certainly be that.

She walked on through alleyways that were unfamiliar and over whatever bridges she came to until San Nicolò dei Mendicoli brought her to a halt, a reminder that she was now almost at the western limit of the city. The open door of the church – beautifully restored, she knew, by the Venice in Peril Fund in London – invited her inside and she sat down thankfully to rest. But the habit of prayer in such surroundings was hard to break and she found herself falling to her knees.

She could argue that the plan in her mind was full of benefits all round; but she was equally aware that the intention in her heart was almost entirely wrong. And she didn't need to be where she was to hear her mother saying that the Blessed Virgin Mary looked into hearts, not minds. She got to her feet at last with the battle still going on inside her. A nudge from Fate was needed, she said rather defiantly to the serene marble face looking down at her, but she suddenly turned back, dipped her fingers in the stoup of holy water and sketched a repentant cross on her forehead.

The way back to her room at the UNESCO office led her towards the church of San

Gregorio, now deconsecrated and used as an artist's workshop. Although it was on her list of places to visit, there'd be no point in calling now, she reasoned; it was past noon and everyone would be at lunch. But the door opened as she walked past and Anna Lambertini came out – Fate's nudge, sooner than she expected.

They both stopped, Anna willing as always to be sociable, but not quite sure whether the girl who now stood facing her was a friend or not.

'Were you by any chance thinking of eating lunch – and, if so, may I join you?' said Claudia, and saw the other girl's face relax into a smile.

'Our local *tratt* is just around the corner – cheerful and cheap!' Anna fell into step beside her. 'Were you on your way to see what we're doing?' she asked. 'Giancarlo told us about your visit to the Magistrato – Daniele still hasn't recovered, apparently.'

'Because it was such an ordeal?'

'No – such a pleasure!' Anna smiled again at the thought and led the way into the sort of unassuming *trattoria* that could be found in any un-touristy corner of the city. Settled at a table with spaghetti, a flask of *rosso* and mineral water ordered, they took stock of each other. Claudia spoke first.

'You've been very kind, attending my brother's meetings; he keeps very quiet about them at home because he knows they worry Mamma, so we aren't sure how the battle's going.' She waited while the waiter delivered their food and then went on cheerfully. 'This has been a morning for meeting people; I bumped into Leif Hansson earlier on. He said he'd be leaving fairly soon, and looked rather sad about it, I thought.'

'Yes,' Anna said briefly. 'But once away from Venice he'll forget us all quite soon, I expect. He leads a very interesting life, and he can't fail to make friends wherever he goes.' That, her voice said, was all she was prepared to offer on the subject.

Claudia wound spaghetti expertly round her fork, considering her next question. Honesty, she decided, was the only option open. 'Anna, forgive a very personal question, please, but it's important or I wouldn't ask. I got the impression this morning that Leif might have lost out to Giancarlo Rasini where you're concerned ... I might get my own muddled life sorted out if I knew that this was true.' Given her behaviour the night of the ill-fated dinner party, she hoped it might seem a reasonable enough enquiry, but it was a relief when Anna's vivid smile lit her face.

'I've been warned about the information network that Battistina and Lucia run between them! I suppose the ladies are waiting to hear that Giancarlo has fallen madly in love with me.'

'It would very neatly keep you at the palazzo,' Claudia pointed out, smiling in her turn.

'Life isn't much concerned with neatness,' the other girl said, suddenly serious again. 'I love all the Rasinis dearly, and I'm happy to know they love me; but I'm not going to be the next Contessa. You probably know Giancarlo's history as well as I do, but he explained it to me once, wanting me to understand. His parents and then his fiancée were taken away from him, and the only other girl who mattered after that married someone else. He's given up on happiness for himself, I think, though no one deserves it more.' She stared at her companion, unable to read the expression on her face. 'Is that what you wanted to know?'

'Thank you ... yes, it is,' Claudia agreed quietly. Then she waved the subject away. 'What about you? I imagine there's work enough here to last a picture-restorer a lifetime. I hope you came prepared for that!'

Anna shook her head. 'I came very unprepared as a matter of fact, imagining that when my three months were up I'd be done with Venice. But it now seems that I can have a job here for ever if I want to. I'm glad about that, because I love working at San Gregorio, and Venice is starting to seem like home. Mostly, of course, I don't want to leave Donna Emilia and Count Paolo. They feel more and more like my grandparents, but even if they didn't Giancarlo needs someone to help him take care of them.'

While Claudia considered this in silence for a moment it was Anna's turn to ask a question. 'You spoke about your own muddled life – does that mean you can't decide whether to stay here or not?'

She was answered with a smile she couldn't interpret. Then Claudia shook her head. 'That isn't what the muddle was about. It's just that I haven't been able to work out what to do next. I know now what I want, but it remains to be seen whether I can pull it off.'

Anna stared at her consideringly. 'Oh, you'll pull it off all right – whatever it may be! I'd say that anything you want to happen, happens.'

'Generally speaking, yes,' Claudia agreed, and saw no reason to explain that just now and again the gods had decided to teach her a probably much-needed lesson. Instead, she signalled to the waiter for their bill.

'The spaghetti's on me – your turn next time. Now you must get back to work and so must I. I haven't achieved very much so far today.'

But that was a lie, she reflected when they parted company outside the *trattoria*. Her report might not have made much progress – although she had seen the inside of San Niccolò – but, thanks to Leif and Anna it had been a busy and productive morning's work. She would share with Marco the news that when Leif left Venice he would go alone; the rest of what the morning had confirmed she must keep to herself.

Eighteen

Venice was suddenly in the grip of election fever, and a contest that had seemed no contest at all had become real. Excitement was seeping through the alleyways and squares because the outsider in the race, in Llewellyn's terminology, was coming up strongly on the inside. Maria had grown accustomed to seeing her son's face smiling at her from posters all the way to the Rialto markets, but Llewellyn and Claudia now reported that he was being talked about in other parts of the city as well.

On the night of the final rally before voting day Maria waited for Llewellyn to come home. 'Well?' she asked anxiously. 'How did the meeting go? Did the people listen to Marco?'

'Of course they listened – they were being offered a future for once instead of stagnation. It's a brilliant idea that he and Nathan have hatched between them – not the old "market place between the morning and the evening lands" but in today's terms a geographical and cultural meeting place between East and West. Instead of trading in spices and silks and precious stones, here is where information should be exchanged and different creeds learn to co-exist. Venice would have a purpose again.' Llewellyn thought back to the scene in the crowded hall. 'Our son had the audience in his hand – I couldn't have done it better myself.'

Letting this pass, Maria nodded sadly. 'So he's going to win, isn't he? I'm sure Venice needs him, but I wanted a different life for him, *amore* – a normal life, with a wife and children to take care of. He doesn't even have time to meet a girl and fall in love.'

Llewellyn hesitated for a moment, uncertain whether he was about to give good news or bad. 'With or without time, I think he's managed to do that. There were several hundred people crammed into the hall this evening but Marco was looking at, speaking to, just one of them. It was Anna Lambertini who had to be convinced of what he was saying!'

Maria now looked more anxious than ever. 'But what is the use of that when she's as good as promised to Giancarlo? I know it's what Emilia is praying for – that Giancarlo will finally think about the future; and if anyone can make him forget Jessica, Anna will.' She brooded over this for a moment, then looked at Llewellyn. 'You might have been mistaken ... I remember Marco saying that, facing a large crowd of people, the speaker had to focus on one of them – don't you think that's what he would have been doing?'

He saw the hope in her face and decided on

235

a lie; she had enough to make her anxious at the moment. 'Maybe, sweetheart ... maybe he just looked for the friendliest face he could see. By this time tomorrow it will be almost over anyway, thank God.'

But first there was polling day itself to get through. Maria was already at the breakfast table when Marco went downstairs soon after six o'clock.

'You shouldn't have got up, Mamma,' he said, kissing her cheek. 'I meant to slip out without waking anyone.'

'And without eating either, I expect,' she pointed out. '*Tesoro*, some breakfast you must have – I insist on it.'

She insisted so rarely that he smiled at her, and forced himself to tackle the croissants and coffee she had waiting. While he ate, she glanced at him as often as she dared, trying to find in his face anything more than the nervous excitement and tiredness that she expected. But he seemed the same as always when he looked up and smiled at her – her dear and precious son.

'You've done all you could for your friends,' she said suddenly. 'Now whatever happens will be what God intends, my dear.'

Her faith was unshakeable, he knew, and he saw no reason to say that the day's outcome might also be governed by the ruthlessly organized tactics of his opponents. God might be in his heaven, but the devil still had some of the most seductive tunes.

'Don't worry, Mamma,' he said instead. 'I

236

shan't be broken-hearted if I lose; only disappointed for my friends. But I shall traipse round the polling stations, looking every inch the confident candidate! Try to keep Llewellyn at home – he'll only get tired and overexcited if he comes to the Committee Room.'

Knowing what was possible where her husband was concerned, Maria made no promise, but said she would do her best. She was given a quick hug, and instructed not to wait up for the election result as it would be long past midnight before they knew what it was.

When he'd gone she continued to sit there, thinking about Anna Lambertini. It was true that he'd got angry with Claudia for criticizing her, but he got angry with anyone who was unkind or unfair; and although it was apparently true that Anna had gone to all his meetings, as Emilia had been quick to explain, she was a girl who made a habit of helping people. Probably there was nothing to worry about, but later in the morning, when she and Llewellyn had cast their votes and he, as she'd known he would, had set off in search of Marco, she called in at Sant' Agnese on the way home to pray for her son, because the Blessed Virgin Mary knew all the anxieties that beset a mother's heart.

It was long after midnight, as Marco had predicted, before Llewellyn returned to find Maria, Lucia and Giorgio in the kitchen, drinking coffee to keep themselves awake. A glance at his face told them the result.

'Marco didn't win,' Maria said quietly, not sure whether to smile or weep.

'He lost by a few hundred votes.' Llewellyn took a sip of the coffee she poured for him, and then went on. 'Two losing candidates' names were read out, which left Marco and the outgoing Mayor. You could have heard a pin drop in the room. But Marco's name came next, so we knew he'd lost. I'd like to say the count was rigged, but there wasn't really any chance of that – and anyway the bribes had been made long before.'

'Go on, Signor Matthias,' Lucia begged. 'What happened then?'

'A good deal of shouting and booing and cheering all mixed up together; but when some sort of order had been restored Marco very properly complimented the Mayor on his re-election, and then simply promised his supporters that he would try again. You would have been proud of him,' Llewellyn said unsteadily. 'He was just right – dignified in defeat but ready for a battle next time, which he intends to win.'

'When will he be home?' asked Maria, now openly weeping. 'He needs sleep.'

'Yes, but he also needs to wind down – Elvira had food waiting at the palazzo, and Nathan swept them all off there – Marco, Claudia, Anna, Giancarlo and Leif. They asked me to go, but I said I was too old for midnight feasts.'

'And you remembered we'd be waiting,' Maria said, smiling at him through her tears, and knowing how much he would have enjoyed the midnight feast.

'There was that as well,' he agreed. 'Now, I suggest we all go to bed. When he comes back he'll sleep the clock round, I expect. After that life might return to normal again.'

But the peacefulness for which Maria at least yearned didn't quite return. No sooner had the election hubbub died down than they were embroiled in the excitement of the Vogalunga.

Watching the regatta from the Rasinis' balcony, Llewellyn explained it to Anna – a nicely calculated mixture of tourist spectacle and a genuine attempt to keep traditional oarsmanship alive. The city's canals were being taken over by ever-more powerful motorboats that not only threatened the watermen's livelihood, but also damaged the foundations of ancient buildings with their *moto ondoso*. In short, the Vogalunga – the high spot of the regatta – was both a lark and a serious protest, and it was also extremely hard work for the men who had to row the length of the Grand Canal.

They watched and cheered Marco's crew, not near enough to the finishing line to know who had won, but when he reappeared, hastily showered and changed out of his rowing gear, he reported that they'd managed a creditable second place behind a Cambridge crew already triumphant in England from winning the University Boat Race. Coming second, he explained solemnly, was now getting to be a habit; he was probably too young to be a successful politician and too old to be a winning oarsman, he commented ruefully.

Then, having been called into the dining room, they sat down to Battistina's delicious seafood risotto – seated at the table by Donna Emilia with an ulterior motive, Claudia suspected. She was normally the most adroit of hostesses, but today's place settings left the hero of the occasion talking to Elvira Acheson and his own sister, while Anna was safely anchored between Llewellyn and Giancarlo. But the flaw in the arrangement from the Countess's point of view was that it left Marco facing Anna across the table, and Claudia – still apparently listening to something Nathan was saying – watched the moment when Marco, caught by Anna's glance, suddenly smiled at her. She knew it for what it was: an unconscious but totally revealing confession of love which doomed her brother to great unhappiness if Donna Emilia succeeded in matching Anna with her grandson.

Claudia returned her full attention to Nathan Acheson in time to see him raise his hand in a little gesture that asked for silence. He glanced round the table with his rare, charming smile.

'There's something I've been keeping quiet about while so much else was going on, but I think this is the moment to confess my own piece of news. The Trust is to be given an award for its contribution to the welfare of the city. I tried to refuse it to begin with, but then I realized how unfair that would be, not only to Marco and Jessica, but also to the excellent craftsmen we employ.' He glanced along the table at Marco. 'Can you think of a reason to bring Jess back to Venice very soon? I'm afraid the ceremony is only a fortnight away – brought forward on my account because I've had an urgent summons to go back to New York, and I don't know how long I shall have to be away.'

'There's always a good reason to ask Jess to come,' Marco said at once, 'but I know how busy she is in Paris; and if she scents that there's to be what she would call a fuss, she'll find some excuse to stay where she is.'

'It will be our diamond-wedding anniversary,' Donna Emilia suddenly suggested. 'Would that be enough to persuade her and Jacques to come?' She smiled at her husband Paolo sitting at the other end of the table. 'We hadn't thought of having a party, but what better reason could we have, provided Battistina can manage it.'

Llewellyn glanced a questioning eye at Maria and saw her nod. 'No need to bother Battistina, dear lady,' he insisted, 'and nor should you give the party; we do that. You and Paolo will be the guests of honour.'

With a little more gentle persuasion from Maria his suggestion was accepted, the date fixed, and Marco left to inveigle Jessica and

Jacques into coming back to Venice. From then on while the award was being marvelled at and much else discussed besides, Claudia appeared to be listening but she said so little that Maria, at least, noticed her daughter's silence and feared that she could guess the reason for it. If anyone other than Jessica received an award, Claudia would applaud as whole heartedly as the rest of them. But generosity shrivelled and died where her half-sister was concerned; and matters would be much worse if Jacques came to the ceremony with his wife.

But for once Maria was wrong about her daughter. Unusually quiet though she was, Claudia didn't resent the fact that Jessica was going to be made much of at the award cere-mony; and not even the possibility of seeing Jacques again was upsetting her. Heart and mind were fixed instead on the knowledge that her plan must be put into action far sooner than she'd expected or was prepared for. Thinking about it was one thing; trying to make it happen before Jessica arrived was quite another.

But in fact the chance came two days later. With its usual unpredictability the fine spring weather ended in a sudden rainstorm that caught her and most Venetians unawares. In a thin suit and without an umbrella, she was sheltering in a doorway in the Piazzetta when a passer-by, anonymous because he was under an umbrella, halted and then came back to her. Under its dripping brim she now recognized Giancarlo Rasini.

'If you don't mind a dash round the corner, we could wait out the deluge in Florian's,' he suggested.

Aware that if the right moment was ever going to come it had come now, Claudia breathlessly agreed. With umbrella politely held over her they ran past the streaming flank of the Campanile into the shelter of the café under the Piazza arcade.

Inside, in its steamy warmth, she watched him mop his wet face and calmly waited for him to order coffee. The calmness pleased her – hadn't Llewellyn always said that risks should only be taken with a cool head? But she was well aware that this rain-sodden afternoon might appropriately be looked back on as the most crucial watershed of her life.

'You seem to be making a habit of coming to my rescue,' she said when the waiter had gone.

'But without Leif this time – he flew to Oslo for his mother's birthday,' Giancarlo replied. 'He'll come back, of course, but I shall miss him when he finally leaves – he's become a good friend.'

She waited for the return of the waiter with the coffee; her head, she told herself, was still cool, even though her heartbeat was racing and she couldn't be sure of holding her voice steady.

'I'm glad you came by just now,' she finally began. 'I've been wanting to talk to you.' She stalled for a moment, almost on the point of making some ridiculous excuse to get up and leave. But Giancarlo was waiting.

'Talk to me about what?' he asked quietly.

Claudia took a deep breath. 'I wondered if you'd consider getting engaged to me.' The clatter of cups and the sound of the rain faded away; they were isolated from the rest of the world, it seemed, in a little pool of silence just for them. She had to wait a long time for him to reply.

'An engagement usually leads on to marriage – would that be the intention in our case?' he finally asked in a voice totally devoid of expression.

She glanced at his face, which gave no clue either; she had no idea whether he was shocked, enraged, or just humiliatingly amused by the absurdity of what she'd said. 'It would be easier if you'd let me explain first,' she suggested rather desperately.

He only nodded by way of answer, and she was obliged to go on. 'My brother is deeply in love with Anna Lambertini. He was afraid she might be going to leave Venice with Leif Hansson, but that isn't the case; she seems determined to stay at the palazzo. Anna knows you don't want to marry her but she loves your grandparents and is convinced that you're going to need her to help you take care of them. That makes a problem for Marco: my own problem is that I need a reason to stay in Venice once the UNESCO report is finished.'

Giancarlo interrupted her. 'I thought you disliked Venice – has that changed?'

'I *love* Venice,' she insisted, 'but the point is that I need to be here to help Mamma take care of Llewellyn – he is going blind. He still refuses to talk to me about it in case it stops me going back to New York and I need a reason to stay that has nothing to do with him. Until I can find another job, being engaged to you would be reason enough, and it would also free Anna to marry Marco.'

Giancarlo's face registered the shock of her news about Llewellyn. To think of him was to see him with a paintbrush in his hand, always dissatisfied with what he'd just done, always joyously ready to start again. 'I'm more sorry than I can say about your father – must he give up painting altogether?' he finally asked.

Claudia nodded. 'I think he already has, although he pretends to go up to his studio so that I shan't guess before I'm due to leave. But Jacques told me in New York.'

She sipped her coffee, aware that she'd only dealt with the reasons for her suggestion, not its consequences. Giancarlo now went to the heart of the matter.

'You've mentioned Anna and Marco, and Llewellyn. What about the other people who would also be affected by our shabby little deception – do we allow them to congratulate us, knowing that the engagement is a sham?'

She heard contempt in his voice and it stung her into the sort of recklessness that Llewellyn would have recognized. 'Then why not make it real? We've both failed to get the person we wanted and can't imagine loving anyone else. Settling for second best might be better than staying lonely.'

Had she really said that? Yes, his face confirmed that she had, and revealed all too clearly what he thought of her madness. Rather than wait for him to reply she had to extricate herself somehow from total humiliation. 'Sorry ... it wasn't only a stupid idea; it must have seemed like *lèse-majesté* as well! A Rasini marrying a Matthias isn't to be thought of, is it? We'll forget this conversation ever took place, and I'll find some other solution to my problem.'

But before she could get up to leave his voice held her there, cutting like a lash against her skin. 'We'll end this conversation when you've heard what I have to say. I shall make Anna understand that she's free to marry Marco or anyone else she pleases; it's not her job to care for my grandparents – that's my privilege. Nor do I feel the need to marry to ward off loneliness – I prefer life on my own. But should I ever feel inclined to marry, it wouldn't matter a damn whose family my wife belonged to. It never has mattered, but you've always refused to grasp that simple fact. Llewellyn is my grandfather's dear friend, and my grandmother and Maria rightly love each other; how dare you believe otherwise?'

White-faced now, she still tried to smile at him. 'Another of my many mistakes! I think

246

I'll go home now. It's stopped raining ... you don't even have to share your umbrella with me.'

But his hand suddenly reached across the table to fasten on hers. 'I haven't finished yet. I had to make things clear, but if you'll accept what I've just said, I will agree to the sham engagement for as long as it takes you to find another reason to stay here. I want Anna to feel free to leave, and Llewellyn cannot be asked to bear the additional grief of believing that he's spoiling your life.'

She stared at him, speechless, and very aware of his hand touching hers. But at least there was no derision in his face – rather something that looked strangely like compassion.

'I'll leave you to decide when to start hinting at our new relationship,' he said gravely. 'It had better be a gradual change, I think, or no one will believe in it.' Feeling that she'd now run completely mad, she thought she saw a gleam of humour in his dark eyes. 'I shall, of course, allow you to jilt me when the time comes.'

'*Noblesse oblige*, I suppose,' she managed to say, and then ruefully corrected herself. 'No more poking fun at the aristocracy – I must remember that in future.' She freed her hand and tried to smile at him. 'Thank you ... for helping, I mean.' Then she fled out into the *piazza* before he could offer to go with her.

From sheer force of habit her feet knew the way to the Accademia Bridge; her mind was

247

otherwise engaged. In the battle between astonishment, relief and shame it was shame that seemed to be winning. Her reasons for what she'd just pulled off were good enough to have been accepted by Giancarlo, but a lesson learned in childhood was surfacing in her mind: her motives had been all wrong, and for that she must expect to be punished.

Nineteen

Marco worded his telephone call to Jess carefully enough for her to feel that Nathan was the real recipient of the city's award, and that Emilia and Paolo's anniversary was the main reason for her to fly down to Venice with Jacques.

'Of course I'll come,' she said at once. 'Work is only work, but a diamond-wedding celebration can't be missed. I'm certain Jacques will feel the same, but I can't ask him until he gets back from a trip to London. I'll let you know for sure, my dear, but tell Maria to expect him.'

He gave the message to his mother, who then reported a lengthy tussle with Llewellyn.

'Your dear father thought we should invite half of Venice to the party, beginning with the Patriarch himself, the Prefect, and the

Mayor! I've only just managed to convince him that Emilia and Paolo would prefer a small party – just the people they know best.'

Marco grinned but agreed that she was right, then asked why she still looked anxious.

'When Jess and Jacques came for your father's birthday, Claudia ignored them. Will it be the same this time?' He didn't answer at once, so she went on instead. 'On top of that she's unlike herself at the moment. I know she's working hard, trying to get her report finished, but the house used to be full of laughter when she was here – it's not like that now.'

Marco was tempted to say that the new, quiet Claudia suited him better, but he knew it would do nothing to reassure his mother. 'I asked her once how she felt about meeting Jess again; she said that if there was a problem she'd have to learn to deal with it. We have to leave it to her, Mamma – she's a big girl now!' Then he frowned over what he'd said. 'I think there's another problem as well – she's trying to decide what to do next.'

'What is there for her here, my dear? She's outgrown anything we can offer her.'

But now Marco had real comfort to offer. 'It's not as bad as that; Nathan's going to come to the rescue as usual. He just happened, he said, to bump into the Mayor, who seemed very interested in our idea of developing Venice as a midway information centre. Nathan then suggested that if setting it up required skilled people that the Mayor hadn't got, he couldn't do better than offer the job to Claudia as soon as she finishes her UNESCO work. We haven't mentioned this to her, of course – she must hear it from the Mayor.'

'What a dear friend Nathan is,' said Maria, looking happier now. But she had one complaint to make. 'It was your idea, *tesoro* – yours and Nathan's. I suppose the Mayor's going to take the credit for it now.' It was as close as she could get, Marco thought, to saying something harsh.

'I dare say he will,' he agreed with a rueful smile. 'He's the one in charge at the Commune, not us!'

Maria accepted this, not quite ready to admit how far she'd got in thinking that the right person to be in charge there was her son. Assuming the conversation to be over, she returned to the list of party requirements she was making, but Marco suddenly halted on his way to the door.

'Mamma, do you like Anna Lambertini?'

The question was so unexpected that she had to pause and think for a moment – seeing in her mind's eye a girl with long hair and a liking for rather too-short skirts; a girl whose airy grace and confidence belonged to a generation far different from her own. She thought, too, of Emilia's prayers for her grandson. Then she looked up to find Marco waiting for her to answer, as if he was holding his breath because what she said would be important.

'I like her very much,' she admitted at last, and saw him smile.

'Good – so do I,' he said simply, and then went out of the room.

Left alone, Maria gave a little sigh. Llewellyn had been right – he usually was about other people. Face it: the kind, sensible girl she'd picked out in her mind for Marco would never be their daughter-in-law now. Anna might not be either, but she was the one her son wanted.

By the time Saturday came round the wet weather had been blown far inland and, silvered by the sunlight close at hand, the lagoon lay quiet and sapphire-coloured against the horizon, and the morning's crispness would give way to heat later on. With his boat's engine idling gently, Marco waited at the Palazzo Rasini's garden entrance, not knowing whether what he waited for would happen. His note to Anna had only said that she might like to share a ride out to the monks' island again. He'd wait until eleven, and then leave.

There was no need to keep glancing at his watch; all of the neighbourhood church clocks chimed the hour for him. When the last cracked note had died away and there was no sign of the girl he awaited, he accepted failure for the third time, but the election and the race hadn't mattered as this one did; nothing in the world could feel as painful as this loss did.

He turned the ignition key and the engine sprang to life; the boat, at least, felt anxious to leave. He was just edging it away from the canal bank when the gate on to the path opened and Anna rushed out, waving to him to slow down. She leapt across the small gap and landed safely beside him; his hands steadied her and then let her go.

'I'd just given you up,' he said, trying his hardest to sound casual about it.

'I would have been punctual but Battistina chose the wrong moment to cut her hand, and I had to stop and bind it up for her.' If she minded about nearly missing him, he thought she concealed it very well.

'Thank the Gesuati's clock,' he managed to say. 'It's always five minutes slow! Now, sit quietly while we get out into the Bacino – the Canalazzo will be busy this morning.' He needed to concentrate on handling the boat, but time was also needed to accept what he now knew for certain – if the girl beside him wouldn't – couldn't – marry him, then he'd have to go lonely for the rest of his days; no substitute would do.

They were safely through the morning traffic and heading eastwards across the lagoon before he spoke again. 'I thought you'd decided not to come, because you were bored when we went to San Francesco before but were too polite to say so.'

'Then you should have known that wasn't true,' she insisted rather crossly. But there, it seemed, the conversation could end because she was more interested in watching a cormorant dive into the water in search of food.

He turned to glance at her, dark hair pulled back today and tied with a scarlet ribbon. Without its soft frame he could see the faint hollows at temple and cheekbone that made her face look fragile. She wasn't beautiful, as his sister Lorenza had always been and as Claudia had now become, but he knew he would never tire of looking at her. He wanted to tell her so, but a moment ago she'd chosen, very deliberately he thought, not to prolong a conversation that threatened to become too personal. She was there as a friendly companion, but already instinct warned her that she shouldn't have come because he was liable to misconstrue her kindness.

This time there was no genial monk waiting at the island's landing stage, so Anna jumped ashore with the mooring rope and tied them up.

'Very professionally done – you'll make a boatman's mate yet!' he said with what he hoped was a condescending grin.

She smiled back and some sort of ease was re-established, but it wasn't the magical contentment they'd known before; he could sense her wariness, and thought he could guess the reason for it. When he said that he must call on the Abbot while he was there – the monks had a small technical problem that they were sure he could solve for them – Anna looked merely relieved; not permitted inside the monastery itself, she would wait for him in the church, or wander about the gardens.

He found her half an hour later happily playing with a black Labrador's litter of enchanting puppies.

'Problem solved?' she asked with a friendly smile.

'It wasn't very difficult,' he said. 'Just that the monks haven't quite mastered today's technology! Now, if you can tear yourself away from the puppies I think it's lunchtime.'

They went back to the boat and chatted amicably while they shared Lucia's picnic lunch, but when the last of the coffee had been drunk Marco made no move to start the engine.

'Time to clear the air, I think,' he said quietly. 'When we came before I had the impression you enjoyed being here as much as I always do, but something's been wrong today. I think you're afraid I read too much into a pleasant outing, and wish you'd stayed at home today. It's where you belong, I realize – at the palazzo with the Rasinis.'

She was staring at a rowing boat pulling away from the shore, and what he could see of her face – an averted cheek – told him nothing. Even when she turned round he couldn't read the odd little smile that touched her mouth.

'I'm not as sure of that as you are,' she said finally. 'It's true that, apart from feeling indebted to Donna Emilia and Count Paolo for taking me in, I love them dearly. I'd be happy to stay and help Giancarlo take care of them; but he's gone out of his way to say that I'm not to feel obligated to them in any way. I can leave whenever I want to.'

'But you don't want to?' Marco suggested.

'Why should I? I've been happier there than I've ever been before.' But the memory of her conversation with Claudia made her add something else. 'If things change – Giancarlo might marry – then I think I would have to leave; I'd be rather in the way.'

There was a little silence before Marco spoke. 'I don't understand,' he said at last. 'If Giancarlo does marry, he'll marry you ... it's what Donna Emilia prays for, I'm sure, and what the rest of us expect. I can't believe we've got that wrong.'

Again she smiled that odd little smile, and suddenly he knew that the moment had come to say what was in his heart. Almost certainly she was going to turn him down, but speak he must.

'Anna, I need to know why you came today – if it was out of kindness, you must tell me so, because I desperately need it to have been simply out of love. I thought it was hopeless – first there was Leif, and then I felt sure it was Giancarlo you wanted – perhaps it still is, but at least I have to let you know how dearly and completely I love you. Maybe you can't bear the thought of marriage at all, even though you know it does work for some people, but it is marriage I want, not some brief, pointless affair, and I would try my hardest to make it work for us.'

She didn't answer for a moment, and he waited to hear her turn him down as gently as she could. But she said something else instead, with a wealth of love in her voice.

'Haven't you realized why Giancarlo insisted that I was free to leave the palazzo? He knew why I dragged Leif along to all your meetings and badgered people into voting for you, and I was terribly afraid you'd guessed too, because I'd made it so obvious. I thought today's invitation was prompted by pity for an infatuated creature old enough to make a better job of concealing her feelings! You were kind enough to look pleased when I turned up this morning, but I spoiled the day by thinking that I should have had pride enough to stay at home.'

'And I,' Marco said with feeling, 'should have had more sense than to start this conversation in full view of three interested monks! For the moment I can't convince you that my invitation had nothing to do with pity or kindness, so the sooner we leave here the better.' He lifted her hand, dropped a kiss on its palm and folded her fingers over it – the monks couldn't object to that, surely? 'But there are things to tell you first,' he went on. 'Things that you must know before you commit yourself, my love. I have to stay in Venice and, beautiful though it is, its winters are vile and its summers tourist-ridden, and we can't even be sure that it will see out our children's lifetime.'

'Then they will have to ensure that it does,' she said firmly. 'Of course we stay here – it's where your work is, and mine too.' Then she smiled blindingly at him. 'In between raising the children of course!'

His hand touched her face in a fleeting caress but he still looked anxious. 'There's more, I'm afraid. Lorenza and Filippo must go where his work takes him, and there's no telling where Claudia will finish up. But I must stay because Llewellyn is going blind, and he and Maria will need my help.'

Shocked almost to tears, she managed to say, 'They will need *our* help, Marco ... Oh, poor, poor man; I'm so sorry, my dear.'

His anxious face broke into a smile at last. 'Time we went, sweetheart. I'd be happy to miss the tide and spend the night with you marooned on a sandbank, but you might wish you'd made a better choice of skipper!'

'I doubt if I'd mind either,' she confessed primly. 'But we have to think of Battistina – she sits up at night waiting for me to come in!'

Smiling at the thought, she climbed out of the boat, untied the rope and, being Anna, gave the watching monks a friendly wave before getting back on board again. 'We'll come back here, I hope,' she said softly as Marco turned the boat's nose in the direction of Venice.

'Again and again,' he promised, and then settled to the task of steering one-handed so that he could also hold her hand.

Little was said on the journey back because both of them were content to take in the wonder of what had happened. They were almost home before Anna spoke again. 'Could we not tell anyone until Leif has left Venice? That would be kinder, I think.'

He smiled at the typical suggestion but answered seriously. 'It's the least I can do for a man who is going to have to leave Venice without you, although I can't promise that my mother won't guess the moment I step inside the door.'

But when he'd left Anna at the palazzo gate – still unable to kiss her because Battistina was there, chatting to a neighbour – and walked into the hall of the *pensione* five minutes later, no one took any notice of him at all.

His parents were listening to Claudia explaining how her day had been spent. She'd gone out that morning as usual, not mentioning that her appointment was with the Mayor, but now she could talk about it because he'd offered her what sounded like a fascinating job. Already forewarned by Marco, Maria tried to look surprised as well as pleased. Llewellyn, well-known for disapproving of the Mayor, was able to use him as an excuse for anger.

'*Tesoro*, you're going back to New York, remember? What's the point of even considering a job in Venice, and at Ca' Forsetti of all places?'

Disconcerted by the tone of his voice as much as by the words, Claudia looked at her mother. 'Do you both want to be rid of me, or is it only Papa?' Maria lifted her hands in despair, unable to answer, and Claudia turned to face Llewellyn. 'I'm not going back to New York,' she said defiantly, 'I'm staying here.'

Suspicious now, he caught Maria's agonized glance at Marco, and his unfailing radar where she was concerned registered the message. 'You told her!' he shouted at his wife. 'How could you after promising me you wouldn't?'

Marco moved at once to Maria's side and put an arm round her shoulders. 'Mamma told no one,' he said fiercely. 'I told Jess because I thought she ought to know, and we both agreed that Jacques must tell Claudia when he was in New York. The fact is that we're sick and tired of lying about it and playing this stupid game of make-believe.'

He couldn't guess how Llewellyn would react; his father was equally capable of sulking in silence for a week or rushing outside to announce to the world at large that it would be spared any more of his paintings. But before Llewellyn could make up his mind Claudia went to stand in front of him, her eyes bright with unshed tears.

'Don't be cross, please, Papa.' That was a phrase he'd heard from her often enough throughout her tempestuous childhood. 'I couldn't help being angry with you and

259

Mamma, even though I knew why you didn't tell me what was happening, because it meant that I couldn't come back until I had some work to do here. But now that I'm back I want to stay, because this is where I belong. That's why I'm going to work for the Mayor. Whatever you think of him, he's offering me a worthwhile job – but if you don't want me here I'll find somewhere else to live.'

Maria waited with held breath, knowing that however hard it would be for him to climb down, he could no more resist that appeal than he could fly to the moon. She could feel the moment when he caved in, although he still tried to frown equally at Marco and his daughter.

'It's a fine thing when a man's family conspires behind his back to refuse the one thing he asks of them.' He glanced sadly at Maria. 'I blame my dear wife, of course – she must have raised our offspring very badly.'

But when this lament had had time to sink in, he walked across to kiss her cheek and smile lovingly at her. 'Forgive me for shouting at you, *amore* – I should have known better – and on the whole I have to say that our children are not unbearable.'

The two of them were now standing side by side, just as they had in years long past whenever it had seemed wiser to brave parental wrath together. His mouth twitched at the memory, but he tried to sound stern when he spoke to Claudia.

'I should tan your hide for suggesting that

we want to get rid of you; this is your home for as long as you want it to be. Our impression for the past few years has been that it was you who wanted to get rid of us – that's why you weren't given the news of my little problem until your brother and sister interfered. If you're really content to be here, stay for ever; if not, I want you to go back to your life in New York and be happy there.'

Claudia looked steadily at him. 'I'll stay for ever, please.' Then her old teasing smile reappeared. 'Who's going to get Marco and Nathan's brilliant vision off the ground if I don't hold the Mayor's hand? I doubt if he can do it on his own.'

'Almost certainly true,' Llewellyn acknowledged. 'Now, if that's settled I suggest one of you brings a bottle of Prosecco to the drawing room to calm our nerves before supper. Too much emotion plays havoc with the digestion, and we must do justice to Lucia's *bigoli in salsa*!'

He took Maria's arm and led her out of the hall, leaving Marco and Claudia smiling ruefully at each other.

'Well, thank God that's over,' he said with feeling. 'Now perhaps we can work out how to help him when the time comes. However much he hates the idea, he's going to need help.'

Claudia nodded, but there was a more immediate thought in her mind. 'Do you mind about the Mayor going ahead with your scheme? I had the idea that Nathan might

261

have put my name forward, in which case it seems that at least *he* doesn't mind.'

'And nor do I,' Marco assured her. 'The important thing is that it should happen – the sooner the better. And anyway, if you're there, at least we shall always know what's going on!'

Claudia stared at him for a moment longer. 'You looked happy when you came in, before all that rumpus. Was it nice today, out at the island?'

'It was wonderful,' he answered briefly, and then smiled. 'Now, I'd better go and get the wine or there'll be anguished cries from the drawing room.'

She agreed, not mentioning that she suspected him of being grateful for the row she'd just sparked off. Not only could they stop pretending that she didn't know about Llewellyn's condition, but he had escaped Maria's questioning eye. Still, whatever was engrossing him mattered far less for the moment than her own problem. It was typical of the bloody-minded perversity of Fate that the Mayor's offer of a job had come just too late to prevent her conversation with Giancarlo. She must be grateful that the sham engagement could now be over before it had begun, with no-one but Giancarlo ever knowing the reason for it. That left the issue of what her motives had been, but these she would have to learn to deal with herself.

Twenty

The weekend approached too soon for Claudia. She was tired from weeks of intensive interviews and fact-finding, but that was a professional condition, and nothing she couldn't cope with. Harder to bear was the engagement fiasco involving Giancarlo, and on top of that the bruising confrontation with her father. She wasn't ready to face Jessica and Jacques now as well. It would have been a relief to turn tail and flee for as long as they remained at the *pensione*, but for once it wasn't merely pride that kept her there – she knew that Maria and Llewellyn's pleasure in their visit would be destroyed if she refused to meet them.

The morning of their Friday evening arrival she had to spend in the offices of the Regional Council in the Palazzo Balbi. She emerged at lunchtime and on her way out walked blindly into Leif Hansson.

'My fault,' she apologized at once. 'I was still thinking about the futile conversation I've just had with one of our many bureaucrats!'

He studied her for a moment, registering a change in the high-glossed, self-confident girl he'd first met in New York. She looked tired, but the difference went deeper than that.

'You're in need of a sympathetic ear, I expect, and probably some food as well. Dr Hansson prescribes lunch and a glass of good red wine.'

'Lunch wasn't on my agenda, but it sounds like a good idea,' she admitted gratefully.

Dr Hansson even knew where to go, apparently, and five minutes later they were settled in the sort of pleasant *trattoria* that usually only Venetians could find. With lasagne and wine ordered, she looked at him across the table, remembering their last meeting, when he'd spoken sadly of leaving Venice. She hadn't been able to speak of her own reason for staying there for good, nor could she even now.

'Things have happened since we last met,' she pointed out instead. 'Marco didn't get to be Mayor, and you've been back to Norway. I hope you were glad to be there – found that it still felt like home.'

He was surprised by the comment, and wondered if it was born of some similar experience of her own. 'Did coming back here feel like that for you?' he asked, suddenly curious to know the answer. 'An unexpected homecoming?'

She nodded, aware that it would be a relief to tell this sympathetic ear the truth. 'I thought I was a fixture in New York. I'd made such a song and dance about my successful life there that I couldn't admit, even to myself, how homesick I really was. I missed my family, and yearned for a city that I pretended was a dilapidated ruin on the verge of falling to bits. I even smilingly agreed when New Yorkers raved about Fifth Avenue, instead of saying, "Poor fools, you've never seen the Canalazzo on a Venetian morning in spring!"'

Leif's charming grin echoed her smile. 'And of course, they never had!' He waited while food was set in front of them, and then went on more seriously. 'But you did finally give in or you wouldn't be here now. What happens next? After some life-saving gulps of lagoon air do you head back to Manhattan?'

Claudia shook her head. 'I've been offered a permanent job here, which I shall take. Marco's plan to put Venice on the map again as an information trading centre has been taken up by the Mayor. I think he reckons that by having me involved he'll get Marco's help too. But first I've to finish my UNESCO report.' She sipped some wine and then smiled at him. 'Your turn now.'

Leif gave a sad little grimace. 'Assignment nearly over, I'm afraid. It's been the most fascinating one I can remember, as well as unforgettable in other ways.'

Claudia risked a question he might think intrusive. 'You probably won't ever come back – because that would be too painful?'

He didn't pretend to misunderstand. 'I shall go without Anna, which is certainly painful enough, but of course I'll come back. I can't

265

lose the friends I've made here as well. They aren't to blame for my failure with her.'

She was silent for a moment, then heard herself make a confession. 'That's not how I dealt with my own lost happiness. I decided to turn my back on everyone here. I think the skewed logic behind it was that if I could blame them for what happened it would also be fair to punish them – by staying away. I seem to be taking a long time to grow up, but I'm beginning to understand that what I mostly did was punish myself.'

She couldn't quite admit even now that her unhappiness had been no one else's fault, that life simply arranged its triumphs and disasters with blind impartiality. It still seemed more bearable to blame the woman Jacques had married instead of herself. But the reminder of Jessica brought her mind back to the weekend ahead.

'I must get back to work,' she said abruptly, 'but I'm very grateful to Dr Hansson. His treatment was exactly what I needed.' She stood up to go, holding out her hand. 'You won't leave without saying goodbye?'

'Of course not, but in any case your mother's been kind enough to invite me to the diamond-wedding party on Sunday, so I shall see you all then.'

But when she'd walked away he sat on for a while, thinking of his earlier impression of a change in her that hadn't quite been accounted for in the course of their conversation. He'd become too involved with the Matthias family not to hope that before he left Venice he would be able to solve the puzzle she presented. It was very possible that the intricacies and deceptions of life in Venice would defeat him but he was a man who did like to get to the bottom of things.

Claudia managed at least to avoid Marco's return from the airport that evening with the visitors from Paris, even Maria having been forced to admit that her daughter couldn't ignore a sisterly plea from Lorenza to help entertain Filippo's English colleagues from Covent Garden. But the following morning she steeled herself to go downstairs, only to find the breakfast room empty. The Signori, Lucia explained, were still in their room, and the rest of the household had already breakfasted. Lured outside by another fine, warm morning, Claudia carried a tray on to the terrace, and only then discovered that her half-sister was out there too, pruning a rampant clematis determined to suffocate its neighbouring climbing rose. There was a moment when neither of them spoke, then Jess pocketed her secateurs and came to stand at the table.

'*Ciao*, Claudia,' she said with her lovely, slow smile. 'I decided not to join Jacques and Marco in a strenuous morning walk, but it's too gorgeous to be indoors, and there's work to be done out here.'

'The English passion for gardening,' Claudia commented by way of greeting. 'I know about that from Elizabeth Harrington – but shouldn't the heroine of today's ceremony be upstairs getting ready for the great event?'

Jess shook her head. 'It's Nathan's award, not mine, although Marco certainly deserves a mention. How's the report going? I hope – against all reasonable expectation – that everyone is being co-operative.'

'I'm managing, thanks. Being a Venetian helps.' That seemed to be that; she applied herself to the roll she was buttering, and Jess hunted for another question to ask.

'Maria said you were with Lorenza last night – is she keeping well?'

'Blooming, I'd say; I've never seen her look so happy. Pregnancy suits her very well.' There was a little silence that needed to be filled and ungraciously Claudia managed it. 'When you were last here I forgot to say that I was sorry about your baby.'

The careless comment seemed so deliberately hurtful that Jess felt a sudden shocking urge to shake the girl sitting in front of her.

'Don't bother to say it now unless you mean it,' she pointed out crisply. 'I think what you'd rather say is that Jacques married the wrong woman if he wanted a nursery full of healthy children.'

The bluntness from someone Claudia reckoned to be so boringly peace-loving and gentle left her for a moment with nothing to say. She was aware of deserving what had felt like a slap across her cheek, but she'd thought Jessica the last person capable of delivering it.

Feeling that it was unfair to have been so misled, she spoke exactly what was in her mind, caution forgotten now.

'You are fifteen years older than me. I think I could have made a better job of child-bearing than you.'

'Almost certainly I think,' Jess agreed. But while she wondered whether to take the coward's way out and end an unpleasant conversation by walking away, Claudia spoke again, waving a languid hand as if to dismiss a subject she found pointless.

'Shall we agree not to rake over the past whenever we happen to meet? It all happened so long ago. Lorenza's forgotten that Giancarlo exists, and I never give Jacques a thought.'

Jess wished it might be true, but there was doubt in her face that suddenly seemed intolerable and it spurred Claudia into saying what must convince the woman watching her.

'This is not to be mentioned yet to anyone else, but Giancarlo and I have been discussing our engagement.'

She smiled at Jess's sharp intake of breath; surely it was worth some inner discomfort to have dealt her such a blow – and what she'd said was true; they most certainly had talked about marriage.

At last Jess found something to say. ' "Discussing" sounds rather businesslike! Can't you just decide that you want to be man and wife?'

Claudia managed a careless shrug. 'It's not

as easy as that. I've just been offered a very tempting job here as well, and I have to make a choice. I doubt if even a Rasini by marriage is expected to go out to work!'

Jess struggled to remember that she'd spent years feeling guilty about her own happiness with Jacques. But pity for this strangely altered girl shrivelled and died in the face of her concern for a man she counted as a dear friend.

'Forget the job and marry Giancarlo, please, if you love him enough,' she suggested quietly. 'If not, don't think of involving him in a marriage that can't last – he's had too much sadness already to have to endure that as well.'

Claudia's colour rose, but she accepted the challenge. 'I can make it last if I want to. We all know what Jessica can do, she's everybody's darling, but you shouldn't assume that you're the only woman who can make a man happy.'

'I assume nothing of the sort,' Jess said shortly. 'I'm only asking you to marry for the right reason. It would be quite the wrong reason if it's a way of punishing Giancarlo for not choosing Lorenza years ago, and punishing me because you imagine I'm selfish enough to want him not to forget me and marry someone else. I don't mention my most heinous sin – marrying Jacques – because you've assured me that you never give him a thought.'

It was said so quietly that it took a moment

for its deadly accuracy to sink in. When it did, Claudia realized all over again the extent of her error. This gentle-voiced, grey-eyed woman who watched her now was truly Llewellyn's daughter after all. It had been an enjoyable game at first, when she first arrived in Venice, to mock her for being so different from themselves, so self-controlled, so stupidly English; then, when it became painfully obvious that whatever was different about her was exactly what Llewellyn and Jacques Duclos loved, it had become necessary to hate her instead for stealing away affections that rightly belonged to Claudia Matthias. The terrible truth that must be faced at last was that Jessica had beaten her on merit alone; her own limitations had been the cause of all her failures, and they still were.

The anguish of coming to terms with it was written in her white face, and for once she could find nothing to say. Jess pulled out a chair beside her and sat down, aware that this conversation they'd been avoiding for years had to be finished now that it had been begun.

'Claudia, listen to me, please, and believe what I say. I'm sure that you can do whatever you set your mind to – you're young, talented, and beautiful – but your heart must be set on it too, because nothing succeeds without love. If you doubt that you've only to look at your own mother – her whole life is an expression of love for the rest of us, and love doesn't diminish with being offered; Llewellyn doesn't love you less because he's learned to include me in his family; Jacques still loves you in the way he did, just as I still love Giancarlo. Won't you understand that there are different ways of loving – the Greeks even had five words for it! One way doesn't, cannot, cancel out another.'

She looked at Claudia's face, doubtful of being understood or even listened to. 'I'm sorry,' she said unevenly. 'I expect I'm only making matters worse when I so long to make them better. You'll arrange your life as you see fit, without any unasked-for advice from me. But I'll say one more thing. If you can stay here happily, either working or married to Giancarlo, it will give Llewellyn greater comfort in what lies ahead of him than anything else could, because you're his pride and joy. But if you can't be happy in whatever you decide to do, his coming to terms with blindness will be made much worse. Now, with the lecture concluded, I shall take your advice and go and clean myself up for the ordeal ahead.'

She stood up, feeling defeated by Claudia's refusal to even look at her, and began to walk away, but the sound of the other girl's voice made her turn round.

'Jess ... I am sorry about your baby; if it didn't seem that way then I'm sorry about that, too.'

This time the tone was right, and Jess's sudden smile acknowledged the fact. 'Thank you

... thank you very much,' she said gently, and walked back into the house.

When Jacques walked into the bedroom an hour later Jess had got as far as changing jeans and cotton shirt for an elegant suit of jade-green silk, but her mind wasn't on the task of choosing between the string of pearls in her hand and a gold chain necklace lying on the dressing table. She looked up and smiled at her husband, though, and remembered to ask the question he expected.

'Well, did you discover anything or do men prefer an amicable silence when they go for a walk together?'

'We exchanged an occasional comment,' Jacques said solemnly, 'agreed that it was an exceptionally fine morning, and half a mile further on decided that Venice had never looked more beautiful!' Then he grinned ruefully at Jess. 'The name of Anna Lambertini wasn't mentioned, my love, and I lacked the female guile to know the right question to ask.'

'But do you think Marco is happy ... or are we wrong about that?'

'He's deeply enraptured, I'd say, but not quite ready to tell us why.'

'So at least that's all right,' Jess said with feeling, and went back to staring at the pearls.

'But something else isn't – you were looking despairing when I walked in.' Jacques sat down beside her. 'Tell me what's wrong, please, or shall I just make a guess at Claudia?'

She nodded, regretting for once his un-failing ability to sense her mood or state of mind. 'It was my fault. She wasn't really try-ing to pick a fight, but I suddenly grew tired of pretending we were friends and, of course, she retaliated.'

Jacques touched his wife's cheek with gentle fingers. 'After all this time you still feel guilty, don't you, sweetheart, even though the blame was mine, not yours.'

Jess nodded again. 'I've been so aware of the anger and bitterness locked up inside her. I hoped that all that angst might be released if we could only talk about it honestly, but I expect that I just made matters worse. I could hear myself lecturing her like a pompous teacher trying to instruct a wayward pupil. No wonder I failed.'

Jacques stared at her for a moment, aware of the fragility of her face; he loved her more than life itself and still went cold at the thought of how easily he could have missed finding her. 'You don't fail very often,' he said gently, 'and you must never regret our mar-riage, however much Claudia might want you to feel that it shouldn't have happened.'

She leaned forward to kiss him. 'I've never felt that, and never shall.' Then her smile finally reappeared. 'Now I have to choose between these two bits of totally unnecessary jewellery and you, my love, must get changed – you know how Venetians love to dress up!'

Aware that she wanted the subject of Clau-dia to be dropped, Jacques agreed resignedly that in the matter of personal finery present-day Venetians remained all too true to their fancy-dress-loving forbears.

'Then we'll appear in our own glad rags, sweetheart, and smile at the city's dignitaries, and try to pretend that we wouldn't much rather be skimming across the lagoon in Marco's boat, looking for somewhere to tie up and eat a picnic lunch. My only consolation is that Nathan will be having just as much of a struggle to look as if he's enjoying himself!'

Jess shook her head. 'He'll be happy because Elvira will be enjoying herself. She'll look gorgeous and behave like a Duchess, and try not to tell too many people that the Serenissima has been very slow to give Nathan the recognition he deserves! From now on she may even begin to feel that she belongs here, and that will be all the reward Nathan really wants.'

Jacques' muffled agreement to this came as he began to pull off his cotton sweater. When his head reappeared he smiled at her. 'By the way, I hope you're prepared to be included in today's goings-on! Marco let that nugget of information drop while we were out this morning – you and he are both linked with Nathan in the presentation, and so you damn well should be.'

Looking horror-struck, Jess now sounded plaintive. 'How sly of him to keep quiet about it when he asked us to come. Promise me you'll stay close to Llewellyn, because he's liable to get very above himself; he'll be telling anyone who'll listen that he always knew his children would redeem themselves and be a credit to him in the end!'

Jacques promised to do his best, and went on changing into formal clothes, grateful to know that, for the moment at least, the thought of Claudia had been submerged in his wife's mind by what she saw as an imminent ordeal ahead.

Twenty-One

The award ceremony was passing off as smoothly as its organizers expected. Safely tethered in the audience between Maria and Jacques, Llewellyn was a proud but well-behaved onlooker. Jess and Marco had pretended to enjoy the unwelcome spotlight shone on them, and now Nathan Acheson was responding to the praises heaped on the Trust's work with his usual charming diffidence.

But that wasn't the end of his speech. Quietly as always, he went on to say what he believed with such passionate conviction. The damaging arguments that had been allowed to rage for years over how to safeguard Venice from the sea had to be settled before it was too late. The essential needs of its dwindling citizenry must come before those of its welcome but over-abundant visitors. And the Serenissima, for those who truly loved her, should remain a living city, not a beautiful but dead museum piece. Her proper destiny was clear: to be the new meeting-place 'between the morning and the evening lands'.

He finished speaking and sat down, while everyone waited for the many dignitaries present to lead the applause. But Nathan's criticisms, though tactfully couched, had found their mark, and it was the gentle, courteous, and usually almost invisible Count Paolo Rasini who finally rose to his feet. He was joined immediately by Llewellyn, then by another and another until the entire audience – now including the grimly smiling officials – was standing up to cheer the quiet American.

It was, they agreed over supper at the *pensione* afterwards, a very famous victory, because news of it would travel as surely as the incoming tide into every nook and cranny in the city. Its most respected and generous benefactor had shown the government what it was required to do. But Llewellyn was more inclined to linger over the memory of his old friend's share in Nathan's triumph.

'It wouldn't have happened without Paolo,' he explained to Claudia, who hadn't been there. 'We all knew our weasel politicians were having their noses rubbed ever so gently in the dirt, but it needed someone Venetian-born – which I am not – to make them realize that what Nathan said was right. Thank God for a brave aristocrat, say I, and down with the craven upstarts who rule our lives!'

He smiled at his youngest daughter, waiting for her to defend the people she was going to join, but Claudia only smiled back. Maria was grateful to be spared another argument about the futility of working for the Comune, but Jacques' glance lingered consideringly on the face of the girl sitting opposite him across the table. She looked as he'd seen her in New York – dark hair cut fashionably short to show the lovely shape of her head, clever make-up accentuating her beautiful eyes and mouth – but something was different about her. The word 'chastened' scarcely came to mind even now, but there was a new uncertainty about her, as if what she'd once been so confident of knowing was having to be rethought, and he wondered if Jess's conversation with her that morning might be having some effect.

It was certainly vivid in her mind, but Claudia's chief anxiety was the prospect of Emilia and Paolo's party the following evening. She would have to tell Giancarlo that their temporary engagement was now unnecessary because of her new job. But she'd also have to admit to needing it to continue, because she'd been fool enough to boast about it to Jessica even when she already knew the arrangement could be forgotten. Worse than this, Giancarlo was quite astute

278

enough to work out that her motive in suggesting the engagement in the first place had been different from the reasons she'd given.

The next morning, for the first time since coming home, she went voluntarily to Mass with her mother, but halfway through the service she suddenly got up to leave, whispering to Maria that nothing was wrong – she just needed some fresh air.

Outside, thankful to be free of the clutch of candle smoke and incense, she walked at random until she had to stop, simply because remembered habit had led her to the Punta della Dogana, the Dorsoduro *sestiere*'s most seaward point. She'd loved going there as a child, imagining herself setting out across the lagoon to where adventure waited in the great unknown world beyond. The view was just as it had always been – the Campanile's tall finger pointing towards Heaven across the Bacino, and ahead of her the lovely composition of San Giorgio Maggiore floating on the water. But she scarcely saw any of it now. Instead, she was hearing Jessica's voice again, explaining the true nature of love.

She wanted to argue with that voice, insisting on what she knew. Hadn't the last seven years been filled with the joy of loving Jacques Duclos and the pain of losing him? But even that wasn't true; what she'd nursed so carefully all that time was simply jealousy and a thoroughly Venetian desire for revenge that had brought her to the dire straits she was in now.

She'd quoted, not altogether ironically, to Maria, 'love is patient, love is kind', but could she measure up against any of them – Elvira Acheson, doggedly conquering her real fear of being surrounded by water simply because Venice was Nathan's chosen home? Or Maria herself, accepting Llewellyn's illegitimate English daughter into her own family without the slightest reproach? Or even Giancarlo, refusing to offer his love to Jessica in case some jealous god took her away to join the other dead people he'd adored and lost? Love wasn't only patient and kind; it was above everything else unselfish, and about that she had known nothing at all.

She tried to recreate in her mind the Claudia Matthias of her New York days – clever, confident Claudia, made much of by some for her beauty and for her connections with Elizabeth Harrington, and shied away from by others for her self-assertion and single-minded ambition. But that image had been shattered now – like Humpty Dumpty in the nursery-rhyme Llewellyn had read to them as children, that Claudia had had a great fall, and it would take more than all the King's horses and all the King's men to pick up the pieces and put her together again.

The neighbourhood clocks chiming midday reminded her that it was time to go home; Maria would be back from church, wondering about her, and needing help with the evening's preparations.

She felt vulnerable without the protective shell of self-assurance that she'd grown used to, and as tired as if some cathartic episode had been lived through. But she felt oddly peaceful as well, all passion spent, but with passion had gone the anger and resentment that had been bottled up inside her for so long. The evening still loomed ahead, and Giancarlo had to be faced, but now she could see a time in the future when she might begin to recognize in herself again the girl who'd been in love with life before she'd met Jacques Duclos.

Elegant in black lace, Maria waited for her guests to arrive, wondering why what was intended to be an especially joyful occasion should involve quite so much anxiety. She had no worries about her part in the evening – the rooms looked beautiful, and the menu had been chosen to please her discerning but frail guests of honour. The other guests, including Emilia's only remaining cousin – an elderly Marchesa brought over by Giancarlo from the mainland – were not a problem either; it was her family who troubled her. Claudia had returned from her walk looking as if the fresh air had done her very little good; Jessica, normally a serenely calming influence on everyone, was on edge; and even Marco, when he thought his mother's eye wasn't on him, seemed to be away in a world of his own. But at least Llewellyn – relieved of the horror of sitting down thirteen to dinner by the presence of the Marchesa – was his usual exuberant self. Resplendently dressed for the occasion, he made his guests welcome, and ushered Emilia to her seat with the tender, reverential air he kept for her alone.

Giancarlo brought up the rear of the party from the Palazzo Rasini. He kissed Maria's hand and then her cheek, and offered Jess the same affectionate salute. Glad of some last-minute instruction for Lucia, Claudia could slip into the room almost unobserved and miss the flurry of greetings. But the moment came when, slender and graceful in a dress of aquamarine silk, she had to face Giancarlo. She looked composed enough, but her hand felt cold when he, correctly, bowed over it.

'I need to talk to you,' she murmured in a low voice. 'Our arrangement's unnecessary now – Llewellyn knows that I've been let into his secret, and I've been offered a job by the Mayor.'

'So we've become un-engaged, is that it?' he asked with the calm air of someone who was only faintly interested.

'Not quite ... not yet,' she said desperately. 'I was stupid enough to ... to boast about it to Jessica.'

He considered her for a moment, surprised to find himself thinking that, whatever else it might be, life with Claudia Mathias was unlikely to have been dull. 'Then, as your still-temporary fiancé, I'd like you to look less miserable,' he said solemnly. 'It's bad for my self-esteem!'

Astonishing though it seemed, she thought she could see an unexpected gleam of humour in his eyes but there was no time to be sure because Leif Hansson, for once unusually well turned out in dinner jacket and black tie, had come to stand beside them.

'Lovely,' he said, looking appreciatively at her dress. 'The colour of the lagoon on a fine early morning. Don't you agree, *amico mio*?' he asked Giancarlo.

The question seemed to require some thought. 'Not quite silvery enough perhaps,' the answer blandly came before he excused himself and turned to Elvira Acheson instead.

His eye for colour was truer than Leif's, Claudia decided, and obviously he'd done for civility all that was required; she needn't look for any charming compliment as well. But at least Jessica would have seen them together, and for that she must be grateful. Breathing more easily now, she could notice that Marco was pinned into a corner by the Marchesa. She walked across to them in time to hear Emilia's cousin bewailing the Serenissima's downward slide towards vulgarity.

'You don't notice, I expect, because you live here,' she was saying earnestly, 'but each time I come back there are more shops selling beribboned straw hats, and glass gondolas, and cheap carnival masks ... so tawdry and distressing, don't you agree?'

Marco did agree, but pointed out a problem that he thought might have worried the elderly lady more if she wasn't living safely in

Padua. 'Another shop selling tourist trash means one less butcher or shoe-mender for the people who belong here, Marchesa, and that's even more distressing.'

It was true enough but bluntly put – not quite, Claudia thought, how her brother normally spoke to anyone who failed to understand the city's real problems. But with her own protective shell dismantled, she was aware of the impatience Marco was doing his best to hide. He didn't allow himself to glance at Anna Lambertini, now engrossed in conversation with Giancarlo, but Claudia could feel in her own bones his longing to change places with the other man. Miniskirt abandoned for once, she was a boyish Aphrodite come to life, in a pleated tunic of white silk – no, not boyish, Claudia decided. What she was looking at was feminine grace personified, a quicksilver girl who was hard to pin down. How she would fit into the complicated family life of the Mathiases it was hard to predict; but Claudia had no doubt that Marco intended her to be part of it from now on.

The seating plan had caused Maria much thought and even now, she feared, she hadn't got it right. Concerned with looking after her elderly guests of honour – as well as the Marchesa and the Achesons – she'd had to leave the younger generation to fill the other side of the long table, and she couldn't help being uneasily aware of undercurrents of emotion that seemed to leave them with less

284

than usual to say.

It was Llewellyn's privilege to propose a toast to Emilia and Paolo, and he did it with the warmth and grace that she, of all people, most seemed to inspire in him. Maria was his beloved wife; Donna Emilia was his liege lady, looking, in her black gown trimmed with exquisite white lace, as if she'd stepped out of a seventeenth-century Dutch portrait.

Then it was Paolo's turn to speak, first to thank his wife for the sixty years they'd shared, and then their grandson and their friends. So much happiness known together, such unquestioning confidence in each other; how fortunate he and Emilia had been, and how especially grateful they were to dear Maria and Llewellyn. Almost unaware of doing so, Claudia turned to look at Giancarlo beside her, expecting to find his eyes fixed on her to remind her of her cheap and silly jibe about the social gulf between their families. But, although he was looking at her, he wasn't frowning now, only inviting her to laugh at the absurdity of what she'd said. Of all her past mistakes, her determination to see him as a snobbish, humourless aristocrat had to be one of her worst. His only sin in previous years had been not to see through Llewellyn's flamboyance to the man beneath the disguise, but she could scarcely blame Giancarlo for that – her dear father had enjoyed misleading people, and had probably gone out of his way to do it.

In the drawing room again after dinner they

found a surprise awaiting them. Llewellyn's most recent attempt to capture on canvas the lagoon at dusk, hauntingly lit by a rising moon, was now propped up on a table against one wall. He led Emilia towards it and asked her and Paolo to accept it as his anniversary gift.

Only his family knew that it was the last attempt he would ever make, but Giancarlo felt certain he could guess why there was suddenly so much emotion in the room that Maria's face was wet with tears. Emilia sensed it too and looked uncertainly at Giancarlo, sadly at a loss for the first time.

Praying that he was about to do the right thing, he spoke first to Emilia. '*Cara*, I think you should know what it is you've just been given – Llewellyn's last and most beautiful painting.' Then he turned to Llewellyn, who was now white-faced and speechless. 'Forgive me, but wasn't it time for your friends to know? This isn't the moment I'd have chosen, but somehow it seemed to choose itself.'

There was a long pause in which Giancarlo tried to imagine what might happen next. With Llewellyn anything was possible at the best of times, but what was this if not the worst of times? He saw the Welshman's face flush with angry colour, but, seeing it too, Maria went at once to stand beside her husband and link her arm in his. He looked from her tear-stained face to Emilia's shocked one, then shook his head free of anger and began to speak in his still-beautiful, lilting voice.

'Giancarlo's right, my friends; it's time to confess to you that macular degeneration doesn't respond to treatment, and I can no longer tell Venetian red from Prussian blue – so there will be no more "Llewellyns".' He turned to Emilia apologetically. 'Dear lady, Maria and I both wanted you to have the painting, but I should have known better than to give it to you this evening – I've spoiled your and Paolo's party.'

She shook her head and forced herself to speak through the lump in her throat. 'Nothing is spoiled – how could it be with such dear friends and such a gift?'

It was all that she could manage, and she was thankful to hear Nathan Acheson's voice asking the question that was in all their minds.

'David, are you quite sure nothing can be done?' The use of the name was typical of Nathan, Jess realized, and quite deliberate; if Llewellyn, the artist, was no longer to exist, they would become familiar with the name David Matthias instead.

He dealt calmly with the question. 'I probably shan't live long enough to go completely blind, but no, nothing can be done.' Then he smiled at their shocked faces. 'My dears, you mustn't look so tragic. The truth is that there are only so many times a man can paint the Rialto Bridge or the sunset behind San Giorgio Maggiore! I shall retire to the comfort of my armchair and drive Maria and our children mad with unwanted and probably wrong advice until the day comes when they can stand it no more and deposit me on some uninhabited island in the lagoon.'

Some immediate response was needed, and Anna provided it. 'Where I, at least, shall come and visit you,' she said with a tremulous smile, blowing him a kiss. 'I'm always in need of advice.'

The well-timed arrival of Lucia and Giorgio with their after-dinner coffee broke the spell of sadness in the room, and everyone strove to remember their reason for being there – they were celebrating, not attending a wake. But while the others crowded round to admire the painting, Giancarlo edged close to Jess. 'Tell me, please – was that a dreadful mistake?'

'It was brave, and right,' she insisted quietly. 'Our dear father had become fixated on keeping his secret – chiefly for Claudia's sake, but also because he's terrified of becoming an object of pity. He needs us to treat him as we always do, not too respectfully, just with all the love we have for him in our hearts.'

She stared at the man beside her, torn between hope and uncertainty for him; more than anything she wanted him to have the joy of a happy marriage but, believing she knew Claudia's motives for even considering it, happiness seemed much too doubtful a prospect. He saw in her candid grey eyes all the anxiety she couldn't put into words.

'You look worried, Jess ... Don't be,' he insisted gently. 'I'm not sure what's going to happen next, but I promise you that I won't let harm to come to anyone here. Will you try to believe that?'

Her transfiguring smile appeared as she answered him. 'I do believe it – and I believe something else as well. They are being amazingly discreet about it, but Marco and Anna are at the stage of being unaware that the world contains anyone but themselves. It can't be long before they have to give in and share their secret with the rest of us!'

'Llewellyn's very taken with her already, but what about Maria?' Giancarlo asked. 'I suspect that Anna, lovable as she is, isn't the girl your stepmother would have chosen.'

'Perhaps not, but Anna will make her son happy, that's all Maria will ask of Marco's wife.'

He glanced round the room at the people gathered there. 'You and Jacques will leave tomorrow, I suppose; the Achesons must set off for New York, and by the end of the week Leif will be back in Oslo. How much nicer it would be if you could all just decide to stay here!'

She smiled at that but her eyes were sad. 'Llewellyn especially will miss us, I'm afraid. Could I ask you as a dear friend to help my family take care of him? Maria and Marco have had time to accept the idea of his blindness, but it's hard for Claudia, and she loves him so much.'

'Did I not say a moment ago that you were to stop worrying?' he reminded her almost roughly. Then the rare charming smile that swept away severity lit his face. 'Don't the English have a phrase for it – something about muddling through? We shall do that and emerge victorious!'

'I do believe you will,' she agreed as Maria came to say that the Marchesa and Emilia were beginning to look tired, and it was time to bring the emotional evening to an end.

Twenty-Two

The first official day of spring, the fifteenth of May, was well past, but in fact Venice seemed to have leap-frogged straight into the summer season. The tourists were beginning to arrive in ever-increasing numbers, and Leif could see now why they represented such a very mixed blessing to the city. The way to avoid them was to do what the Venetians did: stay well clear of the area around the Piazza San Marco, which was where they congregated, along with the pigeons that, as unobtrusively as possible, the Comune tried to cull.

As his own stay was now measured in days only, he'd formed the habit of getting up very early to walk about the empty alleyways and squares; as many images as possible had to be securely fixed in his memory before he left. He especially liked to loiter in the Rialto markets, watching the traders arriving at dawn to set up their stalls – it was surely a peculiarly Venetian skill to transform heaps of humble fish and vegetables into such colourful works of art. And then there was the Riva degli Schiavoni to stroll along, to be entranced again and again by the opalescent, changing colours of lagoon and sky as the sun rose to begin another day. Elizabeth Harrington had been right that evening in New York to warn him that he wouldn't leave the Serenissima the same man he'd been when he arrived. He said as much to Giancarlo when they were out in the launch making what would be their last inspection together of the *murazzi*. His companion smiled at him.

'My grandfather would quote his beloved William Shakespeare and say you'd "suffered a sea-change into something rich and strange". But have you identified the difference?'

'Not entirely,' Leif answered slowly. 'But it's certainly something to do with becoming more richly alive. It will sound odd if I describe a city as sensual, but I'm aware as I never was before of colours, textures, sounds, and of course the endlessly changing play of light on water. I realize that some of the effects are just illusions – enough of the staid, sensible northerner remains to be still aware of that! But it makes no difference to what Venice actually is – a city like no other that I can imagine finding again.' He was silent for a moment, looking at the island-dotted

291

seascape around them. 'Can it survive? Are we doing enough of the right things?' he asked with sudden urgency in his voice.

Giancarlo finished carefully photographing a section of sea wall that showed signs of damage, and then sat still with the camera in his hands. 'I can't be sure, of course – I'm not God Almighty, who Maria Matthias would tell you with certainty knows all things. But short of some global catastrophe that we can do nothing to prevent, I believe Venice will survive. It isn't fashionable to say so, of course. Listen to the most extreme of the environmentalists and the frustrated, would-be modernizers, and they'll tell you the Serenissima is doomed, but I refuse to believe it. More slowly no doubt than we should, we are being allowed to get on with what can safely be done, most especially of course with the lagoon barrage.'

Leif nodded, realizing that his confidence in the man beside him was such that it seemed safe to feel reassured. 'What about you?' he asked, changing tack. 'Are you the next Magistrato when our *caro collego* retires?'

'I expect so,' Giancarlo agreed ruefully. 'There has to be someone other than the officials in Rome to blame when things go wrong!'

He stared at Leif, whose attention seemed to be caught by a clam-fisherman's boat chugging past them. The Norwegian's blunt-featured face was already browned by the lagoon sun, but he thought he detected more

of an alteration than that. Leif hadn't mentioned Anna in his list of Venetian awaken-
ings, and Giancarlo wouldn't have expected
him to, but he wondered how much it was
costing his friend to remember that he was
still a wandering man, content to travel alone.

'You'll stay in touch, Leif, I hope – maybe
even come back for good one day when you
get tired of inspecting the world's oceans,' he
said. 'We all feel you belong here, so as the
probable next Magistrato I'll promise you
now employment for ever and a day!'

Leif's withdrawn expression warmed into a
smile. 'I may hold you to that. But I'll come
back in any case – there are so many other
things I'll want to know, leaving Venice itself
aside. Will Llewellyn cope with going blind?
Will Nathan decide he's done enough to keep
the leaky ship of international finance afloat?
Will Marco become Mayor next time round?
I assume, of course, that he'll be married to
Anna by then.' His voice dried up for a
moment, but he cleared his throat and went
on. 'And what will become of the remarkable
girl I first met in New York who is already so
different here?'

For a mad moment Giancarlo was tempted
to suggest that he could answer the last question at least. Claudia Matthias would, if all
else failed, settle for becoming the next Contessa Rasini. But just in time he remembered
that this wouldn't happen, because their engagement was not only temporary but ficti-
tious in any case. Disconcerted by something

that felt like unexpected but sharp regret for a mistake that should have been avoided, he smiled ruefully at Leif.

'Claudia will probably remain what she's always been – a riddle concealed in a puzzle and wrapped up in an enigma! She is a mystifying force of nature to the rest of us.' But the surprise in Leif's face suggested that he'd spoken much too vehemently and now he tried to sound off-hand. 'Let's hope the Mayor knows what he's taking on – she's going to work for him.' Then, turning the ignition key, he started them moving again.

With Jessica and Jacques already back in Paris, it seemed too soon to be having to say goodbye – probably for the rest of the summer – to Elvira and Nathan, and then to Leif as well. Maria was happy enough with a quieter life but she knew that Llewellyn had never relished tranquillity. Where, he would say, is the fun and challenge of never being sure what is going to happen next? Even more, though, he now needed other people to talk to and laugh with if he was to go on pretending that the future didn't fill him with frustration and dread. Her heart ached for him as he set out each morning – the necessary dark glasses only in place, he claimed, to give him a mysterious air – to walk round the neighbourhood and end up at a café on the Zattere where he could sit etching the colours of the sky and the lagoon into his memory.

For the moment Claudia was still away for

long hours, toiling at the completion of her report in the UNESCO office, and it became Anna Lambertini's self-appointed task to entertain Llewellyn at the *pensione*. She would drop in on her way back to the palazzo from San Gregorio, and Llewellyn learned to look forward to visits that usually began with a discussion about whatever she was working on and somehow always ended in a spirited argument over the rival merits of Tintoretto (his favourite) and Veronese (hers), or Canaletto versus Longhi and Guardi.

Now and then she was persuaded to stay for supper, by which time Marco and Claudia had returned home. Each evening she shared with them convinced Maria a little more that here was Marco's chosen companion – the chemistry between them was unmistakable – but nothing was said about marriage, and at last she anxiously consulted Llewellyn on the subject.

'I know what it is,' she said despondently. 'Emilia told me about the Lambertinis' dreadful life together, and Anna has made up her mind never to marry.'

Llewellyn refused to believe that any son of his could be so lacking in the necessary powers of persuasion but undertook to enquire – with what he was pleased to call his usual finesse – what was holding matters up. It was harder than he expected, given that Marco could now side-step leading questions with the skill learned from politicians, and he was finally driven to abandoning finesse altogether.

'Why not marry, or at least live together?' he asked crossly. 'God knows it's easy enough to see that you love one another.' Marco didn't answer at once, and Llewellyn rushed on, horrified by the idea that had just occurred to him. 'If you're about to lie and pretend that it isn't because you have some half-baked idea of staying here to look after me, then don't lie and don't stay either.'

Marco's mouth twisted in a rueful grin. 'That's a pity – Anna and I had just decided how easy it would be to convert the attic floor into a self-contained flat! But if you and Mamma refuse to consider the idea we shall have to find somewhere else to live.' It was Llewellyn's turn to pause, registering the fact that in the mater of finesse, his son had just won hands down. But Marco misread the hesitation, and now hesitated himself. 'It would mean using your studio ... perhaps we shouldn't even have thought of it.'

One of Llewellyn's theatrical gestures waved that aside. 'My dear boy, I wasn't going to put up a blue plaque! Of course you must use it; what's the point of wasting space in Venice?' Then a beatific smile spread over his face. 'I told your dear mother there was nothing to worry about but she would have it that Anna probably jibbed at the matrimonial hurdle, and you were too noble to consider anything else! I said both her conclusions were certain to be wrong.'

'And you were right as usual,' Marco

agreed. 'We were just giving you time to get used to Anna being here. That was her idea, of course – it's obvious to me that you already love her nearly as much as I do.'

His father's answering hug ended the conversation, leaving Marco free to go and explain to Anna that she must now consider herself part of the Matthias family, and to very properly ask Count Paolo, in *loco parentis*, for her hand in marriage. Llewellyn, meanwhile, carried the good news straight to Maria. She happily considered the conversion of the *pensione*'s top floor, then offered a suggestion of her own.

'*Amore*, why don't we and Claudia move up there? Marco and Anna will surely need more space than we do before long. We could say that you'd prefer it, having your studio become our new sitting room.'

Llewellyn ruined the effect by smiling, but tried to sound severe. 'It's catching – Marco's getting as cunning as a cartload of monkeys and now you're just as sly. Still, for all that it's not a bad idea, but you'll have to sell it to Anna.' He saw a shadow cross his wife's face and thought he could guess the reason. 'You're afraid Emilia still has hopes of Anna for Giancarlo?'

Maria shook her head. 'I think she's given up on that. No, it's Claudia who is on my mind. She'll be the odd one out even more now, with all the others happily settled. I love Jacques almost like another son, and I couldn't wish that he hadn't come to Venice,

297

but will she ever get over adoring him? I don't think so.'

Llewellyn had no opinion to offer, knowing that the mysteries of the female heart defeated him. But what he did know wouldn't comfort Maria very much either – he believed their daughter was engaged on some lonely journey of discovery that she was having to make alone. At home she was always kind enough to laugh at his jokes, sweetly affectionate to her mother and on the friendliest terms with Anna, but his conviction was that at some deeper level she wasn't connected with life at the *pensione* at all. Something or someone else absorbed her heart and mind, but she was intent on the rest of them not knowing about it, and he supposed it was because whatever it was would worry them.

He stumbled on the truth accidentally one Sunday morning when the two of them were out in the garden, waiting for Maria to come back from Mass. Claudia was hacking away at a honeysuckle that had already finished flowering, aware that neither she nor Llewellyn – who was theoretically advising her where to cut – had the slightest idea whether their pruning was correct or not.

Without thinking, she suddenly said, 'We need Jess here. I think the English are born knowing what to do with growing things – I suppose it's all that rain they have.'

He didn't point out that it rained fairly continuously in Venice from November to March, being diverted by astonishment at what she'd just said. It was the first time in his hearing that she'd referred to Jess as anything but Jessica, and the first time in anybody's hearing, he felt sure, that she'd suggested that they could do with her presence there. While he was still torn between wanting to comment on the change and fearing to say the wrong thing, he saw Claudia begin to smile at him.

'Yes Papa, I did say "need"!' She abandoned the honeysuckle to its own vigorous devices, and came to sit down beside her father. 'We had a talk when she was here last – straightened a few things out.' Then her dark brows drew together in a frown. 'Well, that's not quite true. My gentle English sister made a fairly thorough job of demolishing me for one reason and another. I didn't admit it at the time but I knew even then that she was right. It was like having a swelling lanced to release the poison inside – painful but effective! The odd thing is that I shan't ever mind her coming again.'

'And ... and Jacques?' Llewellyn ventured.

'They're one and the same – Mamma pointed that out to me, and she was right as well.' Claudia hesitated and then said something else. 'There's one more thing I have to clear up, so I hope she comes back soon. Couldn't she help with the alterations upstairs?'

'Of course, *tesoro* – Marco's probably been trying to pin her down to a visit already.' Convinced, now, that he'd got to the bottom of things, Llewellyn smiled lovingly at his daughter. 'I think you'd better have another go at that poor plant – Jess will say it looks terrible as it is.'

But later in the day Marco reported that they'd have to plan the alterations without Jess – it would be another month before she'd be free to return to Venice, and they couldn't wait that long to start work. Claudia nodded and went to her room to write two letters. The one to Jess admitted that the engagement to Giancarlo was false and gave all the reasons – good and bad – that had led to it; the one to Giancarlo explained that they were finally and firmly disengaged because Jess now knew the truth about the whole charade.

There was one more truth that she acknowledged only to herself, with a mixture of astonishment and despair: she'd made a point of avoiding Giancarlo since the night of the diamond wedding party, but out of sight had been anything but out of mind. The almost unbelievable fact was that the more she told herself she could forget about him, the more persistently he stayed in her thoughts. She saw him in a glimpse of some man, tall like him, ahead of her on a crowded *vaporetto*; she remembered the way his mouth stayed solemn when his eyes were amused, and the feel of his hand on her own. She might go out of her way not to bump into him, but the truth was that it made no difference at all; he seemed to have become the daily companion of her mind.

He answered her letter with a formal little note, courteously phrased, in which she could find no trace, however hard she looked, of any regret or disappointment; if anything she suspected him of being faintly amused. In all fairness she couldn't blame him, and that, she told herself, was the only reason she wanted to weep – no one liked to have been seen to be quite such a fool.

She finished her report and handed it in with a sigh of relief. Not due to start work at the Comune until the beginning of October, she was free to take a holiday, escape the worst of the summer heat and crowds; she planned to go up into the Tyrol, walk in the fresh mountain air, and find peace of mind again. But there was a wedding to help plan, the burden to share of rearranging the layout of the *pensione*, and above all there was Llewellyn himself, never demanding companionship but needing it all the same. So she abandoned the idea of the Tyrol and stayed where she was.

There was no hope of avoiding Giancarlo altogether now; with so much communication between *pensione* and palazzo, she had to learn to greet him as both neighbour and childhood *bête-noire* turned family friend. Well, it could be done; she was long past openly revelling in the sort of adolescent enchantment that Jacques Duclos had inspired. No one else need know, Giancarlo least of all, the self-control required to smile and pretend that she wasn't aware of him in every nerve-end of her body. Perhaps one day she'd come to appreciate the perfect irony of it, that if she'd broadcast their 'engagement' he, being the man he was, would almost certainly have honoured it. But this time round love was adult and unselfish, as Jess had warned her it had to be, and this time round there was no one to blame except herself. Jacques had known that sooner or later she'd grow out of the infatuation she'd lavished on him, but he might have expected her to have more sense than replace him with a man who'd chosen his solitary life with the happy certainty of a medieval hermit. He was content alone, and she would somehow have to learn to live without him.

Twenty-Three

Marco and Anna chose a small-scale, intimate wedding, despite Llewellyn's disappointment. Given a free hand, he'd have invited everyone they knew to fill the vast interior of the Frari, the acknowledged setting for high-profile nuptials. But Maria had pointed out more firmly than usual that the mere father of the bridegroom had nothing to say in the matter. It was for Anna to make her wishes known and, among the churches in the neighbourhood, San Sabastiano had been her choice. So on a hot, still day in late September they gathered in an unimportant church whose walls nevertheless glowed with the humane, warm genius of Anna's favourite painter; and Llewellyn forgave her choice because he loved her as well as Veronese.

Uncertain until the last minute about the arrival of her parents, Anna had explained to Maria and Llewellyn that it depended whether or not the wedding date coincided with one of the short-lived seasons of goodwill between her separated mother and father. In the event they were both there and she could present them to Marco's family confident that at least they *looked* parents to be proud of. With Donna Emilia's eye upon them they behaved very well and, made happy by Llewellyn's evident relish for escorting so elegant a mother of the bride, Gina Lambertini even concealed her disappointment that Anna had chosen Marco instead of the next Conte Rasini.

The bride, attended only by Claudia, wore a simple white organza dress, with tiny white flowers in her hair. Simple, but ravishing enough to make Marco catch his breath at the sight of her, and Maria weep at the expression on his face. Claudia, beautiful though she was in rose-pink, seemed content to be noticed as little as possible, and it seemed to Jess, watching her from a nearby pew, that her face looked sad when she forgot to smile.

There had been no chance for the sisters to talk alone since Jess's arrival late the evening before, but Claudia had been waiting with her parents when Marco brought them back from the airport. Claudia had hesitated, but not Jess, who walked towards her half-sister with arms outstretched, and so for the very first time the two of them had hugged each other. Then Claudia had kissed Jacques too, in the friendly, affectionate way a brother-in-law could expect to be kissed. Watching them, Maria realized with great thankfulness that what she'd said to Llewellyn had been wrong – the child so determined never to let go of her treasured balloon had finally allowed the string to slip through her fingers; the balloon was free to float away at last.

The wedding ceremony was followed by a buffet luncheon at the palazzo – presided over by Battistina, of course, but helped by Lucia and Giorgio from the *pensione*, and Bianca and Beppe, borrowed from the Achesons next door.

It was then that Giancarlo, in the role of best man, thought it permissible to share with the bridesmaid a window-seat that would only accommodate two. They agreed that it had been a lovely wedding. Then Giancarlo suggested that having Marco and Anna at the *pensione* would be a comfort to Maria and a great help to Llewellyn. Claudia agreed again, not pointing out that the *pensione* was still her home as well.

'My grandparents will miss Anna very much,' he said next. 'For the past few months she seems to have breathed fresh life into both of them.'

'I'm sure she still will,' Claudia contributed. 'They won't be forgotten now ... neither Anna nor Marco would allow that to happen.' If this was what Giancarlo wanted to be assured of, she prayed that he could now get up and leave. She was too conscious of him beside her, of his shoulder touching hers; she wanted to weep for the pain of not belonging there while Anna always would, even though married to Marco.

Then Giancarlo's brown hand gestured to the guests clustered at the small tables that were set out around the great room. 'I'm not sure why it is,' he said calmly, 'but one wedding always feels as if it should lead to another one. Don't you think we should take the hint and re-engage ourselves?'

Suggested with rather less eagerness than if he'd been proposing a stroll before tea, the question still left her for a moment wondering whether her heart had stopped beating. No, now it was racing to make up for lost time, propelled mostly by anger, although much hurt was mixed up in it too.

'I did apologize for embroiling you so stupidly in my affairs,' she managed to say at last. 'There was no need to remind me of something you probably found farcical.'

She watched his hand clench on his knee, as if he'd been made angry in his turn, but when he spoke his voice was still calm. 'At least my proposal was more serious than yours – I was thinking of a real engagement, leading to an actual marriage. Does that sound farcical?'

'Why?' she asked baldly, ignoring his last question.

There was a little pause; time for thought was needed, she supposed.

'Mixed reasons,' he finally answered. 'Partly for my grandparents – I realize now how much it meant to them, and especially to Emilia, to have the company of a young woman living in the house. Partly for your own sake – you were hurt by what happened in the past, but decided your parents needed you back in Venice, only to find that Anna is going to be living at the *pensione* anyway. And lastly for my own sake, of course – I should be proud to call you my wife.'

On the verge of insisting that he didn't want a wife, she understood the significance of what he'd just so carefully said. She would be called his wife – social custom still preferred a man to be married, especially if he was destined to be one of the city's high officials – but she would only be *called* his wife, and he needn't worry about jealous gods destroying her, because love wasn't involved this time.

'I realize, of course, that you would want to continue working for the Mayor,' he said quietly. 'What you are going to do for him at the Comune is important.'

She suspected mockery again, but his eyes were fixed on her when she looked at him, and there was no derision in his grave face. If it hadn't seemed so unlikely she might have thought he looked sad, until a wry smile suddenly touched his mouth instead.

'It was a serious suggestion, but I can see it doesn't appeal! Shall we consider it unsaid and go on as we were ... at least until the next time one of us feels like proposing again?'

He made it sound as if it was a little fever they suffered from occasionally, but she was being gently invited, she realized, to laugh at the awkwardness they found themselves in – trust a Rasini to know how to handle any situation, however embarrassing. She had never in her life felt less like laughing but she summoned up something that might pass for a smile.

'I think I'd better say yes now, to save us any more trouble!' The words had been said – she could still hear them echoing in her mind, and whatever madness had put them in her mouth, they couldn't be retracted now; matters had gone too far for that. The expression on his face was unreadable. She couldn't even be sure of seeing relief that at least she'd be taking Anna's place at the palazzo. There was one more thing to say and she managed it quite calmly. 'I'd rather leave you to announce our news when you think everyone's had time enough to recover from today's excitement.'

'Of course. I must speak to your father first in any case, but tomorrow, unfortunately, I have to fly to Stockholm for ten days – yet another conference on climate change. With your permission, I'd like to tell Donna Emilia, though, before I leave.' A smile suddenly melted his formality. 'I'll warn her not to confide in Battistina!' Then whatever else he might have said was lost because Beppe arrived beside them, carrying a tray of champagne. It was time to drink the toast Count Paolo was getting ready to propose.

For the rest of the long afternoon she was only properly aware of the moment when they waved Marco and Anna into the launch that would begin their honeymoon journey to Greece. She needed the reminder of how a newly-wed couple ought to look – utter happiness underpinned with a kind of reverence for each other – a reminder too, therefore, that marriage was a sacrament. When their own time came would she and Giancarlo still be treating each other with the polite formality they did now? Would anyone else know that she meant the vows she took even if he didn't? She shivered at the thought, despite the warmth of the afternoon, but Jess was watching her, and she had to produce a smile instead.

'Ghost walking over my grave! Isn't that what the English say?'

Jess nodded but, instead of answering, just linked her arm in Claudia's, and the friendly little gesture was enough to quell the panic she could feel rising inside her. It was even possible to get through smiling goodbyes for Donna Emilia and the Count, but she faltered when she came to Giancarlo.

'Safe journey ... and not too many boring speeches in Stockholm, I hope,' she managed to say, holding out her hand. He bent to kiss her cheek, and held her hand for a moment, then politely released it. Courtesy would be the death of them, she thought, unless he could ever bring himself to behave to her as anything but an acquaintance just met in the street. She could walk home certain that her family had no suspicion of the bombshell in store; it was a comfort in one way, and yet in another way it was something to weep over.

After the hardships of the summer – heat, crowded *vaporettos*, mosquitoes, and too many malodorous side canals – it should have been time for the Serenissima to relax gratefully into the most pleasant season of the year. Instead, a stifling blanket still lay over the city, like the wrath of God, Llewellyn said. He'd given up sneering at the idea of global warming and bewailed instead the daily heat haze that blotted out the Dolomites, which were usually visible on the northern horizon, promised freshness there at least. People meeting in the dusty alleyways and squares raised their eyes to heaven, asking each other if it would ever rain.

Claudia, walking among them to the Rialto markets to shop for her mother, waited not for rain but for Giancarlo to return from Stockholm. Then he would speak to Llewellyn and she could, for better or worse, move out of the unreal limbo state she seemed to inhabit. But, two days after Marco and Anna's wedding, a note from Donna Emilia jolted her into remembering something that had barely registered at the time – Giancarlo had said that he would speak to his grand-mother before he left Venice. The Countess's note briefly suggested a late-afternoon visit; the day didn't matter as she was always at home then. Not one to shirk something that promised to be unpleasant, or at least un-comfortable, Claudia set out for the palazzo that afternoon, saying merely to her mother that there was someone she had to meet. Maria, immersed in their removal to the top floor of the *pensione*, merely waved a hand by way of goodbye.

At the palazzo, Battistina loitered watch-fully at the open door as Claudia climbed the staircase towards her. The Signora Contessa was *un po' triste*, it seemed, so perhaps an un-expected visitor would do her good. Claudia registered the fact that the invitation hadn't been mentioned, and smiled in spite of herself; for once the *rio*'s information chain hadn't been set in motion.

She was led not into the great *portego* but to a smaller side room that she'd never entered before. Looking out into the garden at the back of the house, it was shadowy and cool – the Contessa's private sitting room, obvi-ously, and a proper setting for its fastidious owner. Knowing Battistina's inclination to linger, Donna Emilia dismissed her handmaiden gently but firmly, and then smiled at her guest.

'Thank you for coming so promptly, my dear,' she said, wasting no time in social niceties. 'We have something to talk about, do we not?'

But having made that brisk start, she hesitated a moment, wanting to see how the girl facing her would behave. In the little pause that followed she acknowledged to herself that, on the surface at least, her grandson had chosen well. Claudia looked right, and the Countess placed proper value on that. In addition, she already knew something about Llewellyn's youngest daughter. Lorenza had been content to grow up in the shadow of her larger-than-life father; Jessica had been her own woman long before they even met; but Claudia had seen it as a joyful challenge to compete with him. She was competing now, in a way, waiting calmly for her opponent to make the first move.

Slightly ruffled by that word 'opponent' in her mind, Donna Emilia spoke more abruptly than usual. 'My grandson told me of your engagement ... It came as a complete surprise, I have to admit.' Ingrained courtesy made her hesitate again and Claudia suddenly felt moved to pity for this elderly woman who couldn't understand why her much-loved, clever grandson should be making a mistake he would always regret.

'It's not a surprise you like, I'm afraid,' she suggested honestly.

Donna Emilia met frankness with frankness. 'The reason for it is what troubles me. I don't count Giancarlo's concern for us here, precious though it is, as a reason for marrying; and I can't help remembering that you're much younger than he is, and you've always seemed rather to dislike him. But perhaps you think I have no right to ask what your reasons are.'

Claudia decided that since they were talking at all they might as well risk facing together what they both knew. 'You also remember how much Jacques Duclos meant to the girl I used to be. And for Giancarlo you think of his dead fiancée, and of Jessica whom you would have welcomed as a daughter-in-law.'

The Countess nodded, making no attempt to deny what Claudia had just said. 'Young people change, I know that. They cannot, must not, live in the past as the old are inclined to do. I suppose it's just that you both strike me as being very constant in your affections. It ought to be a virtue, but in this case it must be a handicap to your happiness together.'

Claudia managed a faint smile, wondering how much more of this conversation she could bear. 'I expect my parents will say exactly the same thing when Giancarlo gets back and breaks the news to them. I shan't be able to promise them, any more than I can you, Donna Emilia, that he and I will make each other happy. But the alternative is to be

312

lonely, and we've both been lonely long enough.' Her face beneath its summer tan was pale now, and her voice wasn't quite steady. Any more questions, she thought, and she would disgust this self-disciplined aristocrat by bursting into tears. But suddenly Donna Emilia lowered her sword.

'Loneliness is a reason for marrying,' she admitted gently. 'Forgive me for not realizing that it applied to you as well.' Then her charming smile reappeared. 'I'm quite sure Maria will be happy about it. I might not have been able to say that of Llewellyn once upon a time, but I think that he and my grandson have gradually learned to appreciate each other!'

She stood up, and it seemed to Claudia that the gruelling interview was over. What came next? How was she expected to leave? With a friendly wave, a smile, a curtsey? But Donna Emilia solved the problem by simply holding out her hands, and without any more thought Claudia grasped them in her own and leaned forward to kiss her. Then she turned away and walked out of the room, to be escorted back to the staircase by the ever-vigilant Battistina, who would now be sure to return to her mistress to discover whether the visitor had cured her *tristezza* or, unforgivably, made it worse.

Twenty-Four

It was Friday, the first day of October, and a relief to set out to start work at Ca' Forsetti; the nervous anticipation of Giancarlo's return was getting to be more than she could bear. She'd tried her hardest to behave as if the only thing that mattered was getting her parents comfortably installed in their new quarters upstairs, but she longed for her own suspense to be over as much as she dreaded it at the same time. To be made to think about her new job, and have a good reason to escape from the *pensione*, was the only comfort available.

The heatwave still hadn't broken and despite her apprehension she climbed the steps of the Accademia Bridge aware of something else as well: the heavy and expectant feel to the air. From habit she paused to stare down at the broad waterway between its flanking palaces. The view could never be less than beautiful but its colours looked faded now, and even the canal itself seemed to flow reluctantly towards the Bacino and the lagoon. The storm they needed so badly surely couldn't be long in coming.

She was made welcome at the Comune,

met her new colleagues, and then left alone to confront a heap of files. As the Mayor rightly said, there'd been other dreams in the past of revitalizing the life of the city, and she had to learn what had been proposed before – some plans realized, and even more abandoned before they could start working together. With a long weekend ahead she selected the largest file to take home with her at the end of the day, grateful for the excuse it would give her to stay working in her room.

The first intimation of the storm ahead came as they were still at the dinner table, when they heard the faint rumble of thunder, still far away over on the mainland but just audible. By midnight it had begun to rain, large slow drops promising the deluge that was heading their way. By morning it was breaking over them from a grey, low sky in a downpour that blotted out every other sound. But in waterproof cape and wellingtons, Claudia still splashed her way to the Rialto; certain habits ignored climatic disturbances, and Venetians had to buy vegetables fresh in the market every day. She met Battistina there, more concerned to shelter her basket than herself under a huge umbrella. They agreed that the night's thunderstorm had been dramatic, and what a mercy, Battistina said, that at least Signor Giancarlo had got home safely before the worst of it had reached them.

Feeling her stomach lurch, Claudia stared at Battistina's homely face. 'Got home?' she queried too sharply. 'But he was to be away for ten days, he said.'

The servant nodded. That was very true, but the signorina probably knew what such conferences were like – too many speeches, too much eating and drinking. '*Questa robaccia non piace al Signore*,' she finished up severely.

Well, no, 'that rubbish' wouldn't please him at all, Claudia realized; he'd have left as soon as he could. 'Then perhaps we'll see him soon at the *pensione*,' she suggested faintly, only to watch Battistina frown and shake her head. No, that wasn't likely, because the young man who'd brought him back to the palazzo last night had collected him again early this morning. There was anxiety about conditions out in the lagoon. He had to be there with his men, of course, but in her opinion they should all be here on terra firma. Claudia looked down at the streaming puddles in which they nearly floated, but found nothing to smile at in what Battistina had just said. How could the conditions do anything but get worse out on the water? The wind was noticeably stronger even since she'd left home and, like any Venetian, she knew the danger of a high tide driven in by the sirocco meeting the rain-swollen river waters trying to empty themselves into the lagoon. Battistina was right: no one should be out there trying to keep the rest of them safe, but that was Giancarlo's job, and she could see now with aching clarity why he wanted someone else

316

living at the palazzo, to make sure his grand-parents were looked after.

She said goodbye to Battistina, struggled through her shopping list, and fought her way back towards home against the wind. But the door of Sant' Agnese was open and on instinct she went inside. The last time she'd been in a church on her own was on a morning in New York, only a few months ago, which now seemed to belong to another life. She'd been angry then – she could recall that clearly enough – and offhand with the gentle priest who'd wanted to help her. This time at least she was there to pray to the compassionate God her mother believed in, to beg him to watch over Giancarlo and his companions. Then she fought her way home in the teeth of the wind, to the sound of sirens already warning of the danger of flooding.

Her white, strained face made Llewellyn stare at her. '*Tesoro*, you shouldn't have gone out,' he said anxiously.

'You're right,' she agreed, trying to smile at him, 'but then I wouldn't have bumped into Battistina and learned that Giancarlo got back safely from Stockholm last night.' Then her voice wavered and broke. 'The only trouble is that he's not very safe now – he and his men are out in the lagoon.'

She read in her father's face the alarm she would have expected, but also astonishment as well. Fearing the question that was going to come next, she mumbled something about changing her wet clothes and fled upstairs.

317

When she emerged from her room, dry and under control again, he was just replacing the telephone. Maria waited anxiously beside him, but she too now stared at her daughter. Llewellyn spoke to Claudia, rather than to his wife.

'I tried the Magistrato's office – no reply,' he explained briefly. 'So I rang Paolo Rasini. All he knows is what Giancarlo said when he left early this morning. They were worried about the sea wall at the far end of Pellestrina – that's where they are, sandbagging it – but at least they're working inside the lagoon, thank God. They're too experienced to be swept out to sea there.'

Claudia nodded, not sure that she could trust her voice. Then Maria risked the question that Llewellyn baulked at. '*Tesoro*, does it matter to you so much?' she asked gently.

There was a pause before the answer came. 'I was leaving it to Giancarlo to tell you first.' She tried to smile at Llewellyn. 'He insists on doing things properly! But I'm going to marry him. We decided the day of Marco's wedding, but he had to leave straight afterwards for Stockholm.' The disbelief in Llewellyn's face was almost enough to make her smile. 'Giancarlo told Donna Emilia before he went to Sweden – I'm afraid her reaction was the same as yours.'

At last Maria found something to say. 'Our reactions don't matter, *tesoro* … It's just … are you sure?'

'Yes, I'm sure,' Claudia answered, and the

318

certainty in her voice couldn't be questioned again. 'Now, I think I should go to the palazzo ... if I'm not needed I can come home again.' She saw what Llewellyn was about to suggest and shook her head. 'Stay here with Mamma, please – no need for two of us to get wet!' She pulled on boots and the still-dripping cape again, blew them a little kiss, and let herself out of the house.

When the door closed behind her Maria collapsed into the nearest chair. 'I didn't imagine that conversation! Our daughter did say she's going to marry a man she seems to have done nothing but dislike?'

'She's just confirmed it by going to take care of Emilia and Paolo,' Llewellyn pointed out. 'You weren't here when she came in and said where Giancarlo was – she wasn't talking then of someone she disliked; she wanted to be out there with him.'

It relieved one of Maria's anxieties but made another much worse. 'God must take care of him, but not only for Claudia's sake – think what Emilia and Paolo are going through, remembering how Giancarlo's parents were taken from them.'

'That was forty years ago, sweetheart; things are better organized now.' He didn't truly believe they were – probably no one living in the entire peninsula had that amount of faith in the system that ordered their lives – but at least Maria was able to drag her mind away from the idea of disaster and think instead about her daughter's shock announcement.

But there were too many questions she couldn't answer and, as always when she was distressed or puzzled, she took comfort from the unending task of looking after the well-being of her family.

Claudia arrived at the palazzo out of breath from her tussle with the wind and dripping water, but Battistina smiled a welcome, and Donna Emilia even kissed her cheek.

'It's no day to be out of doors, my dear, but thank you for coming. Now Paolo will feel obliged to leave his library and at least pretend to eat something with us in the dining room.'

He did emerge to sit with them, but he hid himself away again when the brief meal was over. Claudia and the Countess were back in the sitting room listening to the long-case clock chime the slow passing of yet another hour when an anxious Battistina reappeared to report the arrival of someone whose name Claudia recognized. He was too wet and dishevelled to leave the hall but he hoped he might speak to the Countess there. Looking at her face, now sheet-white, Claudia asked if she might go instead, seeing that she'd already met Daniele Monti at the Magistrato's offices. He stood dripping water on the marble floor of the hall, and fear of what he'd come to say made her voice sharp and unfriendly. 'If you're back, why not Giancarlo?'

'Because he's still out there.' Daniele smeared away the rivulets that trickled down from his wet hair, and she saw the tiredness in his face.

'Forgive me,' she said more gently. 'I should have asked you to take off your wet things and sit down.'

He smiled faintly, but shook his head. 'It doesn't matter, signorina; I only came to let you know what's been happening. We did what was needed out at Pellestrina – banked up the sea wall with sandbags in case things got worse – and were just about to make our way back. But there was a noise we could hear even above the wind and waves; a fishing boat had gone aground on a sandbank out on the seaward side of the wall at the Porto di Chioggia. We had to go and help, of course, and found the boat full of Albanian refugees. God knows how they'd made it that far – the boat wasn't fit to be afloat and they'd got into the wrong channel altogether.'

He wiped a hand across his wet face again, and this time Claudia took his other hand and led him into Battistina's kitchen. She told him to take off his waterproof, then poured wine and, while he sipped it, waited for him to go on.

'We got them across to our boat – I don't quite know how we managed that in those conditions – but then Giancarlo, who was on the trawler handing them over, sent the last one across with a note. We were to bring our load back to be checked at the hospital; he was staying on board with an injured man and a woman who wouldn't leave him – the man's wife I suppose.'

'And that's where he still is?' Claudia managed to ask.

Daniele nodded. 'We didn't have a stretcher – couldn't have used it anyway. There's not a thing we can do for them until the wind drops and daylight comes.'

Claudia took a breath and forced another question out of her mouth. 'Are they safe where they are? I need to know ... I have to tell Giancarlo's grandparents.'

He hesitated but her eyes asked for the truth. 'They're safe for as long as the boat doesn't break up. But it's a hulk, and it's taking a pounding. We just have to pray for the sirocco to blow itself out.' Exhaustion and fear for a man he idolized made his voice waver, and Claudia leaned across to grasp his hand for a moment.

'Thank you for coming, Daniele,' she said gently. 'Go home and rest. I'll ask Battistina to show you out while I talk to Donna Emilia and Count Paolo.'

She found them both in the little sitting room and told them what Daniele had said – Giancarlo was all right so far, but there was the night to get through. Most other people she knew would have railed to Heaven against the injustice of knowing that their only precious link with life was being risked for the sake of an illegal Albanian immigrant and his wife, but what Donna Emilia finally said was, 'Poor people – terrified and hurt, but desperate enough to make that dreadful journey. Of course Giancarlo had to stay with them.' Then she turned to stare at Claudia. 'You look tired, child. I shall ring Bianca next door and ask if Beppe can see you safely home.'

Claudia knelt down beside her chair. 'I'd rather we were together, Donna Emilia. Unless you and the Count don't want me here, may I ring my father and say I'm staying ... just till Giancarlo gets back?' Her dark eyes, shadowed with too much anxiety and stress, now made no secret of the dread she'd tried to hide, and suddenly the Countess's drawn face was full of kindness.

'Dear child, of course stay – but speak to Llewellyn first, and ask Maria to help us with her prayers.'

'She won't need asking,' Claudia said unsteadily, 'but I'll ask anyway, just to make sure.'

Darkness came and slowly the interminable hours crept by until, worried by the exhaustion in his wife's face, Paolo begged her to lie down. To relieve one of his anxieties, Emilia agreed and even swallowed a sleeping pill, and to comfort Battistina she asked the heartbroken servant to sit with her. Left alone with the Count, known from childhood but not really known at all, Claudia discovered to her astonishment that she could not only talk to him but could do so with the ease of an old friend. She even found herself speaking of Jess and the sharpness of their quarrel in the *pensione*'s garden.

'I was angry with her then,' she confessed,

323

suddenly wanting this wise, gentle man to understand. 'I reckoned I knew all about love. I knew nothing at all, but I'm learning now.'

Paolo smiled at her, then quoted his favourite English poet. '"It looks on tempests and is never shaken; it is the star to every wandering barque, whose worth's unknown although its height be taken." That, my dear, was written by a man who knew a great deal about love.'

She nodded, thinking of the tempest outside, but then relapsed into silence, seeing that at last the old man's eyes were closing. Now was the time to face alone a future that might not include Giancarlo. She had wondered how to bear being a wife who wasn't loved, but all she could ask of God now was to be allowed to live with him on any terms he liked.

She was still wide awake when the first grey light of dawn crept into the room. It dragged her stiffly across to the window, and then she realized what else had changed outside: the rain had stopped, and the garden was no longer being flailed by the wind. The storm had passed. The Count was still quietly asleep in his chair, so she left him undisturbed and went to check on Donna Emilia. A tap on her door was answered by a soft invitation to enter. The Countess was sitting up, pretending to read, while Battistina dozed in an armchair by the window.

'It's dawn,' Claudia whispered. 'There'll be some daylight out in the lagoon by now, and the storm is over.'

'I know, but we must still wait for the sea to quieten.' Donna Emilia spoke calmly, but the despair in her face made Claudia want to weep.

'Count Paolo is sleeping,' she said, as if that was good news at least, 'and I'm about to make some tea.' She even tried to smile. 'Your grandson once told me that it's what you always recommend in times of stress!'

In Battistina's beautifully ordered kitchen it wasn't hard to find what she needed, and she was laying out cups and saucers when a foot-fall sounded in the hall; the Count had woken up, it seemed. But it wasn't his frail figure in the doorway a moment later. It was Giancarlo she was staring at – unshaven, face grey with weariness but there, unharmed and safe. Anything in her hands would have smashed on the tiled floor; as it was, she ducked her head against a wave of faintness and felt his hands gently guiding her to a chair. When she was able to look up, he was busy at the stove apparently intent on filling the teapot.

'Count Paolo was asleep a moment ago, but your grandmother is awake, and expecting some tea.' She was pleased with herself for sounding calm. The night, dreadful as it had been, was over and normal life could be resumed. But then she spoiled it when her voice trembled. 'Your appearance will come as a shock ... we expected to have to go on waiting.'

'So did I,' he agreed with at tired smile, 'but my intrepid rescuers must have set out well before dawn.' He stared at her drawn, white face, now devoid of make-up and as plain as it was possible for her to look, but somehow all the more precious for that. 'Stay where you are,' he said gently. 'I'll be back.'

She poured tea for herself and sat with her cold hands wrapped round the cup. There was no need to be there now; she could go home. But she'd been told to stay, and so she would. Her mother would certainly remind her to thank God Almighty, and she'd do that as well.

Giancarlo returned at last, to report briefly that his grandparents would rest until normal breakfast time arrived. Battistina, happy tears mopped up, was back in her own room. Claudia scarcely waited for what else he might say; she was ready with a question it was reasonable to ask.

'What about the Albanian – did he survive?'

'Yes, he did, poor devil. His wife would have died of fear rather than leave him – he has that to be thankful for.'

'He has you to be thankful for,' she snapped. Now that he was safe it seemed reasonable to want to shout that he couldn't – mustn't – hold his life so cheaply again because they weren't able to manage without him.

She was staring at her empty cup and didn't see Giancarlo smile. 'By the way, I saw Leif in Stockholm,' he said gently. 'He sent his love to everyone but especially to you – he seemed to think you needed it most.'

'Northerners,' Claudia tried to explain, 'so much more romantically minded really than we are – contrary to popular legend.' She glanced at her watch and tried to sound casual. 'It's time I went.' But even to her it seemed ridiculous – as if she'd been invited to dinner and stayed too long.

'It's time you stayed for good,' he corrected her. 'My grandparents think so, too.'

She managed a bright smile. 'If you're going to feel obliged to play the hero every time we have a storm, I think I agree with them.' But now her voice wobbled. 'I hope you knew last night that I'd take care of them if you didn't come back – out of love, not just because it was part of our arrangement.'

He frowned at the open door behind him. 'This is not a conversation to have when Battistina will be here at any moment. Allow me to walk you back to the *pensione*, wife-to-be; there's an interview with your father outstanding anyway.'

Pale cheeks suddenly flushed, Claudia shook her head. 'They know already at home – I had to explain why I was coming here.' She wasn't sure what Llewellyn's reception would be even now, but tried to sound hopeful. 'They'll have had enough time to get over the shock.'

Giancarlo's mouth twitched but all he said was, 'In that case we shan't need to dawdle. I've told Emilia that I would see you home.'

With nothing else to put on, she got into the unglamorous cape and wellingtons she'd arrived in, caught sight of herself in the hall mirror and hastily looked away again. But the morning they stepped out into was beautiful, even though the gutters still ran with water. The air smelled fresh again, and the sky was tinged with the faint pink glow that promised a fine day. She was about to turn right at the palazzo gate, but was steered in the opposite direction instead.

'This isn't the way home,' she pointed out.

'It's not the most direct way,' he agreed, 'but there's a bar along here that ought to be open by now, and it offers the best coffee in Venice.'

The bar was open and Giancarlo was greeted like an old friend. Once served, they were left alone while the *padrone* went away to discuss with his wife the arrival of the signore so early in the day with a beautiful but tired-looking young lady.

'I haven't thanked you for staying with Emilia and Paolo last night,' Giancarlo began gently, 'and there's a lot more to say, but you look almost too exhausted to listen. Are you following me thus far?'

'Faint but pursuing,' she agreed, too intent on spooning sugar into her coffee to see him smile.

'Well then, I spoke to Emilia before I left for Stockholm but I couldn't blame her for scarcely believing me – it didn't sound real, it didn't feel real, and I knew why. I was pretending it was the sort of second-best arrangement you suggested that rainy day at

Florian's, but I knew even then that it was a lie. I didn't want to marry you as a substitute for Jessica, and I refused to be a pale imitation of Jacques Duclos for you.' He stopped speaking, halted by the memory of the past night's maelstrom of wind and water in the lagoon. 'All I could think of on that damned boat was that I might never have the chance to tell you the truth: that I wanted you for my wife, "to have and to hold as long as we both shall live" as the marriage sacrament says.'

She could hear the conviction in his voice, but he'd said himself it was the truth they needed now, and there was a question to ask. 'Isn't the past still getting the way – me loving Jacques, you loving Jess. Doesn't that still matter?'

She stared at him as she asked the question, but saw only certainty in his face. 'Of course it matters – we are what the past has made of us, they're a part of it, and still part of us.' He reached across the table to take her cold hands in his warm ones. 'My dear, I know I'm years older than you, and I know we've been at pains to misunderstand one another for years, but ever since you came back to Venice I've known how much I need you at the centre of my life. I didn't dare say that when I asked you to marry me in case the jealous gods were still listening.'

Her dark eyes, over-large in the pallor of her face, asked the question she put into words. 'Aren't they listening now?'

Giancarlo shook his head. 'I take last night's

reprieve to mean that they're finally prepared to leave me alone! We're being allowed our chance of happiness this time if we're prepared to take it. Are you? Or am I asking too much?' He waited for her to answer, fearful that he hadn't said enough, hadn't yet put aside the habit of solitariness that made it hard to put feeling into words. Her eyes were full of tears, and he thought he could guess her answer – for her the past was still in the way. But then a smile began to tremble on her mouth.

'I told Mamma's God last night,' she began unsteadily, 'that all I prayed for was for Him to bring you safely home. I said I'd be content to be the wife who wasn't loved and never ask for more. But I'm sure He knew how big a lie that was!' Her fingers entwined themselves in Giancarlo's. 'Let's take our chance of happiness, please.'

He lifted her hands to his mouth, but couldn't answer before the *padrone* reappeared in case more coffee might be required, but he suspected that his question scarcely registered on the couple in front of him. Then the girl thanked him and shook her head.

They walked back to the *pensione* hand-in-hand, both silently aware of the need to make haste slowly with a new relationship that would yield great happiness if they got it right and unending pain if they didn't. When they were nearly home Claudia found something to say. 'You value solitude, privacy. Will you mind a shared life?'

330

He halted and turned her to look at him so that he could see the anxiety in her face, and she could see the certainty in his. 'My dear one, does a condemned man mind being offered his freedom? I've had my fill of solitude.' And then his mouth on hers confirmed the truth of what he'd said.

Llewellyn, alerted by a telephone call from the Countess, was on the lookout and watched them arrive at the garden gate. Then he turned to smile at Maria. 'Your wandering daughter is nearly home; shepherded by someone who looks like a tramp but will probably turn out to be our prospective son-in-law!'

'We must thank God he's safely back,' Maria said, but she still looked anxious. 'So much has happened – to both of them. Do you think they'll be happy at last?'

Llewellyn's grin faded into seriousness. 'You'll know the moment they walk in. Now I'll ask you a much more doubtful question: is it too early in the day to drink champagne?'

'Breakfast first,' Maria decided firmly. 'Then champagne.'

And reluctantly he agreed that, as always, she was right.